I0730958

Steadfast
Patricia Boyer-Weisman

WORKBOOK PRESS LLC
187 E Warm Springs Rd,
Suite B285, Las Vegas, NV 89119, USA

Website: https://workbookpress.com/
Hotline: 1-888-818-4856
Email: admin@workbookpress.com

Ordering Information:
Quantity sales. Special discounts are available on quantity purchases by corporations, associations, and others.
For details, contact the publisher at the address above.

Library of Congress Control Number:
ISBN-13:   978-1-958176-02-3 (Paperback Version)
              978-1-958176-03-0 (Digital Version)

REV. DATE: 06/04/2022

The shot came from the hill across from the guard office at the entrance of the gated subdivision. Marcus had purposely put it in place to protect all the homeowners that lived there. The truck was red and the man inside was wearing a hat and what look like part of army fatigues. Marcus had just come through the gate on his Harley, he had on his signature helmet, leather jacket, and chaps. It was cold outside and had just snowed. The roads were slick, but that wouldn't stop Marcus. He wanted to embrace the elements. Mike was in the black security van just behind him and saw the man fire but could not signal Marcus in time. The bullet ripped through Marcus' chest causing him to lose control of the bike. The bike flipped over and slid down the road, throwing him off. His body sliding on the ice, his head hit the pavement.

It was a sickly sight to Mike, and a dilemma. Did he go after the red truck or stop and see about Marcus? He quickly got on the radio and tried to talk to Marcus, no answer. He called the paramedics, more of his security team, and the police. People were stopping and seeing what they could do to help. Mike stopped to see about Marcus, his lifelong friend. He knew that Marcus would want him to catch the man that had been threatening the Matthew family for months.

It just so happened that Dr. Majors, from the neighborhood, was just coming through the security gate and stopped to help. The security guard had drawn weapons and had already called the police and paramedics. Marcus' helmet came off during impact and his legs crumpled under him. He was bleeding from the opening in his chest. Dr. Majors was applying compression to the area. Marcus was unconscious but breathing. He looked dead.

Mike turned to the security guard and Dr. Majors, "I am trusting you to help him. I am going after the red truck and the man who did this." All of this was handled in split second decisions.

"Go!" said Dr. Majors. "I got him."

Mike quickly got back into his van and started following the path that the red truck went. He was setting on the hill across from the entrance to the subdivision, so he was off road. Mike had four-wheel drive and his van was equipped to handle any terrain. As he climbed the hill, he could see the red truck. The driver was having difficulties maneuvering the snowbanks on the undeveloped property. The red truck finally hit a snowbank and was unable to go any farther. The man in the truck was gunning his motor, but the wheels could not get any traction to climb the snow and ice bank. Suddenly, he got out of the truck and begin to run toward the road, slipping and falling along the way. Mike knew he had him and sped up until he was right behind him. Mike put his car in park, jumped out and tackled the man. Mike was in top physical shape whereas the old man looked haggard and worn out. The old man tried to wrestle Mike off. It was apparent he had military training at some point in his life. He was dressed in Army fatigues. Mike recognized him as the same man who had been the original contractor on the development that Matthew Construction had purchased from the bank.

Mike picked him up and punched him hard in the face. "You piece of shit!" yelled Mike. "If my friend dies, I will kill you myself." Then he punched the old man again. He was just about to land another punch when his arm and body were held back by two of his security team.

"Come on Mike," Anthony said, "You will kill him. Let's take him to the police, man. Let's get back to Marcus."

By that time a police cruiser came up the hill and two policemen got out with guns drawn. They went towards Mike, his security guys, and the old man. The police were very aware of the strength of the Matthew's security team and knew the relationship between Mike and Marcus. Officer Beck was the first to speak, "Mike, we will take care of him now. You go to Marcus. The family will need you. You can come later to the precinct."

They took the old man from Mike and handcuffed him, then put him in the back of the patrol car. A second patrol car was checking out the red truck and had located the gun. Mike jumped back into the van and headed back to the scene where Marcus would be lying in the road, on the cold snowy ground. There was an ambulance loading Marcus into the back. He was on a backboard with a collar around his neck. They were giving him oxygen and had an IV started in his arm. He looked pale and lifeless. Mike leaned over Marcus and said, "We got him man, hang in there." With that, Dr. Majors got into the back of the ambulance, and it sped away. Mike radioed his team to secure the doctor's car and to make sure that no one called the Matthew's family except him. He debated in his mind who to notify first, but just as he reached for the phone, John Marcus Sr. called. "What the hell is going on, Mike? I just got a call from a reporter that there was a shooting and Marcus was hit. On his motorcycle."

"Sir, that's true. The man who shot him was on the hill across the street to the entrance to the subdivision. Sir, I was right behind him when it happened. He is in custody now. I was just about to call Saul so he can meet Samantha at the hospital. My next call was to you."

"Right, right. Do you know how my son is?"

"He looks bad, sir. It was a bad wreck, plus he was shot in the chest. I need to get to Samantha before someone calls her."

"Okay. His mother and I are on our way to the hospital."

Mike hung up and dialed Saul's number. "Saul, I cannot go into detail, but Marcus has been shot."

The next call was going to be the most difficult. He dialed Samantha's number, she answered on the first ring. "Hi Mike, what's up?"

"Samantha, I am at front of the house to pick you up. Put on a coat, sweetheart. Marcus has been shot. I need to get you to the hospital. I will meet you at the front door." Mike went up the steps to the front door and rang the doorbell. Just as it opened, Samantha ran into Mike's arms sobbing.

"Where is he? What happened? Please, is he alright?" She was now six months pregnant with their second biological child. She was pale and looked like all the wind was knocked from her. She had her coat in her hand and Mike quickly helped her put it on. "Careful, let me help you down these steps and into the van."

Samantha was like a little girl. She became very submissive, and Mike had to lift her into the van. As they were driving to the hospital, she was quiet; just sobbing. She finally found her voice and through the sobs, she asked, "What happened Mike?"

"Samantha, as we were coming out of the subdivision, a man was sitting on the hill across from the entrance and fired a shot which hit Marcus in the chest. You know he was riding his Harley and the impact from the shot caused him to wreck. I was able to catch the old man and the police have him in custody. Dr. Majors was coming out of the development just as it happened and stopped to help. It was all very quick."

"But is he on his way to the hospital in an ambulance?" Samantha asked.

"Was he conscious?" she furthered. Mike hesitated. *What should I say?* He was careful with his words. "No, he was not. But he was breathing, and they had oxygen hooked up to him. That's all I really know."

"Mike, I cannot lose him. I just cannot lose him." Mike reached for her hand. "I know, I cannot lose him either. He is a tough man. I know he has whipped my ass a dozen times. He is my best friend, my brother."

Samantha sank deeper into her coat and looked out the van window. She said, "Are the children safe?"

"Yes, I have security everywhere. All of the Matthew's family has extra security."

"Yet, they still got to him."

"Yes, Samantha, it took someone crazy to climb that hill in an old red truck in this weather. But you know Marcus does what Marcus wants, and no matter how many times we had asked him not to be in the open on his bikes, he did not listen. Samantha, I really think, Marcus has had a plan of his own to draw this person out in the open. I think he was tired of the threat to his family."

"That's who he is. But it has been years since we heard anything from this man. We were happy and everything was getting back to normal," Samantha said, very softly.

"I know," Mike said. She was no longer sobbing; tears were streaming down her face as she continued to withdraw.

"Samantha," Mike said. "Think of his baby. This baby really means a lot to him." Samantha turned to Mike, "I cannot do this without him. I just cannot." They drove up to the emergency room and parked. Mike quickly got out and helped Samantha.

***

"My husband has just been brought into the hospital with a gunshot wound. He is Marcus Matthew, and I am his wife," she said to the nurse at the desk.

"Yes, Mrs. Matthew, right this way. Dr. Majors is in with him. Let me show you where he is." The nurse took Samantha and Mike to an emergency room where they had Marcus hooked up to an IV, tubes, and machines. He was pale and unconscious. Dr. Majors was giving orders to the nurse.

"Samantha, we must get him into surgery right away. I called in Dr. Snowden, a cardiac surgeon." With that, they wheeled him toward the door. Samantha suddenly said, "Stop please. Let me kiss him." She went to the bed and kissed Marcus on the lips.

"Baby, I am so sorry. Please get well. Fight to come back to me and our baby. You're my heart, the oxygen I breathe. I cannot love another. Please, my darling."

"Samantha, we have to get him into surgery," Dr. Majors said. Mike took Samantha in his arms, "Darling, he will make it. He is strong and a fighter. He will make it. Be brave. He wants you to be brave for him, his children, and his unborn child." Samantha collapsed in Mike's arm.

"Nurse!" he said. "I need some help." The nurse brought a bed and Mike placed Samantha on it. The nurse covered her with a blanket. Mike said, "Her doctor is Dr. McCullough. Please call her."

"She is on the floor seeing patients. I will page her."

Dr. McCullough came to Samantha's room within minutes of the call.

"Mike, what's going on?" She went straight to Samantha and listened to the baby. She checked her pulse. Mike quickly said, "Marcus was shot. He's in surgery. Samantha just fainted in my arms."

"Well," said Dr. McCullough. "Wait outside in the waiting room while

I check her out." Mike left the room just as Saul was coming in.

"Mike, what's going on?"

"Sir, Marcus was shot coming out of the development. He was on his Harley and crashed and lost his helmet. He has head injuries, as well as the gunshot wound.

"Oh my God. And Samantha? Where is Marcus and my daughter?"

"Marcus is in surgery and Samantha fainted. Dr. McCullough is with her and wants to check her out."

"And the children?"

"We have security on all the family, as well as you," Mike replied. Margaret came into the room and heard the last of the conversation.

"Saul, I'll go to the children. They need family right now."

Mike said, "I have security around the entrance of the development and security at their house. I also called their nannies and told them to keep them away from the televisions. There are reporters already at the entrance. So please, let's wait to see how their father is before we tell them anything."

"I want to be there for them. Honey, you take care of their mother and father, and I'll take care of the children." Margaret gave Saul a hug and said, "My darling, I am praying for your daughter and Marcus. I am leaving for the house, and I will take the car and the driver. Of course, I'll stay in touch. I love you."

In walked John Marcus and Isabella. "Mike, son, how is my boy?"

"Sir, all I know is that he is in surgery right now. The man that shot him was waiting on the hill in front of the development. Marcus was on his Harley when he was hit, and he lost control of his bike. His helmet came off and his legs were crumpled underneath him." Isabella started crying, "My boy, my boy."

John Marcus said, "Dry those tears. Our boy is strong and a fighter. Mike, I know you did everything you could. Marcus is head strong and marches to his own beat."

"I know, sir. I just wished he'd listened this time. He put himself in plain sight of the shooter."

"Mike, you did all you could. You caught the man?"

"Yes, sir, he was the man who was developing the project when he lost it to the bank. I guess he had a grudge against Marcus for buying the property." John Marcus said, "I know my boy. He probably gave the man money to get back on his feet. But it's been years since we heard anything. Why now?"

"Yes, sir. Marcus was very generous and even offered the man a job," Mike said, "but I think there is more to it than that. The man was dressed in military fatigues. His weapon was military issue. A civilian would not own a gun like that. They have him at the police station. I am going down as soon as I know how Marcus and Samantha are doing." Isabella who had been sobbing quietly said, "What is wrong with her?"

"I do not know," said Mike. "She fainted in my arms. The doctor is in with her now." Isabella went into John Marcus arms. He held her. Isabella said, "He really wanted this baby."

"Sweetheart, let's wait for the doctors before we jump to conclusions. Is Saul with her?"

"Yes. And Margaret went to the children. I have extra security around all the family," Mike said.

"Please call the girls and Phillipe and let them know please," said Mike.

"Of course." He got his phone out to call his daughters and son. Dr. McCullough came into the room, "Samantha is all right and so is the baby. She is weak emotionally, which is to be expected given the circumstances. I'm going to admit her, just for observation. So, they are moving to the Matthew's suite. And when they get her settled, if she wants to see you, the nurse will let you know. I know you will want to wait in the private waiting room."

"Yes," said Isabella. They took the elevator to the ninth floor where the suites for the wealthy families of New York stayed. As they entered the waiting area, the nurse came out. "Give her a few minutes. She is changing into a gown."

"Sure," said Mike. They waited until the nurse came back in, "She'd like to see you."

They entered Samantha's room, she looked withdrawn and pale. There was an IV in her arm. You could see the suffering on her face. Saul said, "She's better. The baby is fine." Isabella went to Samantha and hugged her and kissed the top of her head. "My son would want you to be strong. He is looking forward to this baby." Samantha burst into tears.

"I love him. I cannot lose him." John Marcus said, "Samantha, he will make it. He is a strong boy. He's my boy and he's a fighter, right Mike?"

"Yes, sir, you know how many times he whipped my butt and you had to break us up."

"Yes, when you joined the family at seven, you and Marcus were inseparable."

Dr. Majors and Dr. Snowden entered Samantha's room.

"We'd like to tell you that the surgery went well," Dr Snowden said, "The bullet nicked a lung but missed all other vital organs. He's scraped up, cut, and bruised. His left leg is broken, but he will be okay. The only thing that we are a little concerned about is that he had a concussion, and he is unconscious still. I think he is dealing with the accident and will come to once he has processed his injury. The mind is funny. It will take time, but he will come to and then we will see if there are any mental issues." Samantha seemed to withdraw even more. She looked like a little girl laying in the bed with a large stomach. She was close to seven months. Saul went to Samantha, "Sweetheart, this is good news. Now let's get you something to eat. You want to be in good shape when he wakes up."

"Yes, Dad, I want to let him know how much I love him and cannot live without him."

"Nurse, please bring her a hearty steak dinner with milk." The suite's waiting room was equipped with a coffee machine, snacks, and water. A candy striper was assigned to the Matthew's family. That's what happens when you owned the hospital, and you were the Matthew family.

Dr. Majors said, "Unless you just want to wait around, it could be a few days or so. There is just no way to know. My suggestion is you go home and wait to hear."

"John Marcus, how are you are feeling? I'd like to check you out and make sure your heart is good. Two heart attacks and this stress? You need to go home and rest," Dr. Majors continued.

"Yes, darling, do as the doctor says. I cannot have both my men in the hospital. The car and driver are downstairs."

"Saul, you can leave also. Dr. McCullough has ordered Samantha something to help her sleep. So, after she eats, the nurse will give her something in her IV." John Marcus and Isabella left to go home. Food services brought in her meal and Samantha picked at it and tried to eat a little. She drank her milk.

"That's all I can eat, Dad. I just do not feel like eating. I want to sleep. Maybe tomorrow I will wake up and this will all be an ugly nightmare." The nurse gave her the sleep medication in her IV. Saul kissed her and said to Mike, "Will you take me to the house with Margaret and the children?"

"Yes, sir. I also must stop at the precinct and talk to the DA." Mike walked over to Samantha and kissed her cheek. "I will be back as soon as I take care of all the details." Samantha was barely awake. "Please, he must be okay." She drifted into sleep. Mike and Saul left her room and went downstairs where Mike's van was parked. Saul said, "I want to go with you to the precinct."

"Yes, sir," Mike said and started the van.

***

When they got to the precinct, Saul knew the DA and asked him what kind of charges he was bringing against the shooter. The DA said, "Well Mr. Carr has been moved to the psychiatric hospital. He is suffering PTSD and has delusions. He served four deployments in the Middle East and was a ranger, so he's seen a lot of human tragedy. He believes Marcus is the enemy and he is fighting to get his development back. He was in therapy and on his medications for a few years, that's why things were quiet for you guys. He was getting better. Then he couldn't afford the therapy or medication anymore. I think that lead to this tragedy. Saul, Mike, until he has been evaluated, I'm not sure he is competent enough to stand trial, or even be charged. Give us a few days and I'll call you. Hopefully by then we will know something. How is Marcus?" the DA asked.

Mike said, "He is still unconscious, but the doctors feel like his injuries will heal and eventually, he will be alright."

"Well, I say minimum, Mr. Carr will be charged with attempted murder and stalking. But let's wait to see what the doctors say about Mr. Carr."

***

Saul and Mike headed back to the mansion. At the gate, Mike's security team had the outside of the development covered, but there were several reporters there trying to get information. There was blood still on the road. He radioed Anthony, his next in charge of security, and asked that the blood be removed from the road. He wanted no evidence of the shooting. Marcus' bike had already been taken to a repair shop. The red truck had been impounded. Dr Majors' car had been delivered to his house in the development. Mike said to Saul, "I need to make a statement so that the reporters will leave." Saul said, "Do you want me to do it?"

"No, Saul, that's my job." Mike stopped the van and got out in front of the development and stood on the bumper of the van. He addressed the reporters.

"I know most of you heard that Marcus Matthew was shot leaving his subdivision. The family have been stalked by a veteran who has had PTSD for years. He is in police custody. Marcus is out of surgery; he has a broken leg and lots of cuts and scrapes, as you can imagine in such an accident. He has a concussion, but the doctors said he would heal and regain consciousness. So, I respectfully ask you to go back to your offices now that you have your answers. This will be all the statements made by the family now. Thank you." Mike got back into the van and passed through the gates to pull up in front of the mansion and got out. He and Saul went to the front door. It was quiet; the children must be in the playroom. He and Saul went to the playroom, only to find that the children were in the theater room.

"Uncle Mike!" The girls were always excited to see him.

"What are you watching, missy?" he said to Bella.

"*Alice in Wonderland.* You want to watch it with us?"

"Sure," said Mike. Matilda gave Mike some of her popcorn and he lost all his worries in the movie. Saul went to the library to fix himself a drink, he was worried about Samantha. He knew how delectate she was emotionally. He called Rick and told him what had happened and of Marcus' and Samantha's conditions.

"What can I do?" Rick said.

"What you always do. Take care of the office and contact me if you need help with anything," Saul responded.

"You got it. Tell Samantha we love her and if she wants visitors, let me know. Scott and I are there for her."

"You're a good friend. I'll tell her," Saul said. Margaret left the children with Mike and the nannies and joined Saul in the library.

"Well, love. How is she?" Saul, with a worried look, said, "She is sleeping. She's lost and keeps saying this must be a nightmare. The baby is fine. Marcus's surgery went well. But he is still unconscious. They expect him to regain consciousness and do not think he will have any permanent mental issues. His left leg is broken, and he has a lot of rehab ahead of him. The bullet grazed his right lung, but the doctors felt like he will have no problems with that. He is lucky to be alive. But all we can do now is wait."

"And pray," said Margaret. She went to Saul and hugged him.

"We will get through this. Can I fix you a snack before dinner?"

"Yes, sweetheart. That would be nice. I skipped breakfast and lunch. And a cup of tea would be great, honey." Margaret left the room to prepare the food. She had already set them up in one of the guest suites and had her assistant bring over some clothes and personal items for them. Saul opened a book that Samantha had been reading and began reading it.

***

Samantha woke up in the middle of the night to find Mike in the room with her. "How do you feel?" he asked.

"So, it is real, Mike? My husband is clinging to life?"

"Samantha, you heard what the doctor said. Marcus is strong and will recover." She started crying again and Mike went to her bedside, sat down beside her, and put his arms around her. He held her until she was able to stop crying. "Samantha, concentrate on the baby. Marcus's baby. You know he keeps nothing from me. I know that Joseph is the biological father of the twins, and the girls are adopted. Bella is his first biological daughter, but I know he wants more. That is why he is over the top about this baby, his first biological son. He is looking forward to more children that the two of you make. He loves all his kids and he's a good father, but you must understand what it means to him, this little boy is his. I think he said that you and he were going to name him after his father. So, you must take care of yourself and have his baby. Until he recovers, I'm here for you. Anything you need just ask me. Marcus is my brother so that makes you my sister-in law. I checked in on him and there has been no change. But he will wake up to you."

"Mike, I love him so much and I just do not want this life without him in it," she said.

"He will be in it. You know he wants a big family so I'm sure he will want another one or two. So, let's get you a snack and something to drink. Then I will take you to see him. Samantha, news has reached Joseph. He's offering to come down and help with the boys. I told him you were in the hospital, just for observation, and I told him about Marcus' condition. He said he is praying for him and his family. At least we have removed the threat to the family. I thought all this was behind us, now I think it finally is."

"Nurse, could you send down for some soup, cheese and crackers, water and milk? I'll have the same thing. Except I'll have coffee."

"Yes, sir," the nurse said. She told the candy striper who was on duty to call the kitchen and tell them it is for the Matthew suite. The food came up and the chicken soup smelled wonderful. Mike pulled up a table for Samantha and he put his food next to hers and held his soup in his hands.

"Come on, girl. Eat up if you want to go see your husband." Samantha began to eat and suddenly realized that she was hungry. The baby was kicking. Samantha and Mike talked a little about Mr. Carr and his diagnosis and his mental health. Samantha said, "Marcus will want to help him and his family. Marcus will not file charges against him."

"I know, but it will be up to the DA, I am sure. Now let's go see your husband." Mike said. They went into intensive care and a nurse and doctor were in the room with Marcus hooking him up to a ventilator.

"Mrs. Matthews, the lung that was grazed by the bullet has collapsed so we are putting him on the ventilator to inflate his lung. He's not in any danger. So, if you would come back after we're finished, I think it will be better for you," the doctor said.

Mike said, "Samantha, let's let them do their work and we will come back in an hour." Samantha went over to Marcus' bed and said, "My darling. I am so sorry this happened to you, but please return to me." She kissed his lips and left with Mike. It was after eleven when Samantha and Mike went back into Marcus's room. He had a private nurse with him.

"Mrs. Matthews," she said. "He's doing well, and his lung will be inflated by morning and then we will take him off the machine. Would you like to sit with him?"

"Yes, please." The nurse moved the chair close to the bed and Samantha had a seat next to her husband.

"Mike, tell Joseph if he wants to come down that is fine with me. I think he can help with the boys."

Mike said, "If you are good, I am going back to your house, so I'll be there in the morning when the children are eating breakfast."

"Tell them I will be home for dinner tomorrow. Thank you, Mike."

"Samantha, I'd give my life for Marcus. He's the closest to family I've ever had. I love him like a brother."

"I know you do Mike, and he loves you the same," she said.

***

It was going on midnight when he decided to call Joseph. The phone rang once, and Joseph picked up the call.

"Hey Mike, what's going on?"

"I hope this isn't too late to call, but I just left the hospital."

"No, man I stay up and get some of my reading done while the house is quiet," Joseph replied.

"I talked to Samantha about you coming down to help. She said that the boys would probably enjoy your company."

"Okay, I'll fly in tomorrow by noon."

"I'll have a car there for you, Joseph. You do not need a driver, do you?"

"No, I will be fine with just the car."

"Okay, I'll have one waiting for you when you get in. Will you be coming straight to the mansion?"

"Yea, I think that's best. I'll give Samantha all the space she needs to deal with Marcus' recovery. I can imagine she's about lost it."

"Yeah, but she is doing better tonight. I can see the hope in her now. Well, I am here at the mansion. I'm going to try to get some sleep. See you tomorrow, or today, really."

He texted Anthony and told him to take the Jaguar and leave it for Joseph Claiborne who would be flying in by private jet by noon tomorrow. Mike opened the door to the mansion; all was quiet. He looked in on the girls. They were both snuggled down in their beds asleep. When he went into the boy's room, Jacob had kicked his blanket off, so Mike covered him back up. Jared was sound asleep. Yep, you could tell these were Joseph's boys. They looked just like him. You could tell they were bi-racial the more they got older. But no one would question their paternity and cross the Matthew family. *Man, five kids with another on the way,* Mike thought. He took the elevator up to the third floor where the guest suites were.

He went into his room and took a quick shower. He set his clock on his phone for 6:30 a.m. so he could be downstairs with the children. They would have many questions about their parents, and he wanted to be there to help answer them. Only about four and a half hours sleep, but he had functioned on less. He was asleep as soon as his head hit the pillow.

***

The alarm went off right on time. Usually, Mike was awake before the alarm goes off, but his morning it was hard for him to get going. A quick shower would wake him up, then he'll be ready for the kids. He was glad he never had children. He loved Marcus' children, but every morning to be on the clock, plus nights? No, he did not want children. Denise and he both shared that opinion. Neither of them wanted children. Tonight, he'd go by and see her and let her know what was going on. Samantha would be here tonight, and well, he wanted to get some needs met of his own.

He took the stairs down the first floor to the dining room. The buffet table was filled with fruit juice, eggs, and chocolate chip pancakes. He was going for black coffee. The girls come looking as cute as three young girls could. Both Ester and Matilda were blonde with blue eyes. Bella had dark curls and blue eyes. Marcus had wanted their hair long. Matilda's was straight, and she had it up in a ponytail. Both girls loved to wear dresses. Ester's hair was naturally curly, and she had it up in pigtails. She was still young, but outspoken. Bella's hair was wild, curly, and impossible to tame, just like her. Mike loved to debate with her and Ester. Matilda was much more serious, but the psychologist had said that her demeanor may be because she understood more. She's the oldest and took her biological parents' death more seriously because she could remember them. Marcus had insisted on keeping them in therapy. He did not want to miss anything concerning their mental health.

"Good morning, Uncle Mike," the girls said in unison. Samantha had made sure they knew their manners. The nannies they had were German and French, so the girls were learning these languages, as well as Spanish. Isabella was always talking to them in Spanish. She made sure all her children, and Mike, had learned her native tongue. Only John Marcus did not understand a lot of what she said in Spanish, unless she lost her temper. Then everyone knew what she was saying and knew to scatter.

The boys had not come to the table yet. Margaret was in with them, and their nanny was helping them dress. The girls were out for winter break, but the boys and Bella spent four hours a day, three days a week, in Montessori school. They were smart and needed something to do all the time. They could be exhausting at times, but Marcus always had projects for them to do and took them to work with him often. He was a good dad.

Mike helped the girls with their plates. Each wanted a pancake and cereal. He poured them some orange juice and milk. Matilda was still on the vegetarian kick, so she did not want any turkey bacon. Ester and Bella, however, loved bacon. Mike took a piece off her plate, just to hear her complain.

"Uncle Mike, stop eating my bacon! There is more on the buffet," she said.

"But sweetie, it tastes better when it is yours," Mike replied. She grimaced and said, "No more."

"You can have some of mine, Uncle Mike," Bella said sweetly.

"It's okay, I will get my own," Mike said.

Saul had left for the hospital. He wanted to see Samantha and Marcus first thing. In came the boys, both dressed in corduroy pants and plaid shirts. Today must be school day. Their eyes were blue, and their hair was long and curly, unless Joseph was around, you would never think they were not Marcus and Samantha's biological children.

Marcus was half Spanish and had dark curly hair and blue eyes. He was dark complexioned, and the boys were fair skinned like their mother.

"Hi Jared, Jacob. How did you sleep?" Mike asked the boys as Margaret helped them get their breakfast ready. Jared said, "I had a bad dream about my daddy. Uncle Mike is my daddy dead?"

"Why would you say that? No, your daddy was hurt, but the doctors say he is getting better."

"When will he be home?" Ester asked.

"Well, he needs some time to get better, so I'm not exactly sure," Mike responded. Matilda, who was quiet, asked, "Uncle Mike, are Mommy and Daddy really alright?"

Mike went over and picked her up and wiped her eyes, "Yes, sweetheart. Mommy will be here for dinner. I am sure she will tell you more when she gets home." Margaret interrupted and said, "Boys, you have school at nine. Eat your pancakes and bacon so you will be ready." The doorbell rang and the butler answered the door. In walked Joseph; he was early. He must have left early to be here this soon.

"Hi, Uncle Joseph," said Bella. "Are you here to see us?"

"I sure am, girls. And I here to eat a good breakfast. Chocolate chip pancakes, my favorite." The maid poured him some coffee.

"So, what is on the agenda today, kids?" Joseph asked.

Jacob asked, "What is an agenda?"

Jared answered, "It is your plan for the day, silly."

"Jared," Joseph said "Jacob, or anyone else never asks silly questions. That's how you learn."

"I'm sorry, but I tell him all the time to read more," said Jared.

"Yes, reading is important," said Joseph. "But so is observing and asking questions. So, tell me Jared, what are your plans today?"

"We have school from nine to one and we are working on a science project. Daddy was supposed to help us," he said.

"Well, how about me taking you two and Bella to school and I'll help with the science project. I will be here this week." The children went back to eating; the boys and Bella had chocolate on their hands and face. The maid brought three wet towels in so they could clean themselves up. Ester and Matilda were trying to get Mike to take them skating while the other kids were in school. He had given in and said he would after lunch. The boys and Bella immediately wanted to go, too. Joseph said, "I'll take you to school and then we will see if you have time before dinner." Mike said, "Mommy will be here for dinner, so everyone will want to be here at seven."

The boys and Bella grabbed their book bags and Joseph took them down to the car. He was going to have to drive Samantha's SUV. Sports cars and kids did not necessarily go together unless you had the money to have both. The kids got into the car and fastened their seatbelts. They were chattering away.

Ester and Matilda had asked to be excused and went to their room to work on their cross stitching. Margaret was teaching them sewing. Mike was having a second cup of coffee. He would then help the girls get ready for skating. That meant a dress change into pants and warm sweaters, hats, coats, and gloves. It was work to get them together, but he knew they'd have a lot of fun. So, it will be worth it. And then he sees Denise tonight. His phone rang, he recognized that number.

"Hi Renee, are you in New York?"

"Yes, I came for a shoot, but we got word that Marcus was shot. How is my love?"

"He's doing better. He's still unconscious but they are expecting him to regain consciousness any day now."

"Well, Harry and Elton would like a call from you," she said.

"I'll do it in a few hours. Where are you staying?"

"At the Regent's. When can I see Marcus?"

"Renee, I would wait a few days. Samantha is the one that needs to be with him for a while."

"Okay, my love. I'll see you soon."

"Ciao, Renee."

***

That is all Samantha needed, an old flame of Marcus' turning up. Renee and Marcus lived together in France and were inseparable for a while. Six months exactly. Marcus came home to find Renee in their bed with another woman. Not something Marcus approved of. He was a one-woman man. He left her and went back home to help his father with the business after John Marcus had his first heart attack. He basically called her and told her it was over and left all his things behind. When Marcus was done with a woman, he simply cut it off quickly and never looked back. Many women were left with broken hearts, but Marcus, when he was finished, he moved on. He rarely got involved with anyone seriously, but he also did not do many one-night stands. Sometimes, during a party, he might end up with a woman for the night. But it was aggressiveness that got him there. He leaves before the woman would wake up. That was Marcus, he was very serious when it came to dating. Renee had made it clear that Mike was on her radar. But Mike had always stayed clear because of Marcus. And he knew she was trouble.

***

Joseph was enjoying listening to the conversation between his boys and Bella. The twins he could not acknowledge as his own because of his agreement with Samantha and Marcus. He knew they would have to be told soon. They were ten-years-old now, and very smart.

"Uncle Joseph," Jared said, "so you will help us with our project?"

"Yes, Jared. What is your project?"

"It's electricity. Daddy was showing us how to light a light bulb using lemon juice."

"Jared, I think as long as there is internet, we can figure it out. I know your dad knows a lot about construction and it'd probably be easier for him, but I think I can cover it. We can also ask your grandfather, John Marcus. We will get your science project together. Do you feel all right with this, Jared?"

"Yes. I suppose. I miss my dad."

"I know boys. He will get well and be home soon. I just want to help as much as I can. Is that okay?" Jacob spoke up, "Yes Uncle Joseph. I know you can figure it out."

"I want to help, too!" Bella exclaimed.

"You're too young," Jared argued. "Your science fair is next year."

"She can help," Joseph said firmly. "Bella, your father would be excited to hear you are taking an interest in science.

Joseph got into the car line and the kids' teachers were there to receive them as they got out of the car. The school policy was to let the children be as independent as possible, so no parents were to walk the children in. Joseph liked the school Samantha had chosen. Sophia was being homeschooled. Emily was having a hard time allowing Sophia to become independent. Joseph was making a mental note that he would get more involved with Sophia's education. No matter how close Sophia and her mother seemed, Joseph could come home, and Sophia demanded all his time until she went to bed. She was a daddy's girl.

"See you kids later. Have a good day."

"Bye, Uncle Joseph!" the kids yelled. The teacher closed the door and Joseph drove away. He wished that the twins could have said, "Goodbye, daddy." As he drove, he decided to go see Samantha at the hospital. He knew Saul was there, and he knew Saul would not like it, but he really wanted to see her.

Joseph parked the SUV in the parking lot and took the elevator to the seventh floor. He entered the suite and asked to see Samantha. Saul and Samantha came out of Marcus's room.

"How is he?" asked Joseph.

"He seems better. He is healing and he is moving about. I think another week and he'll coming to."

"Hi, Saul," said Joseph, "I just took the kids to school. So, Samantha will you have lunch with me while I wait for the kids?"

"Sure. Dad, do you mind?"

"No, I'll stay upstairs in Marcus' room," said Saul. Joseph placed his hand on Samantha's back and guided her out the door to the elevator.

"Let's eat at the hospital," said Samantha.

"No, I am sorry. I am getting you out of the hospital. How about across the street, at that little French cafe?"

"Yes, it does look good. And maybe a glass of wine."

"Yes, sweetheart relax a little. I know what it is like to think you lost the love of your life. Talk to me. What is going through that pretty head?"

"Oh, coming so close to losing Marcus, not knowing how he will be when he wakes up. I cannot love again and lose that love." He reached over in the car and gave Samantha a hug and held on a little longer.

"I am sorry, sweetheart. If I had had it to do it all over again, I'd do things differently."

"You mean if you knew that I was pregnant."

"Yes, I'd have you and my boys. I'd have joint custody and we would be friends like we had always been." Samantha reached out and touched his arm, "Joseph we changed, both of us. I wanted a family and children. I wanted to be the center of your world and your parents wanted you to be a politician, you could not decide. We never got to the stage where we were talking about settling down. We were having such an incredible chase. Ours was friendship of competitive love. I love you, Joseph, and always will. Marcus is different, more mature, settled down, and knows what he wants. He is steadfast in his love for me and the children. The children and I are his world. He does not ever ask me to take a back seat. I know it sounds selfless and exhausting, but it works for us, for me."

"Remember in law school, you always had to be the best, number one?" she continued. "And no matter how hard I tried, I was number two. Joseph, you never let me beat you in anything and you never will. It's not your nature to lose, even to your wife. I am number one in Marcus' life. He loves me enough to lose my love. He is steadfast in his love for me. He loves me enough to let me go if that's what I want. So, if I wanted you, Joseph, Marcus would not stand in our way. He'd do everything to make it easier on me and the children. Joseph, is Emily first in your life? And what about Sophia? Please understand, I will always love you, you are the father of our boys. I will always be grateful for your love, but you are who you are. I am who I am. We can make our relationship work if we stick to our plan. I know you'd liked to tell the whole world that you have twin boys. Someday, but not yet."

"Promise. Of course," said Joseph, "I will always do what is right for you and the boys. Now let's go in and get lunch and get you a drink." He came around the side of the car to assist her out.

***

She was getting large, she thought, for going into the seventh month of pregnancy. Maybe she was just self-conscious around Joseph. He's with her like Marcus was when she was seven months pregnant with the twins. Joseph helped her out of the car and placed his hand in the small of her back. They looked like any couple expecting a child, stopping to get lunch, before returning to that well-manicured downtown apartment building. No, that's not Marcus' style of living. Back to reality.

After they were seated, she got her head on straight. *My husband was shot trying to protect his family and I am pregnant with his child,* she thought. She put her hand on Joseph's hand as they sat across from each other at the table.

"I love you, and I always will, but I cannot live another life losing the one I love. You, and now Marcus. I miss you and your touch. But I cannot lose him. He is right for me." Joseph spoke quietly, "I could have been right for you. Just an impulsive act brought me to my senses." The waitress came over to the table, "Can I get you two something to drink?"

"I'd like water and a glass of wine please."

Joseph said, "I'll take a bourbon and coke, with water too."

"Okay," said the waitress and she left to get the drinks. Marcus would frown on Samantha drinking at this stage of the pregnancy, but it would not hurt. Joseph would say nothing about the drinking. He watched her though and made sure she did nothing foolish.

"The lamb looks good," he said to her.

"Yes, I remember how much you like lamb. I think I'll have it also. So how were the kids when you took them to school?" she asked.

"Talkative," said Joseph, "The twins were concerned about their science project. Bella was eager to help, as always."

"Yes, their father was supposed to help them. I told them I'll take his place for the science project, and we would enter it into the fair and we would be fine."

"They asked a few questions about when you and their father were coming home. I told them soon. I like their school. I'd like to find a similar one for Sophia."

"Tell Emily to call me. I can help you and her with finding a school." He put his hand on hers, "I know you will. You're a good friend to Emily." The waitress placed the food before them and Samantha was suddenly hungry. Joseph noticed that she looked pale.

"Are you sure you are okay, sweetheart?"

"Yes, I am. But I have not been eating correctly. But Marcus is out of the woods, except for coming to."

"Yes, and that'll just be a matter of days. So, eat up and let's surprise the kids. The two of us can pick them up from school." Samantha agreed. "Yes," she said shaking her head. "Let's get the kids and I'll go back after dinner to see Marcus." Joseph paid the bill and helped Samantha down the stairs of the restaurant. It was beginning to snow and Joseph wanted to make sure he got Samantha into the car without mishap. He was getting to help her with some of the things he missed when she was carrying his babies. Now she is carrying Marcus' baby and he wanted to help her and return the favor that Marcus had done. Yet, during her seventh month with the boys, neither Marcus nor Joseph knew whose babies they really were.

Joseph turned the heat higher as he noticed Samantha was shivering. He turned out of the parking lot and headed toward the kids' Montessori school. Joseph pulled into the pickup lane where the boys and Bella were standing with their teachers. Samantha waved to them, and you could see the happiness on their faces. The teachers opened the doors and the kids climbed into their car seats and buckled themselves in.

"Hello, Mrs. Matthew. How is your husband?" the teacher asked.

"He is doing better, thank you," Samantha said. The teachers closed the doors and waved to the boys. Bella said, "Mom, we did not know you were coming to pick us up."

"Well, Uncle Joseph came and took me to lunch. I had planned to eat dinner with you children and then go later to see your daddy." Jacob asked, "How is daddy?" Samantha said, "he is doing better, but he needs to stay at the hospital a little longer."

"Uncle Joseph, so you will help us with our science project?" said Jacob.

"Yes, Bella and I are going to help you and we are going to win that science fair, Jared, at least we are going to try."

"I love you, guys," said Samantha.

"It is snowing, so instead of skating, let's play in the snow, kids. How does that sound?" said Joseph.

"Okay," said the kids. "We can try to build a snowman." Joseph headed toward the mansion. Mike was pulling up with the Ester and Matilda.

"Hey girls," said Joseph. "We are going to play in the snow for a while. Do you girls want to play with us?" Mike rolled up a ball of snow and threw it at Matilda.

"Hey, Uncle Mike, that is not nice!" Samantha ran toward the house.

"Careful," said Mike. "It's slippery and we do not want a pregnant lady to fall." Mike grabbed Samantha's arm and guided her to the door of the mansion.

"Bye, kids, I'll see you inside. Have fun with your uncles!" Samantha went into the kitchen and knew Margaret would be there.

"Hi Margaret," said Samantha. "Yum, that smells good. Is Dad still at the hospital?"

"Thank you," Margaret said. "Glad you came home for dinner; those babies need you. Dad is in the library grading papers and projects. Making up lesson plans. You know, finding a reason to drink sherry in the library."

"Yeah. Never hear an objection to that," Samantha said.

"Why would I object to the perfect man? Now, go help your dad," Margaret said.

"Hi, Dad," said Samantha as she took the sherry glass from him and drained it. He pulled her down beside him and put his arms around her, "Yes, he is moving a lot and they had to take him off the respiratory. He is breathing on his own and is just on oxygen. So, after dinner, Mike and I will go back. I just wanted to see the kids."

"How was your lunch with Joseph?" Saul asked.

"Well, it went as well as expected. He understands we will always love each other, but my heart will forever belong to Marcus. And I told him our love had always been a competitive love and that Marcus loves me enough to let me go. And I told him to be fair to Emily."

"Good girl," Saul said. Samantha walked over to the desk and poured herself another drink.

"Yes," Samantha said, knowing Saul still had more to say.

"Well," Saul said. "I think Joseph has hope. He wants to fantasize about what could be."

"Maybe, but it's because of the boys," Samantha replied.

"He loves to think that way, but you're wrong, girlie. Like you said, competitive love."

***

Dinner went well as everyone was talking away after they found out that Dad was doing better. Chatting about the science project and falling on the ice. Joseph said, "Okay. You five kids, let's watch a movie. Your Uncle Mike needs to take Mommy to the hospital." So, they rushed to get showers and got ready to watch a movie. Anything to stay up later than their 8 o'clock bedtime.

"Thanks, Joseph," said Mike. "I'd like to get to the hospital, and I know Samantha would, too." Saul and Margaret said, "Let us know if something happens. We are going up to relax a little. Oh. Samantha, I talked to Isabella today. She said John Marcus is having heart problems but refuses to go to the doctor until Marcus wakes up."

"I understand, Dad." Mike and Samantha put their coats on and left for the hospital.

They went up to Marcus' suite and there were nurses paging the doctor. There was a strange, foreign woman standing in Marcus' room.

"Mike, something's going on," Samantha said. Mike stopped a nurse, "What's going on?" She said, "Mr. Matthew has come out of his coma. He woke up with a lot of aggression. He seems angry. Mrs. Matthew, this is normal behavior. He has confusion. The last experience he had, like the wreck and the shooting, he just may be trying to figure out what is going on. We are giving him a shot to relax him and help him to sleep. I know you want to talk to him, but right now, you need to go home and let's help him get a good night of sleep. Tomorrow we will see how much memory he has and if there is any other damage to his brain. Mike said, "Samantha, I'm going to have a driver take you home. Call the family and let him know that he is awake. John Marcus needs to get his heart checked out."

Samantha just noticed the woman who was in the room and went over to her and asked who she was. Mike intervened in the conversation.

"Renee, I told you I'd let you know. Samantha, this is an old friend that knew Marcus when we were roaming Europe." Renee extended her hand to Samantha.

"Well, if Marcus did not tell you, we lived together in my flat in France. We were together about six months. I came to see how he was." Samantha dropped her hand. "You have no business being here. Mike, how did she get by security?"

"Samantha, I'll take care of escorting Renee out and caution security to do a better job of screening people. Renee," Mike said. "You need to leave." Mike called Anthony, "Make sure only family is allowed up to the Matthew's suite. Make sure we have security downstairs and upstairs. I'd like you to take Mrs. Matthew home, please. I am going to stay the night here."

"Yes, sir," said Anthony. He came and got Samantha and drove her home. Samantha called John Marcus first.

"He is awake, Dad. Now go check your heart out. Marcus will need you well."

"Tell me darling, how is he?"

"He's confused and seems very aggressive. The doctor said that was normal and that they'll know more tomorrow," Samantha replied.

"Thank God. Thank you, sweetheart. I'll be at the doctor's tomorrow. Can we see him?" John Marcus asked. Samantha said, "We will know more tomorrow. The doctors do not want to overwhelm him. They want to give him time to sort out his thoughts and emotions and make sure there is no permanent brain injury. Mike is staying with him."

"That's good. Go home dear, rest, and take care of his baby."

"Yes, I am on my way home to tell the family. Good night, John. Get some rest and send Isabella and the girls my love."

"I will, goodnight."

***

Mike went to Renee and took her by the arm and escorted her to the door.

"Renee, I told you to stay away. I will let you know how he is and if he wants to see you. Renee, I know you, you're here to cause problems. So leave."

"Mike, darling. I just wanted to check on the love of my life myself."

"Renee, Marcus left you and he is happy. He has five children and another on the way. So go. Or do I need to get someone to see you to your hotel?"

"No, darling, my car is downstairs. So, Mike are you involved with anyone?"

"Yes, I am and I am happy. Go. Now." Mike went back into Marcus' room, and he was much calmer. Marcus seemed confused, so Mike pulled up a chair to set next to his bed. Mike said, "Marcus, do you know me and what happened to you?"

"Not really. It's all vague. But yes, I know who you are. You are head of security for the Matthew's construction firm. My best friend, you are like a brother to me."

"Good. You were stalked, and on your own, you decided to take a risk and draw him out. So, you rode your Harley out in the subdivision where you live. The stalker shot you from the hills across the road and you lost control of your bike and were injured pretty bad. You've been in a coma for three weeks. Samantha has been here every day, worried sick."

"So, the hot French woman who was practically trying to get in bed with me is not my wife?"

"No, it's an old girlfriend. Who is trouble," Mike replied.

"My wife is pregnant."

"Yes, with your sixth child. And if you remember, this is your first biological son. Do you remember who Joseph is? And your two daughters that you adopted, Ester and Matilda? And Bella?"

"Yes, it is all coming back. Did you catch the stalker?" asked Marcus.

"Yes." said Mike. "It is Mr. Carr, the man the bank foreclosed on and brought you in to buy the development."

"I paid him well, what is his beef?" Marcus asked.

"He suffers from PTSD and is in the psychiatric unit at the hospital. He was deployed four times and sees you as the enemy. He was in therapy for a while and taking is medication regularly. That's why we didn't hear anything for a few years. But he could no longer afford therapy and had to stop. He is also off his meds. Saul has talked to the DA about prosecuting him, but we wanted to wait until you woke up before anything was done."

"Mike," said Marcus, "have Saul talk to the DA about helping him recover. He served his country and I believe that it is our responsibility to help him get well. What about his family?" asked Marcus.

"They are divorced, and she is raising their two children. We offered her a job at one of our construction offices and we are helping her with housing and care for the kids. This was how we finally found him and were able to track him." Marcus grimaced from the pain in his broken leg.

"Yes, I remember the plan. Just keep everything the same with the family and hopefully we can help Mr. Carr get well."

Mike said, "I thought you'd feel that way. I'll talk to Saul in the morning. Now, how about your wife? She is the love of your life, and you are very excited about this baby boy." Marcus laid back on his pillow, "I am tired, Mike. I need to rest. Let's talk tomorrow."

"Marcus, Samantha is going to be here in the morning expecting you to be the loving husband and father you have always been."

"Yeah. I'll do my best Mike. But I need time to figure out my injuries and how they will affect me. You understand that, don't you man?"

"Yes, but you had a very sensual relationship with your wife. You never screwed around. You've always been a one-woman man."

"And Renee?" said Marcus.

"Past trouble. You lived with her in France for six months and you came home to find her in bed with another woman. You left France and came back to the States when your father had his heart attack. He has had one more, so you took over the company and your dad hired Samantha's firm to handle the legal issues that were plaguing the company. You declared love for her at first sight."

"Yes, I remember everything. I'll see you in the morning." The nurse came in with some sleeping pills.

"Mr. Matthew needs to rest. The doctor will be running tests tomorrow." she told Mike.

"Okay, see you tomorrow. Call your, Dad. Marcus, he is waiting to go to the heart doctor after he's heard from you."

"Leave your cell phone and I will call him."

Mike said, "You and Samantha are naming your son after your father. He will be John Marcus, III. You guys are going to call him Trey for short. Sleep well, man."

Mike left his phone with Marcus, and as he closed the door, he heard Marcus say, "Dad, I am getting better. I need you to see the heart doctor, and then you and mom can come by the hospital and see me. Yes, Samantha was here, but I sent her away. I need time to sort all this out. Mike just left. Get some rest, Dad, and I will see you tomorrow. The nurse gave me something to help me sleep. Goodnight." Mike finished closing the door to Marcus' suite. He was not ready to go back to the mansion. Without his phone, he could not call and tell Denise he was coming home to spend the night. He needed her tonight. He wanted to feel her touch.

His Jeep was parked in the hospital parking lot. He got in and headed to the house they shared together. She would be glad to see him, even if it was after midnight. He was tired, but he knew what he needed. He drove to his house and opened the door. All the lights were off. He made his way to the bedroom to find Denise asleep. He undressed as quietly as possible, but she said, "Sweetheart, what's up?"

"Marcus came out of his coma," Mike said. "I need you tonight." She opened the covers of the bed, "Come tell me about it." Mike slid into bed and immediately pressed his body up next to hers and said, "I'd rather not talk." He then engulfed her mouth with his.

She could feel his desire as he was already hard. He wasted no time with foreplay, but simply pulled her to him and parted her legs. He slid his cock into her and began to thrust as if he was angry. The tension he had been carrying for weeks was with every thrust. Denise knew tonight that he needed her and her body. She put her arms around him and pulled him on top of her. They would talk later, but right now, she knew he needed comforting. Mike had almost lost his best friend, his brother. He began to thrust faster and was leaving her behind. She unselfishly thought of him and his need for her. He came with one last forceful thrust.

"I am sorry," he said.

She said, "Hush my love. Get some sleep. It has been along few weeks. Would you like me to get you up early?"

"Please," he said. "I'd like to go by the mansion and talk to the kids and take Samantha to the hospital." She sat the alarm for five and then put her arms around him to hold him. Mike fell asleep immediately. He needed her and that was all she cared about. There would be a lot to sort out. She was holding the business down and knew she needed to give Marcus an update on everything when he was ready.

"Sleep darling," she said. "Sleep."

***

Mike woke up before the alarm went off. Denise was still asleep, and he knew that when he got out of bed, she would wake up. Finally, he found a woman who understood him. Denise wanted the same things he did; children were not in their plans, neither was marriage. They had both tried it before and just did not like how people changed after marriage. Neither one of them wanted that in their life and were content with living together. If things changed for either one of them, then there was no legal hassle. He loved her independence and the fact that when he showed up after being gone on an assignment, it was okay with her. She was not needy nor possessive. They were both devoted to the Matthew family.

He tried to ease out of the bed, detangling himself from Denise's arms. "Sweetheart, can I make you some coffee for the road?" she asked.

"If you do not mind, that would be great," Mike responded.

"I will make it to go. I know you want to get to the mansion before the kids get up."

"Yes, I also want to talk to Samantha about Marcus. He is going through something and cannot explain it to even himself. He is not the same man," Mike said.

"He needs time. What he has gone through has to have changed him," Denise responded.

"I know, but something is going on with how he feels about Samantha. He did not want her with him last night. Marcus could never keep his hands off her. They had one of the most passionate and loving relationships I have ever seen. She is right for him, but he thinks now, for some reason, he is not right for her."

"Get your shower. Time is what is needed. He has a lot to do physically, as well as emotionally, to get himself to understand all that has happened to him," she said.

"You're right. If that couple fails, then no couple will ever make it." Denise leaned over and kissed his shoulder and got up to make his coffee. It was ready by the time he was out of the shower and dressed. He kissed Denise passionately and patted her butt. "I am sorry the sex was one-sided last night." She put her fingers to his lips,

"I understand there will be time for us once this ordeal gets settled. Go, darling. I will see you when I see you." With that statement, Mike let himself out of their condo and Denise went back to bed. She had a few hours before she was to be at the office. Sleeping a couple more hours would be what she needed. She had a long day a head.

Mike started his Jeep and let the engine warm up; it was freezing outside. He had dressed warmly, but still felt a chill. He knew it was not about the weather; he just knew that his best friend was in trouble, and he was feeling the chill from that. He put the car in gear and directed it in toward the mansion. When he pulled into the driveway, it was time to put his game face on for the kids and Samantha. He let himself in and Peter came out to greet him.

"Mr. Mike, can I get you anything, sir?"

"No, Peter. Is the family up?"

"No, sir, I have not heard anyone stirring yet. Breakfast will be at seven. Mr. Joseph is not down yet but I know he will be down soon. He tries to be downstairs before the children start stirring."

"Thank you, Peter. I am going to check on the girls." Just as he was entering the girl's room, he heard sobbing. Matilda was awake and crying. Ester was in her bed trying to comfort her. "What's going on girls?" He pulled both girls to him. Ester being Ester said, "Matilda thinks Daddy is dead and everyone is keeping it from us. Uncle Mike, Daddy not dead, is he?"

"No, my angels. Your daddy is trying to get well so he can come home and be with you. He loves you. I'll tell you what, after breakfast write him a get-well-soon card and I will take it to him."

"I told you so," teased Bella from her bed on the other side of the room.

Matilda, wiping her tears away with the sleeve of her pajama said, "I want to see him. I want to see if he is alive. Why can't we go to see him? Does he not want to see us?"

"Sure, he does," said Mike, "but the doctors do not want him to have visitors yet."

"We are not visitors," Bella said, "We are his children and we all want to see him. The boys want to see him, too." Mike said, "How about a video chat with him? When I take your mother to the hospital, I will set up a video chat and then you children can see him and talk to him. Is that a good deal? "Yes, Uncle Mike. For now."

"Okay, you girls get ready for breakfast." Kelly, their nanny, came into the room with a happy, "Good morning."

"Girls, let us get ready for breakfast and make plans for the day," she said. Ester spoke up. "We want to write daddy a letter."

"Then you to need to get dressed, eat breakfast, and then we will get to the letter. Now scoot." With that, the girls went into their dressing room to choose their clothes for the day, dress, and brush their hair. Kelly said, "I will be right in."

"So, Mr. Mike, they are having a rough night, they have lost parents before and they need so much reassurance," she said where the girls couldn't hear.

"Yes, I got that. I'm going to set up a video call from Marcus to them. I will call you when I get it all set up from the hospital."

"That is a great idea and I think a visit to their psychologist would be good too," she responded. Mike said, "Good. I am going to check on the boys."

"Mr. Joseph is there helping them dress. They do not have school today, so he is trying to work with them on the science project."

"He is great with them," Mike said.

"I know it is none of my business, and of course I'll never say anything, but I can see that he is their biological father."

"Yes, when he is around it is clear that he is their father, but the boys do not know. Only a few people know the story, and when Marcus and Samantha feel that the boys can understand the whole story, they will tell them. The few of us that know, keep quiet."

"Yes, I understand. They are smart boys and I hope they are told before they figure it out for themselves."

"You and me both," Mike said. "See you at breakfast." And with that, Mike left to find Joseph.

Joseph was trying to get the boys to put their clothes on; the nanny had stepped out. They were completely ignoring him, and he had gone as far as to try and wrestle them into their clothes. They were had just turned ten and sometimes acted like they were four years old. Mike said, "Man, you need a hand with them?"

"I do. How does Marcus get them to listen?"

"Well, Marcus will be firm. He does not raise his voice, but he will give them a choice that they never refuse."

"Okay, tell me the secret," Joseph said.

"It's better to show you." Mike said to the boys, "Uncle Mike is delivering a message from your dad and your mom, so listen. Until your dad is out of the hospital, Uncle Joseph and Uncle Mike oversee you along with your nanny." The boys were both lying on their beds, "So come and face me please." Both boys got up and stood by their bed, Mike bent down so they were in direct eye contact with him. "So, guys here are your choices, you can get dressed and get down to breakfast on time or you can stay in your room in your pajamas and miss breakfast, lunch, dinner, and all snacks. Furthermore, all activities that were planned for you, will be canceled. So, we are leaving now and if you show up completely dressed, face and hands washed, socks and shoes on, hair brushed, and bed made, then we will know you want to go on with your day. Joseph, let us see what the cook has for breakfast, shall we?" Mike left the room and said, "Let's go man. I am hungry and it is seven, if you're late? Well, the girls will have eaten all the bacon and we get left out."

Joseph said, "That is it?"

"Yep, they only challenged Marcus one time. Samantha backed him up and they never pulled their strike again. One day without food and no plans made for growling stomachs and a boring day. They are very head strong and smart. If they think they will make you jump through hoops, they will. Marcus is firm but wants them to make good choices. His dad did the same with him. Isabella tried sometimes to intervene, she falls for the tears and the whining, but that just made John Marcus implement secret number two."

"Okay, tell me what secret two is," Joseph asked

"Toothbrush on hands and knees, scrubbing the tile floors in their many bathrooms. So, Isabella learned to back John and Marcus learned that his dad was firm, but always wanted him to make the right decision."

"So, they will be down?"

"You will see. Now, I could use some coffee, how about you?" Mike said.

"Yes, how about the girls? Does he use the same rules for them?"

"Yep, and they have never had to go through a day or night without food or fun. They watched their brothers make the wrong choice and they knew not to try to pull anything on their dad. I think Samantha backs Marcus a hundred percent in front of the children, and he backs her. They are a wonderful team. They stick together when it comes to parenting. And most other things also. That is what makes their marriage work. There is a true partnership and respect for one another. They come first, then the kids, and then work."

"Well, Emily and I need to get on the same page."

"Yep, or you will find yourself divorced. Denise and I agree that we do not want kids or marriage. That works for us."

They each sat down and waited for everyone to arrive. Samantha had come down and was seated at one end of the table. She looked like she had not slept all night. "Good morning," she said.

"Good morning," Mike said. Joseph said, "Good morning." Next entering the room came the girls. Mike got up and scooted their chairs in. Last to arrive, right at seven, came the boys, elegantly dressed. Bella was still upstairs getting ready in her room. She liked to take her time.

"Good morning." they said in unison just like the girls and sat down into their seats. Samantha said, "Please, let us join hands and say a prayer for your dad. Matilda, would you like to lead us?"

"Yes, Mom." And she began to pray for her dad's speedy recovery, the food, and nature. She had a list. When she said 'amen' everyone joined her and went to the buffet. The girls knew what they wanted to eat and fixed their own plates. The boys could not decide which food to get so Joseph and Samantha helped to fix their plates. The conversation at the table was very interactive. Samantha did her best to be upbeat about their dad. The boys were planning their science project and the girls had plans with Margaret and Isabella. The nannies would work on lesson plans and organizing the children's day. They usually did not eat with the family unless one of the parents had to be out early. Samantha and Marcus had tried to keep from interfering with family time, except for date nights and the occasional overnight stay at Marcus's condominium. He kept it so the two of them could slip away. There were many family outings and trips that usually centered around learning or something like skiing. Then there were overnights with the grandparents and outings with the aunts and Phillipe, Marcus' half-brother. The extended family outings were mostly the entire Matthew clan: boyfriends, girlfriends, husbands and wives, aunts, uncle, nieces, and nephews. Saul and Margaret were always included. The children had not had sleepovers at friends' houses, but Marcus made a point of allowing all their friends over. Mike and Denise were always included in a lot of the outings. And of course, there was always nannies, security, and extra staff when needed. The children also had all kinds of language classes, music, karate, and soccer. The girls had dance and Marcus told the boys when they were old enough, they would be going to ball room dancing classes. Their lives were busy, but every day they had quiet time where they could choose their activity or just chill out. All five children could handle a computer but were limited on the time they spent on it. They were expected to read a book each week and turn in a report to their dad and contribute something interesting at the evening meal. To be children of a very wealthy family, they were learning that wealth created responsibility. Samantha said, "We should leave now for the hospital." The girls said, "May we be excused? We have a letter and drawing for Dad. Uncle Mike, will you let us know about the Zoom meeting?"

"Yes, girls. I am thinking right after your dinner. I want all five of you to be able to talk to your dad."

"I will get my coat and handbag," said Samantha excusing herself from the table. She was well into her seventh month of pregnancy, and she was tired. Joseph said, "Let us get to work on your science project." The staff removed the food and each child had to hand their plate to the server and tell them 'thank you' and send a 'thank you' to the chef. Samantha appeared with her coat and Mike took it from her and helped her in it. Mike said, "All right. We are off to see how your dad is doing."

Mike carefully helped Samantha down the front steps where

the limo was parked; the driver got out and opened the door for Samantha to get in. Mike supported her while she got into the car, helped her with the seat belt, and went around and got into the other side. Security would be following them just for the extra protection. Mike could handle anything that came up, but with all the publicity about Marcus, Mike knew that John Marcus Sr. would have it no other way after the accident. Mike was not going to take any chances. There was extra security on all the family. John Marcus was frantic with fear for the safety of his family. He had ordered Mike to double up on normal security. Not all the family members agreed with him, especially the younger ones; they wanted more freedom. He was frightened for his family as this was the first time any family member had been attacked. He knew he had made enemies, but not Marcus. He was the very man to take over and do the right things by people. They had plenty of money, more than enough, it was important to enjoy what they had. Isabella and he had been talking about an island, maybe to retire there, or at least have a place of refuge for the family. He knew Marcus wanted to stay in New York until the children were grown. He also knew that Samantha was too close to her dad to move far away. And Saul, well he was a Jew and would never leave New York where his connections were. Mike would stay with Marcus and his family anywhere they decided to go. They all had plenty of options as the Matthew family had many homes. Money allowed that. Isabella had a home in Spain, and she wanted to go and visit her parents and her twin sister, just as soon as things settled down. Phillipe had his restaurant in New York, and his mother, and would never leave. So, the Matthew home base would always be New York.

Marcus had been looking at some homes in D.C. It seemed he wanted somewhere his family could stay when they visited Joseph. John Marcus had confided in him that he suspected there was far more to the story with Joseph, but his son was happy, and that is all John Marcus cared about. The driver pulled up in front of the hospital and Mike opened the door to help Samantha out. She was struggling to get comfortable and her eighth month of pregnancy was just around the corner. *She needs to be resting,* Mike thought. But until Marcus was home, she was not going to leave his side.

They rode the elevator to the eighth floor and Marcus was just brought back from physical therapy. He looked defeated and tired.

"Marcus, darling, how are you today love?" Samantha went forward to give him a kiss, but he brushed her off. She seemed crushed, but just sat down beside his bed. Marcus said, "Sam, we need to talk."

"Hey guys, I'll step out and give you your privacy." Marcus said, "Mike, I'd like you to stay and hear me out also." So, Mike sat down on the couch, folded his hands across his lap, and listened.

"Sam, I am not happy with the results of the test that the doctor has given me today. It is going to take many months for me to get back to me, if I even can. I know you want me to come home. Right now, that's not going to be best for me or the children or even you. I will once I can be at home to be with the children. It's going to be hard to put all this behind us, if we even can. I'm going to the penthouse to recover. I know you will have plenty of support from everyone, especially Mike, Joseph, your father, and my family. I know we have great plans for our new baby, and I am still excited about our little boy. I will be there as much as I physically can; delivery and everything. I now suffer from PTSD, have tremendous anger issues, irritability, and cannot, at this time, feel like the old Marcus. Please understand this is not about you but what is best –if I have any chance of becoming who I was before." Samantha began to cry.

"Come here, sweetheart. We will make this work somehow. There are things that I'm not wanting to discuss until I get a better understanding myself." He put his hand on Samantha's stomach and the baby began to move, "This is the most important thing to me. So, I want you to take care of you and him. You're tired, I see it in your face. I'm sure you are not sleeping, and I hope you are eating well. Take no risk to your health or this baby. It will get better, but it is going to take time." Samantha said, "Whatever you need. I am here for you. Like you said, we will make it work. Would you like anything form the cafeteria? I am going there and then to the chapel."

Mike said, "Samantha, you go ahead, I need to talk to Marcus in private, please."

"I see, so anything I can bring anyone?"

"No, Sam, I am good." Marcus said. Mike said, "Good here." And Samantha left the room. Once the door closed Mike said, "What gives, man? That is the love of your life, the mother of your children."

"Mike, I need you to trust me and let me do my recovery the best way I know how. I want you to be there for Sam, the kids, and Joseph when he comes. There are things I am not ready to talk about with anyone but the doctors and the shrinks. Trust me. Assign another security person for me. I want you with the family."

"Well, speaking of family," said Mike, "they are freaking out, so I promised a Zoom call after dinner. They need to see you and you need to make them understand your plan. I know I do not understand it and Sam does not. Can you not see it all over her face?"

"Yes, I can, but for now, this for the best. Please support me in this. The doctors agree. As for Mr. Carr, I spoke to the D.A. and he said Mr. Carr is mentally not competent to stand trial. So, he is in a mental hospital until they can get a handle on his mental health. I want no actions taken against him. He is to receive the best of care. Have Saul handle his case. I want no charges brought. Have Robert check out the family and make sure they receive all the support they need. I understand PTSD, it is serious, and he should not be held accountable for his actions. He served his country, but the VA did not serve him. Also, have Robert set up funding for a clinic just for Veterans. Make it free. The best doctors. I am sure some of my rich friends can donate too. Hell, when your billionaires, money should be there to help."

"Got it," said Mike. "When you're ready to talk more, I am here for you. Just try to be there for Samantha and your children."

"I know it is a mess, but I had to get Mr. Carr before he hurt my family," Marcus said.

"Marcus, you took a great risk," Mike replied.

"Yeah, but he wanted me. I had to give him the chance to come after me. I am here, I will recover. I just need time. The family is safe, and we will get through this."

"Did you talk to your dad?" Mike asked.

"Yes, he went to the doctor, and they said rest and stop worrying. So, I told him my plans and he simply wants me to get better."

Mike said, "We all do."

"How about calling the nurse and seeing if she can give me something for pain and anxiety? I know what Sam's panic attacks are all about now, and they are not fun," Marcus said.

"Okay, I will call the nurse." He went to Marcus's bed and hugged him, "You know we are like brothers. I would do anything for you," Mike said.

"Yes, I know you would. I'm just going to ask you to look after Sam. I cannot talk about my state of mind with her, nor with anyone until the doctors and I can figure out what is going on with my thinking."

"Stop being so hard on yourself," Mike said. "Marcus, just please reassure Samantha and the children that as soon as you get your shit together, you will come home. It is past their dinner so I promised you'd call them by video chat. Here is my iPad. You know the number, call them. I'm going to find Samantha." Marcus dialed the house number and Peter answered the call, "Peter, will you round up the children so I can talk with them?"

"Yes, sir, they are waiting at the dining room table. How are you Mr. Matthew?" Peter asked.

"I think it's too soon to tell. I would appreciate it if you can handle the house responsibilities for Mrs. Matthew."

"Of course. We will keep it running without missing a beat. Now, let me help the children get set up to talk with you." He went to the dining room table where earlier he had set up an iPad so the children could see and talk to their dad.

"Children, your dad will be on the screen in a few minutes. Are all of you ready to take turns talking to your dad?" Joseph came into the room to help if he was needed. Marcus appeared on the screen. Matilda cried out, "Daddy, you are alive! I did not believe it until I saw you." She had tears streaming down her face. Marcus touched the screen, and said, "My sweet girl, Daddy is healing. My leg hurts like hell, but I am getting better." Bella spoke up, "Daddy, you said a bad word, you owe the money jar."

"So, I did," said Marcus. "Will you cover me for the money until I get home?"

"Daddy, it is okay. I am sure you are in pain, and you just slipped on your words," Ester chimed in.

"No, I mean it. My leg hurts like hell. Now I owe another dollar." The girls laughed. "Boys," he addressed the twins, "how is the science project coming?"

Jared spoke up, "We are getting it finished with Uncle Joseph's help."

Jacob said, "But it would go faster if you were here, Dad."

"Jacob, things happen. Be appreciative to your Uncle Joseph for coming all the way from D.C. to help you boys. So be on your best behavior. All of you, help your mother and make sure you do some extra chores to help out if needed. I am counting on the five of you."

"We will, Daddy."

Matilda said. "Can I be in charge?"

"Yes, but make sure you consult an adult if you have questions or need help," Marcus said.

"I will."

"Children, so Matilda is going to help out with you five. She is the oldest and I want you to listen to her and respect her opinions. And Matilda, being a leader is making it so people want to follow you. Everyone got it?" Marcus said firmly.

"Yes sir." There was a unison of young voices.

"Now, I am doing a lot better, but it is going to take time and a lot of work on your old man's part to get back home to be your daddy. I'm also going to need some alone time so I can work extra hard on getting well."

Jared spoke up, "So when will you come home? We miss you, Dad."

"I know you do. And this is what I'm going to do. I will come home and see you every day once the doctors release me. But I am also going to stay some at the penthouse so I can work just with the doctors. Do you understand what I am saying?"

Matilda spoke up, "You mean sometimes you will be staying over at the penthouse by yourself and not at home?"

"Yes, that is right."

"We will miss you," said Matilda, "But I understand. Just hurry home please." Bella started to yawn. "Looks like it is past your bedtime, so I am going to wish you sweet dreams. I love you, my children. I will call you after dinner each day until I can see you in person. Goodnight." There was a chorus of 'goodnight's and 'I love you's.

"Hey Joseph," Marcus said. "Thanks, man, for coming and helping out."

"No problem. We are family and family goes out of its way to help out," he said.

"Joseph? Be there for Sam, please. I am afraid all of this is too much for her and she is going to need to lean on her friends."

"We will take care of Samantha; you focus on getting better so you can be back with your family."

"Goodnight, Joseph. Better take Bella to bed. He looks like he is already asleep on the table."

"I got him," said Joseph as he picked Bella up. Matilda said, "We should all go to bed." Marcus shut off the iPad just as Samantha and Mike came into the room.

"Sam, darling, come sit next to me on the side of the bed." Marcus patted a space next to him. Mike spoke up, "I'll step out and give you two some privacy."

"Mike," said Marcus. "Will you please stay? This will affect you also." Mike sat on the couch in the suite and waited for Marcus to speak. Marcus leaned forward and kissed Samantha on the forehead and wrapped his arms around her. Samantha began to sob uncontrollably, and Marcus just held her and rubbed her back. He kept saying, "It is all going to be alright. You know I love you and the children and am looking forward to our little boy." He put his hand on Samantha's belly and the baby begin to move.

"You see, sweetheart, he already knows his dad's touch." Marcus leaned over and kissed Samantha's belly. This stopped the sobs, but Samantha eyes brimmed with tears. Threatening to erupt again.

"Sam, darling, you are not going to like what I have decided. I have explained it to the children through Zoom and they do not necessarily like what I explained to them, but they accept it. So now, please accept what I am going to tell you. I know you want to spend as much time as you can with me. But, sweetheart, it's just not practical and it is too stressful for you. So, I want Mike to take you home and I do not want you to come back to the hospital. I love you and our baby, so I want you to stay at home and take care of yourself and him. Also, the children need some stability, so having you there is better than having both parents gone. I am going to Zoom call every day after dinner and I will talk to the children, then to you in private. I took this risk, for you and the children. I told you I would die for you and that I loved you enough to let you go if that is what you wanted. You are my lover, my best friend, and the mother of my children." Samantha tried to speak but Marcus put his fingers over her mouth and held her close.

"I will be there when you deliver our little boy. I will be at the house on and off as soon as I am well enough to leave the hospital. I talked to the doctor, and it is going to take time to become the man you love and deserve and to be the kind of father our children deserve. If I cannot get back to that person, then Sam, we will talk about alternatives. Do you understand? I love you and I want what we had, but I cannot be that man right now. I am going to spend nights, and a lot of time, at the penthouse. I need to do what is best for me, which means I am doing what I believe is best for us. Please accept this, I need you to be brave. Now I have asked Mike and Joseph to help you and let you lean on them. They both have agreed. Joseph will stay as long as he can. If something bad had happened to me, and I could not have survived the crash, then I would want you to find another love in time. I know they love me, and I am daddy, but it would have been time to let Joseph step in. That did not happen, so now I must put me back together, as well as my family. Can you understand that?"

"You have so many people who love you and I love you with all my heart." Tears began to run down Samantha's face. Marcus reached over with his fingers and wiped them away. "I'm not trying to hurt you, darling. I'm trying to protect you. I watched you spiral out of control, and I do not want that to happen again. I understand your panic attacks, as I now have them. I experience anger and irritability. I am suffering from PTSD. So, I'm not going to be at my best at times. It has nothing to do with you. I have got to get my head on straight. Now tell me how you feel."

Samantha said, "I'm scared things might change between us."

"Yes, darling, they might. But I'm going to do everything I can for that not to happen." Marcus leaned forward and kissed Samantha passionately and then looked at Mike.

"Take Sam home and take care of her. I'll be in touch with you after I talk to the children."

"When is your next doctor's appointment?" Marcus asked.

"In two weeks," she said.

"So, if I can be there, I will be on crutches when I am released from the hospital. If not, then Mike or Joseph will take over for me, if that is who you want to go with you. It could be your dad or Margaret? But that's only if I cannot get there. I love you and I want to participate, just like I did with the boys and Bella. I know you do not understand all of this right now, but the doctors agree I have a lot of work to do to get back to our normal life. Mike, take her home, please, or I am going to be in tears myself. I love you, Sam. You are my life and I am going to do everything I can to come home and resume our life." Samantha hugged Marcus and kissed his lips.

"I love you, Marcus. I cannot do this without your love."

"Sam, you are a strong woman. You are doing this for us," Marcus replied. Mike said, "Samantha, let me bundle you up. It is cold outside. See you soon, man. I got your family just as any good brother would."

"Thanks, Mike. Goodnight, my love," Marcus said to Samantha. Tears welled in her eyes, "Goodnight."

"We will talk tomorrow," Marcus said to Mike.

"You bet. Goodnight." Mike put his arm around Samantha and led her out of the room, down the elevator, and to the driver who had been waiting patiently for them. Mike helped Samantha into the limousine. The driver had kept the car toasty warm but the look on Samantha's face was that she was not feeling so warm. Her face looked pale, and she was shivering.

"Samantha," said Mike, "You will get through this. I know Marcus seemed harsh, but he has his reasons and is probably is still trying to figure it out himself. He said he was doing this because he wants to get back to the man he was. He said over and over that he loved you and the children and was looking forward to the birth of his new baby." Samantha, with teary eyes said, "I know what he said, but something he is not saying to me makes me believe that he is unsure that he can get back to the man he was. Does not he understand that I love him, no matter what has changed? I cannot do this without him. Why won't he let me help him? Why won't he tell me what he and the doctors are worried about? Why can't I talk to his doctors? It is not like Marcus not to talk to me about his fears. Mike, something else is going on. He practically banned me and the children from the hospital. That is not fair." Mike turned Samantha's face to his, "Honey, Marcus is a man that has to believe he has everything under control. He has never dealt with a situation where he was not in control of himself. He never once said anything about giving up on your marriage or his family. He said over and over he loved you and the children. He wants to participate in the birth of his new baby. Let's take him at his word. He will talk to me, Samantha. I'll go have a chat with him tomorrow and see if he is ready to talk with me. Maybe it has something to do with him being a man. But he is right, you are not taking care of yourself. You are eight months pregnant, Samantha, for the sake of your health and the baby, please just take care of yourself and be there for the children. Marcus knows you're there for him. Sweetheart, I've never seen him so head over heels in love with a woman. You are what he wants. He's just got something going on in his mind; it sounds like fear. Marcus has always been fearless. He is a fixer and now he is fearful he cannot fix whatever is troubling him. Just give him the time and try to stick to the plan he outlined for you. You know the man has to plan his strategies or he is not happy."

Samantha leaned over to Mike and rested her head on his shoulder. "I will try," she said. "To do as he asked." The limo driver stopped at the front door of the mansion; Samantha had dozed off.

"Samantha, honey, we are home," Mike said.

"I'm just so tired," she said.

"I know you are, let's get you to bed." Mike began to move her head off his shoulder. Mike slid out of the car and went to the other door and opened it to help Samantha get out.

"Come, sweetheart, give me your hand." He leaned in to help her out. Samantha was having a hard time getting out of the car, she was so big and pregnant, combined with her emotional state, she seemed like a rag doll.

"What the hell," Mike said as he picked Samantha up in a seated position, held her close as the driver rang the bell. Mike could not get to his key. Peter answered the door.

"Is Mrs. Matthew okay?" he asked.

"She's worn out. I'm going to take her up to her room and help her get ready for bed."

"Can I help?" Peter asked.

"Just push the elevator. She is getting heavy."

"Sure thing, Mr. Mike." Mike got on the elevator with a sleeping Samantha. Mike thought *I've got to talk to Marcus tomorrow. I have to know what he is thinking.* He carried Samantha into her room and sat her on the bed. He took her boots off and looked through her drawers for a gown. He found a long flannel gown and went back to the bed where Samantha was barely awake. Mike thought, *Marcus is like my brother, so Samantha is my sister-in-law,* he reminded himself. He pulled her sweater over her head, exposing her bra. He put the gown over her head and reached under the gown and unhooked her bra and placed it on the chair beside the bed.

"So far, so good," Mike said. Then he unbuttoned her pants and pulled them down and off her legs. He had her in her gown, so he buttoned the back of the gown and turned the covers down and helped her get into bed. He covered her up and leaned down and kissed her forehead.

"Goodnight, princess."

"Mike, you are so good to me and Marcus. You are so good to the children, please do not leave me yet. Wait until I go to sleep, please. Just lie down beside me until I fall asleep. I'm so lonely. I miss having Marcus's body next to me."

Mike thought, *Okay this is a very pregnant woman who needs comforting and I'll do this for my brother. He said to take care of her, he did not say exactly what I was supposed to do. But he had said to put her first.* So, Mike, still fully clothed, laid on the covers next to Samantha. He thought, *Even eight months pregnant she was so beautiful.* And she was so vulnerable. He put his arm around her and cradled her until she fell asleep. He slipped out of bed and looked at the clock. It was after two. He thought it was late, but Denise would be asleep and totally understanding of why he stayed at the mansion. So, he went to the closest guestroom and went to bed. His final thought was, *Marcus had better have a good reason to send her away and hurt her like he did. Yes, I am going to see him for breakfast in the morning.* He set his alarm on his phone for six a.m., but he knew he'd wake up at five. It was habit, a part of the job.

As Mike was leaving Samantha's room at five a.m., he passed Joseph in the hallway.

"So, what is going on, Mike?"

"I am on my way to see Marcus and see if I can find out…"

"Okay, and you were telling Samantha goodbye?"

"Man, you know I would not move in on Marcus' wife."

"Well, that's not what I mean."

"Sorry Joseph. I brought Samantha home last night and she was an emotional mess after Marcus insisted that she not come back to the hospital and that he wanted to try and rehab at the penthouse. She asked me to stay with her last night to comfort her and I did. She's fragile right now, so if you can help her understand what he needs. She is also showing a lot of fatigue. I know you cannot stay too long here, but whatever you can do to help, Marcus said he would really appreciate it."

"Joseph," Mike continued. "You know her as well as Marcus, I think. You also know how devastated she can get."

"I got her, Mike, I will stay another two weeks and then I need to get home to see my family."

"Thanks, I'll see you at dinner. I want to catch Marcus at breakfast at the hospital. I think she has a doctor's appointment next week and he asked that one of us take his place as he will not be out of the hospital yet."

Joseph said, "I'll do it. I missed the birth and the pregnancy of the twins. Marcus was there, so I want to help him now. I know it is different this time. I mean this is Marcus' baby, but I can stand in and help her. I have the experience with my own daughter, so I'd like to help her with his baby. I can say there is nothing normal about our lives; Samantha, Marcus,' or mine. I just want her to be happy. She's had so many hurts. You go see what the hell is wrong with Marcus that he would not want to be with the love of his life."

"See you later," Mike said, "Kiss the girls for me."

"Will do," Joseph said.

Mike picked up his coat from the downstairs foyer closet and headed out the door to his car. He pulled up his collar. It was going to be cold today. He was glad that the chauffeur had already started the car and warmed it up. New York winters were brutally cold.

Joseph headed to the children's wing to check on the boys. They were both fast asleep. He knew they'd be up in an hour. Next, he went to the girls' room and checked on them. Bella was rubbing her eyes and sobbing. Joseph sat down beside her on the bed and asked, "What's wrong princess?"

"I miss my daddy. I want him to come home," she said sadly.

"Sweetie, Daddy's trying his best to get well so he can come home. He had a bad wreck, and it takes time for him to get better."

"I know, but I miss him. He reads me a book at night and does voices for the people in the book," Bella whined.

"How about tonight I read you a book and I do the voices. You can tell me if I do them as well as your dad."

Bella put her arms around Joseph's neck and hugged him. Joseph rubbed her back until he could hear her breathing softly and knew she was back asleep. He missed his Sophia and would call her after breakfast. Right now, he smelled coffee and headed to the kitchen for a cup before all the kids got up for breakfast. He met the chef preparing breakfast and asked him if he would prepare a tray for Mrs. Matthew. She should be waking up now and maybe he could convince her to stay in bed for a while. After the tray was prepared, he took the elevator up to her room and knocked lightly. He heard a very quiet, "Come in." Samantha was still in bed. She looked tired and had been weeping.

"None of that," Joseph said. "You are definitely in your final stages of pregnancy. So, my lady, rest and eat, and I got the kids today."

"Are you sure?" she asked.

"Yes, sweetheart. With two nannies, a nurse, and a house full of staff I think I can handle your herd of children. I know Marcus is Catholic, but you are about to give birth and have your sixth child."

"Yes, Joseph. Marcus and I want a large family."

"Well, I think Emily and I are happy with one child. But hey, whatever you two want to do."

"You know, Joseph, I would have never thought I'd have six children, but I love having this wonderful family. Marcus is a great father."

"I know. I hear all the children's opinion of their daddy's greatness. It's hard to live up to their opinion of him, but I am trying."

"You're doing a great job, Joseph. Thank you."

"Samantha, eat and rest."

"I know I can count on you, Joseph."

"Yes, I will do all I can for this family," said Joseph. "I am on my way to see the children at breakfast."

"Thank you," said Samantha. "Tell them I'll see them in a couple hours."

"I'll tell them." And he leaned over and kissed her on the head.

***

Mike arrived at the hospital just before 6:30 a.m. Marcus was up and talking to the doctors.

"Hey man," said Mike. "Is it alright for me to come in?" Marcus waved for Mike to come in and the doctor said, "Mr. Matthew, it will just take time for your mind and body to heal. You need to be patient with yourself. I am sure you will regain function of your body. So, if there are no more questions, I'll leave you to your breakfast and physical therapy." With that statement the doctor left the room and

Mike said, "How are you feeling?"

"Like shit," Marcus said. "I cannot get my body to function the way it should," Marcus said with anger in his voice.

"Man," said Mike. "You heard the doctor, give yourself a break. You had a major hit to your body, it takes time." Marcus replied, "Yea, I'm not too sure my body is ever going to function like it did before."

"Marcus, don't you need to share your fear with Samantha?" Marcus said angrily, "No, it will change our relationship." Mike said, "So is adding extra worry to Samantha's already fragile state. You think that is fair? She loves you. You know she will stand by you no matter what your condition is."

"No, it is best I work this out before I have to tell Sam," said Marcus. "It will change us. I know my wife, it would destroy us, our relationship."

Mike said, "I think you're selling Samantha short."

"It's my decision, Mike. You would not understand," said Marcus. "Drop the inquisition."

"Would you like some coffee?" Mike asked.

"Sure thing." Marcus asked the CNA if he'd bring an extra breakfast tray in. "So, Marcus, you want to even tell your best friend?" said Mike.

"No, not yet, just drop it and tell me what is going on at the house with my family?" said Marcus. After their breakfast trays had been set before them and the CNA left, Mike took a sip of coffee and said,

"Your youngest daughter, Bella, woke up crying for her daddy. It seems she misses story time with you. The boys, Ester, and Matilda were not awake yet. Joseph was up and going to the kitchen to grab coffee before the kids woke up for breakfast. Your pregnant wife I had to carry up to bed last night and she insisted I lay beside her and hold her until she went to sleep, which I did. Man, but that is where you need to be. Joseph caught me as I was leaving her room. I told him how distraught Samantha is. He said he'd take care of her and the children today and he'd volunteer to go with Samantha to her doctor appointment next week. If you are not going to be able to be there with her?"

"No," said Marcus. "I will not be released by then."

Mike said, "Are you trying to push Joseph and Samantha together?"

"No…well, maybe. I do not know," said Marcus. "I love my wife. I want her to be happy." Mike said, "Happy? How can she be happy if the man she loves, the man whose child she is carrying, will not tell her what is going on?"

"Let's change the subject," said Marcus. "I have my reasons."

"Well," said Mike. "Joseph said he had to go home in two weeks, he has a family he wants to get back to."

"Well," said Marcus. "Maybe by then I'll have things sorted out." He picked up his coffee and had a sip. Marcus said, "Make sure they have the condo ready for the end of the week. They will be releasing me on Friday."

"Should I tell Samantha?"

"No damnit, I will," said Marcus. "Just be my friend and brother and just let me work this out my way, please?" asked Marcus.

"Okay," said Mike. "Just tell me how I can help."

"First, how is Mr. Carr doing?" asked Marcus.

"He is getting treatment and Saul has gotten the state to drop all charges," said Mike.

"Thank God," said Marcus, "And his family?"

"We are taking care of them. Mrs. Carr has quit her job and is home with her children."

"Just make sure they have everything they need" said Marcus.

"It is shitty how this country treats its vets and their family," Marcus continued.

"Well, hopefully your new clinic will help the vets and their family," said Mike.

"Saul got it funded and he found a building and his hiring doctors and staff to run it. Many of your friends have donated so funding will not ever be an issue. Also, Elton and Adele are arranging fundraisers," said Mike.

***

Samantha decided that she had laid in bed long enough. It was sweet that both Mike and Joseph had tried to comfort her. *Today I am going to take care of myself and my children*, she thought as she rubbed her stomach and it started to move.

"Yes, Trey, I know you hear me. Your father has something to work out. I know he loves you and your siblings. I know he loves me. But there is something he's not telling me. The doctors have shown to me that his injuries will heal with time. There is something he is worried about, and I am going to give him his space. When he is ready to share with me, he will. So, let's get out of bed and see what the rest of the family is doing. It is lunch time, and I am hungry. So, let's you and I join the others for lunch." Throwing on a jumpsuit and tossing back her hair, Samantha left her suite and took the elevator to the first floor. Walking into the dining room she could hear laughter. Joseph was telling them a funny story.

"So, what is going on?" Samantha said as she went around the table and hugged each child.

"Mommy," the children greeted.

"You're up. Uncle Joseph has been telling us stories of when you and he were in law school," Ester said.

"And he told us how you and he went camping and he threw you in the cold water," Matilda teased. Samantha looked at Joseph, "Well your Uncle Joseph he had better watch out or I'll have to tell you some funny stories about him. So, what are you having for lunch?" asked Samantha. Jacob spoke up, "We are having hot dogs, baked beans, and potato salad."

"Uncle Joseph said we could have sundaes for dessert," said Bella excitedly.

"Oh, he did. Did he?" said Samantha. "Uncle Joseph would spoil you if I'd let him." Joseph spoke up, "We will eat healthier at dinner. Let me get you a plate. Would you like some milk?"

"Yes, please." Joseph reached for the pitcher of milk and poured Samantha a glass.

"How was your rest?" he asked.

"It was good, thank you. I am ready for lunch and to spend my afternoon with the children. So, what is on the agenda for today?"

Jared said, "We are going to the planetarium." Joseph said, "It is not that cold out so I thought an outing would be the ticket for kids with pent up energy."

"Sounds like a great plan. Can two more join you?" Ester said "Two?"

"Yes," said Samantha. "Me and your baby brother. He's been kicking all morning so I think he could use some exercise too. Now pass me a plate. I'd like one of those hot dogs." Joseph passed her a plate and the hot dogs, beans, and potato salad. The chatter around the table was happy and intense. Samantha thought, *this looks like a happy family. We are going to make the best out of the day. No more mourning about Marcus. He wouldn't miss this with his family, so he must have good reasons.*

***

Mike said, "I'm heading back to the mansion. Marcus, please remember the children are expecting your call after dinner."

"Mike, I will take care of my family and I want you to take care of them also. Tell Joseph I will not be there for Sam's appointment since I won't be discharged until Friday. I know her appointment is Monday. I will be in touch with Sam."

"Well," said Mike. "Whatever is going on with you, I hope you solve it soon or at least talk about it."

"I will," said Marcus. "Just trust me please. I'd do nothing to hurt Sam or my family, they mean everything to me." Mike left Marcus' suite and rode the elevator to the main floor of the hospital. As he was walking to his car, he spotted Renee heading to the hospital entrance.

"Hey, Renee." Mike called out. "What's going on?"

"You tell me," said Renee. "I got a call from Marcus, and he asked me to stop by his room."

"Renee," said Mike. "You really expect me to believe he called you?"

"Well, I do not care if you believe me or not. He called and said I should stop by."

"Renee," said Mike. "Please do not start with your tricks. He is trying to recover and his family, especially his wife, is going through an emotional rollercoaster."

"Mike," she said. "I am answering his call. So, unless you want to get a drink later, I have been summoned."

"No thanks, Renee. I'm good." Mike started his Jeep and sat for a minute thinking. *Marcus cannot possibly want to have anything to do with Renee.* This is getting crazier and crazier. He headed out on the freeway toward the mansion.

After dinner, the children were all sitting at the dining room table, waiting for their dad to facetime them.

"Hey, my loves." said Marcus as his face became visible on the screen. "Daddy!" was the chorus of voices. "Are you coming home?"

"I get released Friday and I will be by to see you. So, how was your day? Did you learn anything today?"

Matilda spoke up, "We went to the planetarium with Uncle Joseph and Mom. I wish you could have been there; it was so much fun."

"We saw so many stars, Daddy!" shouted Bella.

"That sounds like a fun day. Will I get a report on your visit? Can I expect it next Friday?"

Ester said, "Does your leg still hurt daddy?"

"Some, my love, but the doctor will be fitting me with a walking boot this week." Jacob spoke up, "What about where you were shot?"

"I am doing better, and when I get home and the wound has healed, I'll show you my scars."

"Hey, Jared my boy, why are you so quiet?" said Marcus.

"Daddy?" he asked. "What will happen to the man that shot you?" Marcus said, "I will explain it as simple as I can. Mr. Carr, the man that shot me, is very sick. He did not know in his mind what he was doing, so I am going to try and help him get better so he can go back home to his family. Your grandfather, Saul, is setting up a special hospital for people that have suffered some mental problems from the war. These people served their country in war and our country has not taken very good care of them. They need special help. I will take all of you to this new hospital and let you meet these people. Now who called your grandfather, John Marcus? You know he has been sick with his heart, so I expect you to call him and cheer him up." Matilda spoke up, "I will call him after we hang up, Daddy. Grandmother Isabella and Grandmother Margaret call every day. I think Grandfather Saul and Grandmother Margaret are coming tomorrow."

Marcus said to Bella, "I hear you miss our bedtime stories. How about I call each of you at different times so I can read to you until I get out of here and read to you in person? Does that sound like a plan?" In unison, the kids shouted out "Yes!" Marcus said, "It is getting about bedtime and I want to talk to Mommy. I love you guys. Hang in there until Friday when I get home. Goodnight. Sam are you there?" said Marcus.

"Yes, love, I am here. I was waiting for you and the children to finish talking."

"How are you?" he asked.

"Well given the circumstances and being in my last month of pregnancy with our little boy, and my husband will not tell me why he cannot come home to stay: I am hanging in there for you and giving you your space, like you asked."

"Thank you, darling," said Marcus

"I promise as soon as I figure my mind out, I'll tell you everything. I will not be able to attend your next doctor's appointment. I am being released on Friday. I will be at every one after that, and I cannot wait to see our new baby." A tear rolled down Samantha's face. She said, "Joseph is going with me."

Marcus said, "I'll call right after, sweetheart, to hear about the visit. Sam, your health and the health of our baby is what is important to me." Samantha said, "I know that, and you are important to me."

"Courage, Sam. It will work out. I just need some time, that's all. Can we please just leave it like that? And that know I love you and I want to get back to where we were before this nightmare took place. Love, you look tired. I am going to let you go so you can rest. Samantha Amanda Matthew, I love you more than life. Hold that thought in your mind." Samantha said, "I know you love me, and I love you."

"So, goodnight, my love." Marcus blew her a kiss and the screen went blank. Samantha wiped the tears from her eyes and went to help Joseph and Mike with bedtime rituals. Even though they had plenty of help, Marcus and Samantha always wanted to tuck their children in.

Monday's doctor appointment came quick. Joseph was ready and waiting. The appointment was at one and Samantha was moving very slowly. She rode the elevator to the main floor of the mansion where Joseph was waiting for her with her coat.

"Samantha, are you feeling okay?"

"No, I am starting to have pain in my back. I guess, the baby is dropping."

"Well, the car and driver are out front. Let me help you into your coat and let's go." He took her arm and helped her down the steps of the mansion and into the waiting car. Joseph said, "I'm going to call Dr. McCullough's office and let them know we are on our way and you are experiencing lower back pain."

Once they arrived at the doctor's office, Joseph helped Samantha into the building and met Dr. McCullough's nurse who said, "Let's get you straight into a room. Dr. McCullough wants to examine you and do an ultrasound at once." The nurse helped Samantha start removing her clothes. Joseph turned to leave the room. Samantha said, "Stay please. Joseph, I want you here just in case something's wrong." Joseph stood next to Samantha's bed as the nurse began the ultrasound.

Dr. McCullough came into the room, "Samantha, you're having lower back pain?"

"Yes," she said. "All morning." Dr. McCullough turned the monitor around and said, "A good, strong heartbeat. You could see the baby had dropped toward the pelvis into the birth canal." She went to the bottom of the bed where Samantha had her feet in stirrups. She inserted her fingers and said, "Even though you have about two weeks to go, you are dilated to four centimeters. You do not appear to be in labor yet, but I'd say any time you are going to deliver. I am going ahead and admitting you just, for safety's sake. Also, Marcus will already be there if you deliver before he gets out. Nice to see you, Mr. Claiborne, thank you for helping with our girl." Joseph said, "Would you like me to call Marcus for you while you get dressed?"

"No, I will call from the car."

"Samantha, you're going to be fine. I've got you."

"I know. This was supposed to be a happy day for us."

"It will be. You and Marcus will figure it out." Samantha got down off the table with the help of the nurse. Dr. McCullough came back into the room and said, "You're all set. So, I will see you at the hospital later." Samantha nodded her head in agreement and put her coat on as her cell phone rang.

"Hello, Marcus. Yes, darling, I felt that something might be wrong."

"I have been waiting for your call," he said.

"Nothing's wrong," she said.

"If you're supposed to be having a baby in two weeks and you're already dilated to four inches and the doctor is admitting you…" In what sounded like a panicked voice he asked, "Is the baby alright?"

"Yes. She did an ultrasound and said our son has a healthy heartbeat. She's just admitting me as a precaution. She thinks that the baby will come any day now, possibly tonight."

"Sam, I will be there with you. I love you. May, I speak to Joseph?" Samantha passed her phone to Joseph, "Thanks, man. I know this is peculiar for you, but I know she feels safe with you there."

"It is no problem, Marcus. But she wants you: the father of her child."

"I'll be there," said Marcus. "What time do you think you will be at the hospital.?"

"Samantha, do you want to go home first and then go to the hospital?" Joseph asked.

"Home first. I'd like to pick up my bag and talk to the children. I'll call Dad from the car."

"Marcus, I think maybe two hours? I'll call you when we get there and she is checked in."

"Thanks," said Marcus. "I will come to her room as soon as you call."

Marcus hung up and called his mother. "Mom, Samantha is going to be admitted. The doctor thinks she may go into labor early. I'll keep you posted."

"I love you, son. Just take care of your wife and my grandson. I love you," Isabella said.

"Mom, just tell the family that I'll let everyone know as soon as I know. How is Dad today?"

"He is feeling better today, we even went for a drive just to get out. The doctor said just a few more days of rest and he thinks your dad will be fine."

"That's great, Mother. I know Dad had a scare with me and all, but I am healing and everything will be okay. We all just need time. Talk later."

Marcus hung up and called Mike.

"Yes, Marcus?" he said.

"Samantha is on her way home. The doctor is going to admit her to the hospital. Looks like our son will be born very soon. I want you personally to handle security for her."

"You know I will. And are you going to be there for her?"

"Of course," said Marcus. "That is my baby and my wife."

"Well," Mike said. "I just didn't know if you remembered that given your actions this week."

"What the hell does that mean?" said Marcus.

"Renee is what I am talking about. You have had no interest in her since France and she said you called her to the hospital to see you, while you tell your wife to stay at home."

"Look," said Marcus. "I know it makes no sense, but it will. Just be there for Sam." Mike said, "That would never be a problem. I love her like a sister. And Joseph? Is he going to be there also?"

"Yes, he is bringing her to the hospital."

"Of course he is," said Mike. "Man, I just hope you are not pushing her to Joseph."

"Mike, I have my reasons. I know my wife and I am doing what I think is best for her."

"What best for her? Maybe it's what is best for you," Mike said.

"Mike, just please follow my instructions. My only concern is for my wife and son." Marcus hung up.

***

Joseph asked the limo driver to stay parked in front of the mansion and be ready to drive him and Ms. Matthew to the hospital.

"We should be out in two hours."

"Yes, sir." The driver got out of the car and opened the door for Samantha. Joseph slid across the seat and got out behind her, his hand resting on her back as he helped her up the stairs and through the front door of the mansion. The noise of the children was coming from the kitchen. Margaret and Saul were there to see the children, and everyone was involved in making cookies. The boys were covered in flour and girls had aprons tied around their waists and were mixing batter in a bowl. Saul was using his finger to get batter out of an old bowl.

"Well, hi, darling daughter. We were waiting to hear from you."

Joseph said to Samantha, "I'll go get your bag from your room while you talk to your family."

"Dad, Margaret, kids, it looks like your little brother is coming early. I am going to the hospital and Daddy will meet me there."

"Tonight?" said Matilda. Jacob said, "Another brother? I wanted a sister."

"Me too!" said Bella.

Margaret said, "Be glad your mother and brother are well." Jacob said, "I am sorry, Mom." Jared said, "Mom, we will help. We love you and tell Dad we love him."

"I'm sorry, too," Bella said sweetly.

Margaret said, "Samantha, what did the doctor say?"

"She said that the baby's heartbeat is strong and I am dilated four centimeters. So just as precaution she wants to admit me. And I already talked to Marcus. Can you stay over with the children?"

"Of course, darling," said Saul. "I'll also call Rick and make sure the office is okay."

"I am sure it is," said Samantha. "But it is good that you'll tell him what is going on." Joseph came in with the bag and said, "Ready?"

"Yes, just let me kiss the children and my parents."

"Take your time. I'll wait in in the foyer. Kids, hold the fort down," said Joseph. "I will be back as soon as I get your mother settled."

"We will," they said in unison. Joseph helped Samantha to the car.

Arriving at the hospital, they were met by the nurse in charge. "Mrs. Matthew, we have your room ready, and your husband is waiting there for you." Joseph and Samantha followed the nurse to the room. Marcus was in a wheelchair, his leg still in a cast.

"Hi, sweetheart." He rose with crutches to kiss Samantha on the cheek.

"Looks like our little boy is ready to join his family." He looked at Joseph and said, "Thanks, man, I will take it from here."

"Sure thing," said Joseph. He kissed Samantha on the cheek and said, "If you need me, I will be at the mansion for two more weeks to help with the kids, and then I need to get home to my daughter." Samantha said, "You have been good to me and the boys, but you need to go home and see your family. I will be alright; Marcus will see to that."

Joseph looked at Marcus, "Man, you know she needs you right now." Marcus gave Joseph the look that said *I know you'd love to be me, but you're not*. Joseph left as the nurse helped Samantha change into a gown. She said, "If I can get you anything, please push your buzzer. Would you and your husband like to have dinner together?" Marcus replied and said, "Yes, that would be nice." The nurse left the room as Marcus helped Samantha into bed. He felt clumsy as it was hard to maneuver on crutches. He felt like less than the man and husband that he always envisioned himself to be.

"So," he said. "Sam, are you having contractions?"

"No, but I am dilated. And Dr. McCullough thought it would be a good idea for me to come to the hospital, just for precaution. She knows that you are here so she just thought we would like to be together, just in case Trey comes early." Marcus said, "I have called my family. Are Saul and Margaret at the house with the children?"

"Yes, they were there when I stopped to tell the children and to pick up my bag. They agreed to stay until the baby is born." Marcus said, "Your parents are good people." Samantha said, "And yours."

"We are so fortunate to have a loving family and friends. How are you, Marcus?" Samantha said.

"I'd feel a lot better when I can at least get in a walking cast and get discharged from the hospital. I feel useless being unable care for you or the children." He sat down by Samantha and took her hand, "Sam, we will get through this, I promise."

Samantha said, "I just wished you would share with me what is in your head."

"I cannot until I am sure. Just know my heart is the same. I love you like I have always; enough to let you go, if that is what I need to do. You are my friend, my lover, soul mate, my wife, and the mother of my children. You are everything I have wanted. I want to be the man I promised you I would be." He kissed her head, "I know you, Sam, better than you know yourself." Samantha said, "I just do not understand, are you not attracted to me? I know I have gained so much weight in this pregnancy, as much as when I was pregnant with the boys. I know my body has changed so much, but I promise I will get my body back."

"Sam, it is not your body. I love you and have loved every change in your body. I am not a shallow man; it has nothing to do with you. It is me, honey, all me. Let's not dwell on my problem and the fact you cannot understand. Let's enjoy the birth of our baby. This is our baby. I want him born safe and into the love we have for each other, for him, and my family. Please Sam, let's enjoy this time we have together here." As he finished his statement, the orderly brought in dinner for two and set it up on the table in the suite.

"Can I get you or Mr. Matthew anything else?"

"No," said Samantha, "it all looks good." Samantha got out of bed and put her robe on, and Marcus joined her at the table. They both ate, talking mostly about the children and what it will mean to the family to have their sixth child. Samantha knew that Marcus was avoiding something, but she would give him his space, as he requested. Yes, he knew her, but she knew him and believed that he had lost his confidence as a husband, but not as a father. Why? She did not know. So, all she could do as wait and enjoy his company now. After dinner, Marcus said, "Let's Skype the kids and let them see us together. I am sure it will make them feel better."

"Yes," said Samantha, "Let's do that. The girls, especially Matilda, need reassurance that we are together and both ok." The kids had been waiting around the dining room table, Margaret was there with them.

"Hey, you guys," said Marcus. "Mommy and I wanted to let you know that we love you and we are just waiting for your baby brother to greet us."

"Dad," said Bella. "This means I'm not going to be your baby girl?" she asked.

"No," said Marcus. "You will always be my baby girl and so will Ester and Matilda. You may be older, but my love for my girls has nothing to do with who is the oldest or youngest. You three are my heart, just like Jared and Jacob. You five are going to get the chance to be big brothers and sisters, which means you will take care of each other as siblings, just like your siblings took care of you. You are Matthews, which means family comes first. You understand that?" Bella said, "Yes, dad. We know that we can always depend on you and Mommy. You love us. Do you still love each other?"

Samantha spoke up, "Of course we do and our family is the most important things to us." Margaret interrupted, "Dears, if you do not mind, I think it is time we get these children into bed. You two spend your time getting that new grandchild into the world. Samantha, I'll tell your dad when he gets back that you two called. He ran an errand, and Mike and Joseph are waiting to help with bedtime rituals. The nannies have been great, but the children love bedtime with the help of their uncles and grandfather. Tomorrow we are taking them to Phillipe's restaurant where we are going to meet your parents, Marcus. We are going to celebrate the coming of Trey, the newest member of our family. Your sisters are coming also. We even invited Rick, Scott, Joseph, and Mike. I even think Denise is going to get away from the office to join us. So tomorrow we are very busy. But we will expect your call at bedtime, unless your son comes tomorrow. Children, tell your mother and father goodnight."

There was a unison of voices, "Goodnight and we love you!" the children said.

"Goodnight, my darlings," said Samantha.

"Goodnight, we love you. Be good," said Marcus. "And we will talk tomorrow." The picture went dead. Marcus said, "I am staying with you Sam. They have brought in a bed. I wish we could share a bed, but I am afraid my leg makes it hard for me to sleep, but I am here."

"I love you, Marcus." She got back into bed and Marcus kissed her goodnight and got into his bed. Samantha noticed that his kiss did not have the passion or urgency she knew he always had for her. Yep, he had changed. But tonight, they were together. He said he loved her enough to let her go. Now why would he say that to her? She could not wonder anymore.

"Good night, love."

***

At about six in the morning the orderly came into Samantha's room and asked if they would like breakfast for two. Marcus was already up and answered, "Yes." The nurse came in to take Samantha's vitals and said that Dr. McCullough would be in this morning to see Samantha and check the progress of the birth. Samantha was just waking up and was still groggy.

"How are you feeling, Sam?" said Marcus.

"Just a lot of pressure. I can tell that the baby is dropping and I still have lower back pain."

"I am so sorry that you must go through the pain of pregnancy. It sucks to be a woman," said Marcus. "That is why any man that knocks a woman up, or in our case has a baby out of love, is a dog if he does not take care of her. Wife, girlfriend, or just casual sex, no woman should have their body, their lives, turned upside down or left with the responsibility of the baby, in every way, even financially. Health or otherwise. Samantha, I am not the man who would have a few moments pleasure and create a lifetime of issues for a woman. I applaud Joseph for stepping up to the plate with Emily. Even if he did not quite handle it right, he still is responsible for Emily and Sophia. As for Kenneth, killing him would be too good, that is why I put his company out of business by under bidding his contracts. I ran him out of his hometown and I'm not sure what happened to him. I heard he was in Florida where he had gotten another woman pregnant. She had the baby and her father stepped in and took care of her."

"Marcus, through all the excitement, and then the boys and Bella, I failed to say that I saw him at our wedding. He was with a woman, who I guess was invited to our ceremony. I'm not sure how that happened, but he was there."

"Yeah, I knew that Mike had been keeping a tail on him ever since the threat to me and our family was issued. He had moved in with a woman, who was a friend of the family, and lived with her for about a month. I guess he was working her for money or revenge. Anyway, he was ruled out after he left and went to Florida. I'm just glad Saul took care of your father. But let's not waste our time dwelling on the past. We know that Mr. Carr had PTSD and was not in his right mind. So, love, forget all this crap and focus on this happy occasion; our baby being born. You are healthy and our baby is healthy. After breakfast, I'm going to see if they will go ahead and put my walking cast on and get me discharged. Then I will be back to be with you. I love you Sam, and there is nothing I will not do to take care of you." He kissed her on the lips and left the room.

Dr. McCullough came into Samantha's room to check her to see if there had been any changes. "Samantha, you are dilated to five. Are you in pain? Still not having contractions? I'm going to put a monitor on the baby and do another ultrasound. Now, he is mature enough and I can induce labor, or we can give it a few more days to see if he will come on his own, if you're comfortable with that. I am assuming Marcus has been with you?"

"Yes," Samantha said "He's gone down to get a walking cast and ask his doctor to release him. He wants to stay with me."

"Yes, Marcus is a good man, Samantha."

"Yes, I know." Marcus came in with a walking cast.

"Well, I am a free man, darling. The bullet wound is almost

healed, and my lung is fine. I'll need to do physical therapy after the cast comes off. I will need to regain my ability to chase the kids. My brain looks good. I will have to follow up on the PTSD under a psychiatrist, which I will. So, I am good. How are you?"

"It sounds wonderful," said Samantha. "I am good, still have lower back pain and have dilated another centimeter. Dr. McCullough said she can induce labor and get me started or we can wait. She hooked a monitor to the baby to make sure he is not in distress and she did another ultrasound; the baby has dropped more. That is why I am having back pain. Inducing labor causes the pain to be worse and may or may not speed up labor. I am for waiting, and unless the baby is in distress, I say let him come when he decides. At least now, there is time for an epidural."

"I agree. If you and the baby are okay, then waiting it is. So now that I am released from the hospital, is there anything I can get you or have brought to you?"

"No, Marcus. I have you and our baby, and our family at home, so life is perfect right now."

"Well, in that case Sam," Marcus spoke. "I have some cards here and I am feeling lucky at Blackjack, so what should we gamble for?"

"I say you changing all the dirty diapers. I think that is better than money."

"Sam, you play dirty, but alright. Dirty diapers. I have some paper here I'll use as dirty diaper tokens, but I warn you, I'm pretty good. You sure you want to go with dirty diapers?"

"Yes, and nightly feedings. You can also put that on the table."

"Sam, you know I have asked for time to get my mind straight, that is why I want to take some time at the Penthouse."

"So?" said Samantha.

"The nursery is still at the penthouse, or you can stay with all five kids and I will stay at the penthouse, or my apartment. I still have it."

"Deal," said Samantha.

"My wife plays dirty," he said as he dealt the cards. Marcus had made fifty tokens each and dealt the first hand.

"Hit me," said Samantha. Marcus gave her another card. She turned her cards to blackjack; Marcus had bet five dirty diaper tokens. Samantha raked them into her pile.

"My deal, Daddy."

Marcus passed the cards to her with a smile. "So, where did you learn to play blackjack?"

"You are not the only adventurous one. Me and some girl friends went to Vegas. Before I went, I read Kenny Houston's *On Strategies Of Playing*. Not that I was very good, but you know how I like to research everything. That what made me good in moot court. And you, Marcus? Where did you learn?"

"Me and the guys used to play in college for fun. I could usually hold my own, but I may have met my match." With a twinkle in her eye and a smile on her face she said, "We will see. Now do you want a card?"

"No, I will stand," he said. But before Samantha could turn over her cards, she looked distressed and said, "Labor pains have started. Best call Dr. McCullough and the nurse." Marcus left the room and went to the nurse's desk, "My wife in labor. Will you please call the doctor?"

"Yes, Mr. Matthew. Right away." Before the doctor came in, the nurse took Samantha's vitals and checked the fetal monitor. Dr McCullough came in and said, "Let's look. Yep, you're in labor. You are dilated to seven, nurse get an epidural ready. Samantha's babies come fast. Let's make her as comfortable as possible. Samantha, we will just have to time the contractions and wait. If you and the baby are not in distress, we will let nature take its course. Would you like to walk to try and move it along?"

"Yes," she said.

"Marcus, can you manage her walking her up and down the hall?" asked the doctor.

"Yes, I can." As they walked down the hall, they passed Mike. Samantha said, "I thought you were home with the kids."

"I was but I am head of security and Marcus wanted me here. Mason is at the house. I feel all the family is safe now that we know where Mr. Carr is." Samantha kissed Mike on the cheek, "You are a good friend. Thank you."

"You're welcome, that is my best friend's baby. I must make sure everyone is safe and that Marcus is doing his job," he said smiling,

"Yeah, man. I am doing my job as a husband and father; you do not have to worry about that." Mike just gave him a knowing look.

"Sam, how much farther do you think you can walk?"

"I am ready to go back, I am having another pain. And the pressure is crazy." Marcus walked Samantha back to her room.

"Nurse, call Dr. McCullough and tell her the pains are less than ten minutes apart."

"Yes, sir."

Dr. McCullough came in. Marcus was on the floor with Samantha, "So let's look. Yep, you're at nine centimeters and I'm going to break your water. Nurses, take her to delivery and get her ready. Help Mr. Matthew get ready to join us in delivery. Marcus," Dr McCullough continued, "are you ready to welcome number six?"

"Yes, I am." The nurse took Samantha to the delivery room and brought Marcus a gown and shoe coverings to put on.

"Bring me the needle to break her water." As soon as Samantha's water broke, she began to dilate to nine. "Samantha, not much longer," she said.

"I am going to throw up," said Samantha. The nurse brought her a pan. "Marcus, give your wife some ice chips and wipe off her head." Marcus was quiet, but attentive, as he reached for Samantha's hands.

"I love you. You are doing great."

"Marcus, even though I have had an epidural, I feel my anxiety rising. What if something's wrong with our baby?"

"He's strong, like his mother. Just a little while longer and he will be with us. I know, the boys' birth was not easy, but we are prepared for this one, better than we were for them. He is taking his time, so that is a good thing. Dr. McCullough, can you give Samantha something for her anxiety? I think she is about to have a panic attack," Marcus asked.

"Nurse," Dr. McCullough said, "Add some Ativan to her IV, that will calm her down. Once she relaxes, she will dilate and labor will move more rapidly. Talk to her Marcus, she is feeling out of control. You and I have talked about this, Samantha lives in fear, reassure her she is okay, and you are here to keep her safe." Marcus leaned over the bed and whispered in Samantha's ear, "Darling, I told you no matter what, I will always take care of you. You are my life."

"Marcus, please do not leave me. I'll try to work harder, to love you better, to be a good mother, please love me."

"Sam, I do love you and you do not need to do anything except take care of yourself. I will be there no matter what happens. You can do nothing to change my love for you. Now can we get our son here?"

"Marcus, please get ready to cut the cord. The baby is crowning." The fetal monitor when off. "The baby is in distress. The cord is wrapped around his neck. Samantha do not push until I have unwrapped the cord," said Dr. McCullough. Samantha held back and whispered, "Marcus, do not let our son die. I could not bear it."

"Sam, listen to me. Dr. McCullough has him. I have cut the cord. Now one last push and he is here."

"Marcus, would you like to show your son to his mother?"

"Yes. Yes, I would." The nurse handed Marcus the baby and he said, "Look Sam, he is beautiful. His hair is long and curly and his eyes are blue." The nurse then took him to clean him up and swaddled him in a blanket and handed him back to him father.

"John Marcus Matthew III, this is your mommy. You have her big blue eyes." He handed him to Samantha. "He is beautiful. He has your hair and Spanish coloring. He looks like the boys, only he has a lot more hair."

"Sam, I'd like to call him Trey for short," said Marcus.

"I love it, Marcus." Marcus kissed his son and then his wife. His thoughts were on the fact that he now had another child with his wife. There was no doubting this and the only person he ever has to share him with was his mother. He did not realize until she conceived that, even though he loved the boys with all his heart, he knew he had to share them some day with Joseph. As for Ester and Matilda, he loved just as much, but he someday would share them with memories of their dead parents. But Bella and Trey were theirs, and he knew that they would only look like their biological parents. It was a feeling he would keep to himself and later ask his psychologist about. He knew he had a lot of work to do with her. But for now, he wanted to enjoy his family.

Trey was yawning and stretching quietly, but he was hungry. They had agreed that they would use a milk bank and not have Samantha breast feed. Samantha was worn out and needed a break. So the nurse had a bottle ready and handed it to Marcus.

"Sam, may I be the first one to feed our son?"

"Yes, love. I'm just so tired." And with that statement she fell asleep. Dr. McCullough said, "The Ativan, stress, and the physical effort has worn her out. Once the nurse gets her cleaned up, she can be moved to her room."

"After you finish feeding Trey, will we let Dr. Wright, your pediatrician, look him over and then the nurse will bring him in."

"Thank you, Dr. McCullough."

"Marcus, you seriously need to think about Sam now. She's not the type of woman to keep having more children. She's been through too much stress in her life."

"I know, we have talked about it. She knows I want a big family and I am Catholic."

"Well, no sex for twelve weeks."

"That will not be a problem, Dr. McCullough. I have not told anyone except my doctors, but I will tell you. Since the accident, I have not been able to get an erection."

"So that's the mystery?" said Dr. McCullough. "Give yourself time, Marcus. After an incident and injury like you had, that is not unusual. Your health, it will come back. You should tell Samantha."

"I cannot. I feel like if I do, she'd feel sorry for me, and I never want that. Sam needs a whole man in every sense. I am giving myself time to work it out. If it does not come back, I will tell her, but I cannot do that to her. She needs physical love, as well."

"You young people, you forget your vows so easily. Anyway, I know it'll work out." And she finished sewing Samantha up and turned her over to the nurse to finish.

Trey finished eating and the nursery nurse took him in for a checkup. Marcus walked along side Samantha's bed as they pushed her back to her room. Marcus was elated, "We did it, my darling. We brought a healthy little boy into the world."

Samantha said, "We still have to wait until Dr. Wright does the checkup."

Marcus said, "This is our baby. We are compatible in our blood types. You have taken the Rogram shot, your prenatal care has been excellent. You have taken care of yourself. I am confident that our baby is healthy and we will give him so much love. He will be surrounded by people who will love him and take care of him. So, stop your worrying. It only adds stress to your wellbeing. I swear to you I will let nothing or no one harm our family. Now let's call the children first, then your parents and my family."

There was a knock at the door and in walked Dr. Wright and a nurse holding a tiny bundle wrapped in a blue blanket. Dr. Wright spoke first, "Mr. And Mrs. Matthew, you have a beautiful, healthy little boy. He weights six and half pounds and is 19 inches long. His vitals are perfect, so congratulations! He has a head of curly hair unlike most newborns, and we had to cut his fingernails as they were already so long so that he couldn't scratch himself. Samantha, the care you took of yourself shows in the health of your son. I know you had fears because of Jared, but no fears this time, your baby is perfect. Marcus, I know you are just as responsible for the health of your son and your wife. You are a diligent father and husband, so congratulations, well done. Do you have a name picked out?" Marcus shook Dr. Wright's hand and said, "Yes John Marcus Matthew III or Trey for short. Named after his grandfather and me.

"Well," said Dr. Wright. "Nurse, let's let these parents spend time with their son. The nurse handed Samantha the baby and said, "He is clean, diaper changed, and he's full. He has the sweetest disposition. Let me know if you want him to go back to the private nursery."

"Thank you," Samantha said. She was already unwrapping Trey to count finger and toes. Marcus looked on with his eyes glazed with tears. He sat down on the bed next to Samantha. "He is beautiful, just like his mother." Samantha reached for his hand, "I think you and I made a beautiful baby. He has my eyes, but your hair and skin coloring."

Marcus said, "Let me hold my son, please." Samantha handed Marcus the bundle and Marcus took him expertly, kissed him on his head and said quietly, "Little boy, you smell sweetly and your skin is so smooth. Yep, you are a beauty." Trey yawned and stretched and nestle down in his blanket, safe in his daddy's arms. Marcus took him to the rocking chair and sat there and rocked him when a knock came at the door.

"Come in," he spoke. Mike stuck his head in and said, "I do not mean to interrupt but I wanted to see my newest nephew."

"Come on in, man," Marcus spoke. "And meet Trey." He walked over to where Marcus was rocking the baby.

"He is beautiful. He has Samantha's eyes, but your hair and skin coloring." He laughed, "It is a good thing he has a beautiful mother, and a questionably handsome father." Marcus laughed, "We have Sam to thank for his beauty. "

Mike turned his attention to Samantha. "How are you feeling?"

"I feel good. Tired and relieved. Mike, have you been here all night?"

"You know I am not going anywhere."

Marcus spoke up, "Yes man, you need to get some rest. Call someone in to take your place until you get rested. I need you at your best, and thanks, brother. Go get some rest, that's an order," Marcus said.

"Yes, sir. The effects of coffee only last so long. I think I'll go home to Denise. I have not seen her in a week."

"Tell her Marcus said to shut the office down and give all the employees the day off with pay and a bonus. I want them to celebrate with us about the birth of our son, Trey. Have the publicists put a statement out, 'mother and son are doing well', etc. etc. I'm going to call our families. I want Sam to get some rest. Go man, rest, and enjoy your day. I'll see you back tomorrow morning."

"Sounds like a plan," said Mike and he turned and left the room.

"Sam, I going to put Trey in his crib and ask the nurse to take him back to the private nursery. I want you to rest. I am going to call the family and we will call the children later together." He brought Trey to Samantha to kiss the baby's head, placed him in her crib and rang for the nurse. After the nurse left, he called Saul and said, "Samantha and Trey are doing great, both healthy and beautiful. Will you call Rick and Scott? I am calling my parents now."

"Tell Samantha and Trey that they are so loved. Yes, I will call Rick," said Saul. "You two need to get some rest."

Marcus said, "Tell the children we will call them later and please tell Margaret thank you. Both of you have given my family so much support."

"Son, you are the best person who has come into our daughter's life. Thank you."

Next, Marcus called Isabella. "Mother we have our little boy who is in perfect health and so is Sam. Tell Dad and the rest of the family. We want at least a day to ourselves, please. Sam and I are both worn out."

"I'll take care of the family, son, you take care of yourself, Samantha, and my grandson. Love you, my son."

"Mom, I love you. By the way, he weights six and a half pounds, has Samantha's big blue eyes, my curly dark hair and he has the Spanish coloring of your side."

"He sounds beautiful. Goodbye, my love." She hung up. Marcus and Samantha were sleeping when the nurse came in with Trey and spoke, "Sorry to wake you Mrs. Matthew, since it so near to lunch time, I thought you might like to feed your son before you and your husband eat." Samantha sat up and reached for the baby, "Come to mama, my little angel. Let's let Daddy sleep."

"How can I sleep when my most beautiful wife and baby are awake?" Marcus sat on the side of Samantha's bed and watched her feed Trey.

"He is not as aggressive drinking his bottle as the boys were, or at least

Jacob," he spoke. "Marcus, do you think we are making a mistake by not using my breast milk?"

"Sam, I think as long as she is getting breast milk, we are making the right decision. You remember how painful breast feeding was with the boys and Bella? Even though you wanted to continue, it was just too much for you. I think we must take care of you. Some women use formula, at least we are using breast milk, like we finally ended up doing for the boys. They are healthy and there has been no difference. So, sweetheart, let's do what is best for you. I'd breast feed him if I could," he laughed.

"You did the work to get him here. Have they given you the shot to draw up your milk?"

"Yes, right after he was born."

"So, it is decided. Now let me have him and burp him," he said. Samantha handed Trey over to Marcus, "And you may want to change him. He's not smelling so sweet right now." Marcus chuckled. He went to the changing table and began to open the diaper. The nurse came in with lunch trays, "Mr. Matthew, I'd be glad to change him for you."

"No, I got this." Marcus washed his hands and sat at the table with Samantha. "Looks good. Steak, mmmm." When they finished, Marcus spoke, "Let's show Trey to his brothers and sisters by Skype."

"Good idea, I'll call the nurse and ask that they bring Trey back in," said Samantha. In came the nurse with a blue bundle. Marcus sat up the tablet and dialed the Margaret's number. Margaret appeared on the screen.

"Are the children around?" Marcus asked.

"They just got back from Phillipe's restaurant. I was going to give them some quiet time. Let me call them, they will be excited to see you and their new baby brother," said Margaret.

"Margaret, will you get Dad also? I'd like him to see Trey too. I think we are going to stay two more days and then come home. We are going to ask the family to schedule visits at home rather than the hospital. It will be easier. Marcus feels it would be safer if we control the access to the nursery. He's still not himself when it comes to the family's safety."

"Honey, whatever you two decide. We will be here until you do not need us to stay. Do you want me to tell Joseph to come in?"

"No, just the kids and dad and you. Joseph can see him when we get home before he leaves to go back to DC," said Marcus. Margaret got on the house intercom and asked the children, who were in the playroom, to come to the dining room for a surprise visitor. Then she walked into the library where Saul was having a scotch and playing chess with Joseph.

"Saul, please join the family in the dining room. Your daughter would like to talk to you."

"Joseph, pour yourself another scotch and I will be back," he said. When the family had all gathered around the dining room table, Margaret turned the screen so that everyone could see.

"Hi, my darlings," Samantha spoke. "Daddy and I wanted to introduce you to your baby brother. John Marcus Matthew, meet your brothers Jacob and Jared. Your sisters are Ester, Matilda, and Bella. That is your grandfather Saul and your grandmother Margaret," Samantha spoke.

"Kids, we are calling him Trey for short," Marcus said.

"So, what do you think about your baby brother?" Bella spoke up, "He's so small. He looks like a doll."

Ester scowled, "Of course he's small, he's just born."

"Be nice, Ester. She's just a kid," Matilda interrupted.

"He has big eyes," Bella observed.

"Dad," said Jacob. "May we go back to the playroom? He just looks like a baby to me."

"Jacob, be a little more patient," said Jared. "You'd better get used to him.

He's here to stay. Just like Ester, Matilda, and Bella." Marcus said in a stern voice, "You five needed to welcome your brother. Remember what I told you about family taking care of family?"

"Yes, sir," they said in unison.

"That's better. We called to tell you we will be home in two days. Now go back to the playroom, we love you." They all five jumped from their chairs and hurried out of the room. Saul spoke, "He is a beauty like his mother."

Margaret spoke, "And I cannot wait to brush that beautiful hair."

"Thanks, you guys," said Marcus, "Your support really means a lot to us."

"Of course, son," said Saul. "You promised to make me a grandfather, many times over, and love my daughter and take care of her. We are a family."

"Yes, sir," said Marcus, "and I will always live up to my word."

"How are you feeling, Marcus?"

"Good. I've been released and will have to do therapy and see my shrink for some counseling, but right now, I am the happiest man alive."

Margaret said, "Good, but glad he is here."

"We love you," said Saul, "Get some rest."

"Dad, I love you too."

Marcus said, "Thank you sir," and turned off the screen.

The next morning, Dr. McCullough came in early and spoke, "Samantha, how are you feeling today?"

"Like a woman who just delivered a baby two days ago. I feel good. Just a little tired and my breasts are still uncomfortable."

"That's to be expected, but they will dry up. Everything on my examination was good and so was Dr. Wright's report on Trey. I think you can go home tomorrow. How does that sound? I know you have plenty of support and I will stop by and see you since I live in the neighborhood."

"Thank you, Dr. McCullough. I'm ready to go home and join my family. I know they miss me and will be excited to see their new brother."

Dr. McCullough said, "Plenty of rest, continue with your pre-natal vitamins, eat well, and no sex for twelve weeks." Dr. McCullough looked at Marcus and asked, "When will you get your cast off?"

Marcus replied, "Two weeks."

"Well, I am sure you will be able to help out just fine. After all, you have an elevator in your home. But last time the no sex rule did not get followed, so twelve weeks, understood?"

"Yes ma'am," said Marcus. Dr. McCullough signed Samantha's chart and said, "Marcus, could I speak to you in the hallway, please?"

"Sure thing, I will be right back, darling, I sure I am about to get a lecture since I was not a good boy last time." He winked at Samantha and followed Dr. McCullough into the hallway. Mike was there and Marcus asked if he would go in and stay with Samantha.

"Sure thing, boss." Mike said.

Dr. McCullough spoke seriously to Marcus, "I understand that you have issues, and you want to work it out without telling your wife, but in twelve weeks, if you have not regained function, then tell her. I do not want Samantha worried or stressed about anything. I'm not only her doctor, but I care for you and your family."

Marcus spoke, "I promise if I do not have it worked out in the twelve weeks, I will tell her, and we will go from there. I know my wife; she is not the kind of woman to live with a man who she cannot have sex with."

"Marcus, there are several medical things to help with erectile dysfunction."

"I know but I am too young to have to rely on a device or pills. I want my normal self, call it manhood. But that's the way I feel."

"Marcus," Dr. McCullough hugged him. "Give yourself time. You survived an injury that would have killed most men. Time, patience, and good therapy. Samantha loves you."

"I love her, but I want everything to be the same," he spoke.

"Yes, but things are not the same, trauma does a lot of things to the mind and body. You will get through it, do not sell your wife short," spoke Dr. McCullough. "Anyway, I will discharge her tomorrow morning and you can make arrangements to take your wife and baby home. Goodbye and good luck. I'll see her soon."

Marcus went back into Samantha's room, "Mike, Sam's getting discharged tomorrow morning. Let's follow the same arrangement we did with the boys and Bella. The nurse and Trey will leave with you by the side entrance. You send a driver and security, and we will leave from the front of the hospital."

"I will get it set up right now," Mike said. He then left the room.

"So, did you get a lecture about restraining from sex?" Samantha asked. Marcus looked sheepish, "You know I did. My reputation with Dr. McCullough in that department, well let's say is not that good. But I promised her, I will wait twelve weeks. Now you will also have to be patience. Last thing we need is another baby right after Trey."

"Darling," said Samantha. "There are other things we can do."

"Yea, and that could lead to me losing control of myself."

"Tomorrow we will take our son home. You want to call the kids and tell them?" Sam asked.

"No, let's call Margaret and let her know and surprise the children. I will call my parents now and tell them in a few days they can visit their new grandson. They can tell the girls and Phillipe in a week or so."

"I'll call Rick when I get home. He will want to come by with Scott in a few days. He's been such a dear handling my office," said Samantha.

"You call Margaret now and I'll call mother." Samantha picked up her phone and dialed Margaret and told her that they'd be home tomorrow and wanted to surprise the children. Marcus hung up from talking to his mother, "She said to kiss her grandson and when you felt up to visitors to let her know."

"Marcus, are you ready?"

"Darling, I more than ready. I want everything we had back, and more." He kissed Samantha on the lips passionately, the first time he really showed that much passion since the accident. She felt that old stirring between her legs. Samantha said, "Down boy, you made Dr. McCullough a promise."

He grinned, "Yes, I did."

Samantha couldn't resist and kissed him back. A kiss full of passion and longing. As soon as she reached her hand towards his cock, he turned away quickly. Samantha was confused, but understood he wanted to behave himself this time.

The next morning, Dr McCullough had given the nurse the discharge papers and checked Samantha's vitals one more time. "Looks like you're ready, and here are your son's discharge papers signed by Dr. Wright, so you are ready to go." In walked a private nurse with Trey, along with Mike.

"Everything is ready, Marcus. We are going to leave now." Marcus kissed his son's head and said, "Take care of him."

"Man, you know I will. This is my nephew after all. Samantha will see you at the mansion." Mike spoke.

"Your security is in the hall and will escort you down. A driver and another team will follow you," said Marcus.

"I got this," said Mike. Marcus slapped Mike on the shoulder, "I know you do, I guess I am a little paranoid."

"Yep, you are," said Mike, "but we have you." The nurse brought a wheelchair for Samantha and wheeled her to the front entrance of the hospital. As expected, there were reporters and cameras, the security team cleared the couple's path. Marcus helped Samantha into the limo and said, "Let's go home."

"Yes, sir." As they were leaving, the other security van fell in behind them. There were shouts from the reporters, "Where is the baby?" No one stopped to answer. The company's publicist would handle the press. Marcus took Samantha's hand and said, "I'm ready to go home, darling." Samantha smiled at Marcus and said, "You are my true love, and remember we said no lies, that no matter what our love for each other will always see us through. We also said that our family is the most important thing to us."

"Yes, sweetheart. I will never lie to you, but I will protect you with my life, whatever I have to do, I will do it."

"Then Marcus, we have nothing to worry about. We will get through this. You are the last love my heart can open up to. I'd rather be alone if I cannot be with you."

"Sam," Marcus said, then he pulled her head to him and kissed her lips with the passion she knew he had for her. She kissed him with equal passion, searching his mouth with her tongue. He pulled back, "Woman, are you trying to make me break my promise to Dr. McCullough? She said no sex for twelve weeks." Samantha giggled.

"No, but I did not promise her that and it has been so long since I had you inside me."

"Darling, when our time restraints are up, I promise you we will go on a vacation just the two of us and make up for lost time. Right now, please let's be patient, your health is the most important thing to me, and it seems no matter what precautions we take, I always get you pregnant. You must be the most fertile woman I have ever met." Samantha laid her head on his shoulder. The driver finally reached the mansion and pulled in front of the house.

"Come on, darling, our family is waiting, and it looks like Mike has already arrived with Trey and the nurse." He helped Samantha get out of the car as the driver opened the door. Marcus opened the door to the house and Peter met them in the foyer. "Welcome home, Mr. and Mrs. Matthews."

"Thank you, Peter. Where is everyone?" Marcus spoke.

"Well, when the baby arrived the kids got very rowdy and so the nurse, along with Margaret, took him to the nursery. The nanny took Jacob, Bella, Ester, and Matilda to the theater room to watch a movie. Their grandfather is with Jared in the library playing chess. I caught a glimpse of your son, and he is very beautiful. Can I get you something? Maybe some lunch?"

"Yes, have Peg fix us a light lunch and serve it in the kitchen. My wife is tired, but we want to check on the children first."

"Yes sir, I'll tell Mrs. Peggy," Peter said.

"Brace yourself, Sam. Our herd is stampeding." Samantha laughed, "Seems that way. But daddy's home and they will quickly get back in line." Marcus and Samantha first stopped at the library to find Saul and Jared in a heated chess game.

"Samantha, darling, I'm so glad you're home. Marcus, you are looking much better than the last time I saw you." Jared ran to his mommy and then his dad, "I'm so glad you are home. I missed you so much."

"We missed you too." Marcus picked up Jared and said, "Who is winning?"

"Grandfather, but just barely." Saul said, "The boy learns fast. I think we may have a chess prodigy on our hands."

Samantha said, "He's got the best teacher. So, Jared, did you see Trey?"

"Yes, but just for a little while. The other kids were making so much noise that Margaret and the nurse sent us out. He looks like you, Mom. He has your curly hair, but he's dark like me, Jacob, and Dad"

"Well, you finish your game with your grandfather." Marcus put him down so he could return to his chair opposite Saul. "We are going up to see the other children in the movie room before we check on Trey." As Marcus pushed the elevator button, Joseph and Mike stepped off.

"Hey, you two, you have a beautiful son, congratulations."

"Thank you," said Marcus. "For all your support to my family."

"Man, all you have to do his call and I will be here."

"So where are you going? You look like you're packed."

"It is time I get back to my family. Sophia is missing her daddy. Mike's talking to my jet at the airport, and I am leaving as soon as we can take off." Marcus reached for Joseph's hand and pulled him into an embrace, "Thanks man. We are family. Call me if you need anything." Joseph laughed well, "You might need to make another campaign donation. I decided, I am going to run for governor of Virginia. Seems like I might be able to do better there than state senator."

"You got it. Anything else I can do?" said Marcus.

Joseph turned his attention to Samantha, "I am a phone call and a plane ride away, anytime you need me." He took her in his arms and held her a little longer than just friends, he whispered in her ear, "I will always love you." He kissed her on the side of her head. He looked at her with tears in his eyes.

Mike hugged Marcus, "Brother, I'm going to my condo to spend some time with Denise. Mason and the team are here and if you need me, you know how to get me. Enjoy that beautiful little boy. I'll check in tomorrow."

"No," said Marcus. "Take the week off, you deserve it. You and Denise use the jet and go somewhere. Go to Wyoming if you want, hell, go somewhere warm. You two deserve it. I am here. I can handle everything for a few days." Mike turned to Samantha, "Trey is beautiful and now that their father is home, he can get the kids back in line. I am afraid Joseph and I just do not have his touch." He kissed Samantha on the cheek, and they left out the front door of the mansion. Marcus pushed the button on the elevator to the second floor and he and Samantha went into the room where the children were watching a movie. As soon as they spotted their parents, the movie was forgotten, and they rushed for their parents. Marcus picked up Bella and kissed her cheek. He bent over and kissed Matilda and Bella on the cheeks, then hugged Jacob.

"Daddy, you're home!" They were so excited.

"Hey, your mother's home also, and what about that baby brother?" he asked.

The girls went to Samantha and hugged her, "He's beautiful mommy, can we help feed him? Grandmother Margaret said we had to wait. She made us leave the nursery because Jacob and Jared were so loud."

"No, I wasn't," said Jacob. "Mommy, it was the girls."

"She's just a baby, cannot do much yet. How about a hug for your mother? And girls, when he gets a little older, yes, you can help feed him," Marcus said. "And all of you can learn to change diapers, especially the dirty ones."

"Not me," said Jacob, "I will wait until he can do something, like blocks are something." Ester said, "He does not want to play with your stupid blocks."

"Now, finish your movie and then I'd like a report on important women in history and what they have accomplished. Your nanny can help you; I will see it at bedtime."

"Daddy's back," said Matilda. "Yes, Daddy's back. Now go back to your movie, mommy and I are going to the nursery to check on Trey." The nursery was on the third floor where all the bedrooms were. As they entered the nursery, Margaret was giving Trey a bottle. She looked at Samantha and Marcus, "He is beautiful. A perfect combination of the best of the two of you. He looks like his daddy, but has his mother's big blue eyes. How are you both feeling?"

"I think we are both tired and hungry but glad to be home."

Samantha said, "Thank you Margaret, for all your help."

"Would not have it another way sweet pea. Now the two of you go eat and rest, you are going to need it, even with all the help. You got a litter to watch over and teach to be the kind of children that grow into adults that make contributions to this world."

"Yes, Margaret we do. And it takes all of us, family and friends, to shape and influence those minds." Samantha leaned over and kissed Trey's cheek, Margaret said, "Go, you two, you have plenty of opportunities to be the hands-on parents, but you are going to need the strength to do it."

"You heard Margaret," said Marcus. "Let's go see what Peggy has for us to eat and then let's both of us take a nap." They left the nursery and pushed the elevator to the first floor. Peggy had everything set up at the bar in the kitchen, just like old times.

"Peg, what is for lunch?" Marcus asked.

"Turkey sandwiches, salad, and a fruit cup. Mrs. Matthew, I poured you a milk, water, and an herbal tea. Marcus, would you like a beer?" Peggy asked.

"Sounds good to me, thanks. Sam, do you want wine instead of milk? I'm pretty sure it won't hurt you."

"No, Marcus, milk is good. I think I will limit liquor for a while."

"Sweetheart, whatever you decide. Boy, I am hungry. Thanks Peg, this hits the spot."

"How are you, Mr. Matthew?" she asked.

"Well, as soon as I get this cast off, I will be better. The doctor said two more weeks, then six weeks of physical therapy."

"Well, we are glad to have you home, and I got a glimpse of your son, he is a real beauty."

"Thank you. He looks like his mother."

"Mrs. Matthew," said Peggy. "How are you feeling?"

"Tired, but glad to be home. Thank you for all your help with the children."

"You're very welcome. They are a cute bunch of kids, just a little on the rowdy side. But I think that they are so smart and of course they have been missing their dad. It is good you're both home. Children need both their parents," she spoke.

"Well, Sam, if you're finished let's go up and catch a nap before duty calls. Peggy, please tell the cook to prepare a family dinner tonight. Sam's parents will be here, and of course, just our family. I'd like it served in the dining room. Tell him to make it a celebration of the new baby and us being home."

"Of course, Mr. Matthew. I will tell him to prepare something special."

"Sam, let's go up," said Marcus.

"Thank you, Peggy," Sam said and walked with Marcus to the elevator to go to the third floor where all the bedrooms were. Samantha said as they entered their bedroom, "It has been so long since we shared a bed, with the accident, your hospitalization, and then the baby. I'm not sure I know how to restrain myself."

"Darling, I know, but the time will pass fast. Now, it's so damn hard to get my sweat pants off, I'm just going to remove my shirt and lay down," said Marcus

"Well, I'm going to get comfortable and pull out a gown out to put on."

"Hey you," said Marcus, "Nothing sexy."

"How about a flannel granny gown, will that work?" she asked.

"Perfect, now come and lay in my arms and let me kiss you and then let's get some rest." Marcus took Samantha in his arms and kissed her passionately. Normally, he would have gotten hard, did not happen. Frustrated, he said, "Sleep well. I love you." He laid there and thought about his problem; Sam, however, was fast asleep. *How would I tell her this problem?* He thought, *I will get it back like the doctor said and then I will tell her.*

Pretty soon, he drifted into sleep, but woke up suddenly from a bad dream where he was being shot and his family was in danger. The shrinks he was seeing said this would happen. He got up and looked in his bag for the anxiety medicine and pain pills the doctors had prescribed. Sam was still asleep, so Marcus decided to visit Trey in the nursery. The nurse was changing his diaper and had a bottle ready to have fed to him.

"Hello, Mr. Matthew," she said. "Would you like to feed your son?

"Yes, I would. I can't get enough of his sweet smile."

"Each baby is their own person, and he seems to be a sweetie, but that can change as he gets older. That is what is so neat about children; they are their own person," she said. "Nurture only plays so much as genetics play a major role also."

"Do you have children?" Marcus asked as he took Trey in his arms and sat in the rocking chair and began giving him a bottle.

"No, sir. I've never been married, never found the right man, but being a private baby nurse has always been enough. I do have my cats. I guess I will be a cat woman."

"Well take a break. I've got him. His mother will probably be up soon."

"Thank you, sir. I won't too be long." She left as Marcus was having a conversation with Trey. She thought, *Now if I had ever run into a man like that…* she did not finish her thoughts.

***

"Let's go have dinner with the children and then we will come and tuck Trey in," said Marcus. Samantha took Marcus' hand and rode the elevator to the first floor where the children had gathered around the table with Saul and Margaret. It had been months since the family was all together. Since Marcus left on his motorcycle and had been attacked by Mr. Carr. Marcus took his seat at the head of the table and Samantha at the other end of the table. The boys were sitting between Margaret and the girls were sitting between Saul.

"Before we begin our blessing and meal, I'd like to thank each of you for doing your part to keep our family supported during this unexpected threat to the safety of our family. I want you children to know that family and health come before money and power. There is a responsibility to having great wealth and power. You are never untouchable, but you cannot live your life in fear. You do everything to protect the ones you love, and life moves forward, changing, but it is what you make it. Now bow your heads and be thankful for our blessings: family, health, our new baby. Someday you will each have your own family and I want you to learn what is important under God's plan. Thank you for the food that has been prepared for us and teach us, oh Lord, to be humble. Amen." There was a chorus of 'amens' around the table.

"So," Marcus said as the meal was being served. "Did each of you complete your reports?" Matilda was the first to answer, "I'll have mine before bedtime."

Ester spoke up, "Bella and I are finished, Daddy, and so is Jacob."

Jared said, "You did not assign me one, so I worked on my chess strategy with grandfather, and we found a tournament that I can enter."

"Sounds like you have all been busy. Your mother and I took a nap and visited with your new brother. Let's plan an early night tonight, as school starts back tomorrow."

Samantha said, "I hope all of you are ready. I guess your daddy will have to take you since I cannot drive yet."

"So," Marcus said. "Be ready to leave by 8:15am. I'll drop you off on my way into work. Uncle Mike and Denise have the week off, but I will pick you up after school." he said.

"I think your grandmother and grandfather will be going back home tomorrow, so I am counting on each of you to fall back in line; studies, extra activities, your chores, and help out with the baby. Can I count on you?" Marcus continued.

"Yes," came from all around the table. The rest of the dinner went with idle chatter and after dessert, the children went to their rooms to finish up their reports and get ready for bed. Margaret and Saul retired to their suite after kissing each child goodnight. The nannies went into the children's room to help them finish up for the night and get ready for bed. Samantha and Marcus visited the girl's room first. Marcus took their reports and said, "I'll read them tonight and we will discuss them tomorrow."

"Are we getting a book tonight?" Bella asked.

"I tell you what," said Marcus. "Since this is the first night home for me and your mom, can your nanny read you a book? I want a hug and a kiss, as I am sure your mother does too."

"Goodnight, my sweet girls," said Samantha, and she kissed each girl on the cheek. Marcus leaned over and gave them a tickle, kissed their heads, and said,

"Sweet dreams."

"Goodnight, Mommy and Daddy. We love you."

"We love you more," said Marcus. Then they went to see the boys. Their nanny was having a hard time getting them to settle down. It seems like they wanted to have a pillow fight.

"Hey," Marcus said. "Are you ready for bed"

"Yes, sir," came the answer from both. "Now tell your mom goodnight and cut out the monkey business."

"Goodnight, Mommy." Samantha kissed them on the cheek and Marcus did their favorite fist bump.

"Night, boys," he said. "Love you."

The night nurse was coming on to take care of Trey. He was already bathed, fed, and curled up in their cribs. Marcus and Samantha looked down at him quietly and blew him kisses. Marcus said quietly, "Love you, little prince." He told the night nurse that he and Samantha would not be getting up with the baby tonight and she was to handle Trey and check in on the other children.

"I think we can both use an uninterrupted night tonight."

"Yes, sir. That is probably best. I can handle the children tonight and their nannies are up in their rooms, so if I need them, I'll call them. But I am sure all will be quiet. Trey went down easy. He seems to be an easy-going baby as long as he is fed and dry." Marcus laughed, "I hope it stays that way. He has Matthew blood in him, and that sweet disposition may not last long. Sam you look tired, let's go to bed. It will be an early day and my foot is throbbing. I need to rest it."

They went to their room and began to get ready for bed. "Samantha, I'm going to stay here at home as much as possible, but there may be a night that I'll stay at the condo, simply to work on my therapy."

"Whatever we need to do, love. We will make it work." He turned out the lamp beside their bed and she did also. Marcus put his arms around her and kissed her on the head.

"Goodnight, my love."

"I am so glad you are home, darling," said Samantha. "I could not do this without you."

"You will not have to. Get some rest."

The next morning, as the alarm went off, Marcus hit the button, kissed Sam, and said, "Darling if you want to sleep in, I'll handle the children." Samantha kissed him passionately on the lips and said, "You're a brave man. No, I'll check on Trey and if he has not eaten, I'll bring him down and we will all have breakfast together." Marcus kissed her back, and said, "I offered. See you downstairs."

After a quick shower, he put on jeans, a linen shirt, and suede work boots. These were his favorite go-to shoes and he quickly laced them up, slapped Samantha on the butt, and said, "See you downstairs."

Samantha got up and took a long, warm shower. She hated the post-baby effects on her body and could not wait to get her body back in shape. Maybe then they would resume their electric love life. She missed the feel of Marcus inside her and hoped he would break his word to Dr. McCullough and resume their very satisfying sex life. She dressed hurriedly and went to the nursery to check on Trey. The morning nurse was just getting there and preparing a bottle for Trey, who was fussing in his crib.

"Good morning, Mrs. Matthew. We have a very hungry little boy here. He slept four hours at a time before he needed feeding," the night nurse said. "So, he's ready now."

"Let me take him downstairs, please. I'd like the two of us to have breakfast with his father and the children. I think it is important for us all start getting use to be a family again."

"Certainly, Mrs. Matthew. Let me wrap him in a blanket and give you the bottle."

By this time, Trey was starting to cry. Samantha took him from the nurse and placed the bottle in his mouth as they rode the elevator to the first floor to have breakfast with the family. The children were promptly there at seven, dressed in their Catholic uniforms for school. Marcus got up and pulled out Samantha's chair and kissed Trey on the head, "Good morning, my little angel." The other children were chattering away about back to school. Marcus spoke sharply to them, "Your mother and brother have joined us. How about a good morning to each of them?'

"Good morning, Mommy and Trey," came their reply.

"Good morning, my loves. Are you excited about getting back to school?"

Jared said, "Yes, mom. I want to sign up for the chess team."

Jacob spoke up, "I'd rather go to work with Daddy."

"Not today, son," said Marcus. "The first day of school is important."

Ester said, "I want to see my friend Missy. She got a new dog over the holidays."

Matilda said, "I missed art class, Mommy. You know I want to be a famous artist someday."

"I want to be a world-famous dancer and actress. And a lawyer, too, like Mommy," said Bella.

"Well," Samantha said, "first things first, get a good education and you all can do what you want. Now finish up and brush your teeth, get your backpacks, and meet Daddy in the foyer." As they passed by, they each gave Samantha a kiss on the check. Ester patted Trey, "See you later baby brother." Marcus asked, "Sam, do you and Trey have plans today?"

"Just the usual, eating and sleeping and waiting for the family to get home."

"Well, I better get the children out to the van. It is warmed up and ready. Going to be a cold one today. February is going fast. I hope spring comes early; I am tired of this cold weather."

"We may have to plan a quick getaway. Sources say my dad has got his eye on buying a small island. Wants me to check it out as soon as I feel up to it. The cast will be off this week. Then physical therapy starts and hopefully I can get back to doing what I love; building projects and having sex with my wife." He kissed Samantha passionately and said, "Trey, I hope you let your mommy get some rest."

"Sam, you have plenty of help, two nannies, a nurse, and Peg and Phillip to run the house."

"I know, darling, but do call your parents and sisters and set a time for them to visit. I'm going to call Rick and see what is going on at the office."

"Sam, next week my parents can visit and the following week, my sisters and Phillipe want to visit their nephew. My family is different from yours; calm and quiet is not their nature. See you after I pick the children up from school."

"Marcus, their karate teacher will be by this afternoon. I think it is time that they start going to his classes so they can be with the other children."

"I think you're right. Let's talk to him after their private lesson. Now you and Trey go lay down. He is already asleep. Sam, I am amazed at how beautiful he is, we make pretty babies together." He kissed Samantha on the head and left to take the children to school.

The week passed quickly. Isabella and John would be there for Sunday dinner, Penelope, Paige, and Phillipe the following Saturday. Margaret and Saul dropped in, checking to make sure everything was going smoothly. Rick stopped by with papers for Samantha to sign and said the new attorney was really picking up the slack, and that all the clients knew that she was on maternity leave.

"I asked everyone not to send gifts," he said. "But there are a few, so here are the ones that are not flowers. I had the paralegal take the flowers to the other offices throughout the building. Scott sends his love, and after a few weeks when everyone calms down, we will come by and see our nephew. So, Joseph has gone back home?" Rick asked.

"Yes, he has a family and Mike has the week off."

"Well, you look tired. Rest, I got the office."

"Rick, why don't you and Scott take a vacation?"

"We will as soon as your father-in-law closes on the island retreat. That might be some time, but we can wait. I'm good now and Scott is watching his precious stocks. You know he cannot leave them right now. Anyway, see you soon," he said and let himself out.

Peg came in with lunch on a tray, "I thought I'd take this to your room so after eating you can rest. The nurse has Trey."

"Yes, I think that is a good idea," said Samantha. "I have so many cards to sign, so some quiet time will be nice."

It was hard to believe that Trey was ready for his first month's appointment with Dr. Wright. Marcus was going to meet them there, and a driver was going to pick up the children with Mike. Mason was going to drive Samantha and Trey. As they pulled up to the doctor's office, Marcus' car was already there. He was waiting in the doctor's foyer and took Trey from Sam's arms. He was so loving towards him. Trey had an easy smile and sweet disposition. Marcus was convinced, though, that he would change as he is part Spanish. The nurse took them right in and asked them to undress Trey for weight and measurement. He had gained two pounds and was 20 inches long. Dr. Wright came in and exchanged conversation with Marcus.

"Samantha, he is in perfect health. Keep him on a regular diet of breast milk. How is he sleeping?" Dr. Wright asked.

"He has just this week started sleeping six hours at a time."

"Well, you got a sweet one here. Hopefully by next month, he will be sleeping all night. Next time he is here, we will need to start his shots." Marcus was helping the nurse to redress him. He shook Dr. Wright's hand and asked, "Sam, would you like to get lunch before we go home? There is a cafe in the building."

"That'd be nice. Do you want to send Mason home or have him wait?"

"I think he can take my car and go home. We will take your SUV home because it has his car seat in it." This was the first outing that Trey had had. It was nice to be out just the three of them. The server said, "Sit anywhere you want and I'll bring a seat that holds the baby carrier."

Marcus had covered his face with a baby blanket. He did not want anyone to sneak a picture of him, just in case they recognized us. Lunch talk was mostly about his new project and going to see the island that his dad wanted to purchase.

"How's the physical therapy going, darling? You have not talked much about it." "It is going well. I hope to be released from it in another week. There are no problems with my leg or foot. It appears to be good as new." "How about the counseling? Marcus are you able to come to some resolution with your PTSD?"

"I am getting there," he said.

"Well, you know it has been a month, do you think we could do more than play around? I miss our sex." "No, I promised Dr. McCullough twelve weeks and we are going to stay the course. Sam, I want what is best for you, so be patient." "It just not like you to want to wait." Marcus brushed off Samantha's comments with, "Waiting will just make it more exciting. I wanted to tell you that Renee is in town, and she has asked if she can stay at the condo. I wanted to ask you before I gave her an answer." Samantha felt uneasy but did not want to appear jealous. "I guess that's all right. Why the condo?"

"I think she thinks it will be more private. I told her the staff was small there and she would have to hire her own. She said her agency would take care of everything and even pay rent if I wanted. I told her to give the money to charity, we did not need her money."

"Well, I guess that is settled," Samantha said. "I do not want to appear jealous of her, but she is your ex-lover."

"Yes, Sam, but she does not have the standards I would ever be interested in. I have what I want: you and my six children. She was a fling. She probably has had a dozen lovers since, of both sexes." Marcus leaned over and kissed Samantha, "You are more lover than I can handle. Let's pay the check and head home. Trey is starting to squirm; he is probably getting hungry or wants to get out of that baby seat." He picked him up, paid as we went out, and fastened him in the car seat. He opened the door for Samantha. "Have you driven yet?"

"No, I think I will start next week. I am taking things slow. I thought I might drop in on Rick next week, just to see how the firm is going. I think we have a few new clients, and I really should make an effort to see them."

"Sam, you know if you want to quit it is fine with me."

"I know, but I like the stimulation, Marcus."

"Well, darling, it is up to you. I know your plate is full with work, the children, charities, and all the other things you try to do. What would you think of The Matthew's Group being your only client? We certainly keep your firm busy with this new project. I'd like you and the children to be able to travel with me. Dad suggested it and I think he is right, but it is up to you."

Samantha spoke, "Let me think about it. I'd like to talk to Dad. I'd have to sell the practice to someone that I thought very highly of. It is my reputation."

"Well maybe the new lawyer that you said was doing so well. They might be interested in your firm."

"I'll have to work her into it and then she probably could not afford to buy me out. It took me years to build my practice." "I know, sweetheart, you could work a loan out for her and she can lease from Saul."

"You really want this don't you?" Sam asked.

"Well, it may be a little selfish but after last year and with the accident, I'd like to keep my family close to me, if possible." Samantha kissed him on the cheek, "Let me think your proposal through. No discount for family," she laughed.

"But lots of fringe benefits. Let's get our son inside where it's warm." As they entered the house, they could hear the chatter of the children who had just gotten home from school and were heading to the kitchen for a snack.

"I'll take Trey up to the nurse," Marcus said. "And then join you and the children in the kitchen." He kissed Samantha on the head and pushed the elevator button to the second floor.

Marcus entered the kitchen where the children were eating apple slices and took one off of Ester's plate.

"Hey Daddy, get your own," she said.

Matilda said, "I will share, Daddy."

"That's okay. I'm just bugging Ester. I can cut another apple for myself."

Jared spoke up, "Ester whines about everything."

"No, I don't," she said.

"You do, too! You never stop," argued Bella.

"Okay, no more arguing, kids. Tell me what happened at school today."

Jacob spoke up as he dipped his apple slice in peanut butter, "We got a second-place ribbon on our science project."

Samantha spoke up, "Did you do your best?"

Jared spoke up and said, "I did the report and Jacob and Bella did the poster and that is where we lost points. She said it could have been neater."

"Well, could it have been neater?"

"Yes," said Jared, "but Jacob waited to the last minute and Bella isn't great at art."

"That's not nice!" Bella shouted.

"Well then, I think second is a good place to be," said Marcus. "You three know if I could have been there, I would have. I do not like the tone of the conversation this afternoon. So, before bed I want thank you notes to your grandfathers, Uncle Joseph and Uncle Mike, and your grandmothers thanking them for all the help they gave to you while me and your mother were in the hospital. And I'd like one to our staff: Peter, Peggy, your nannies, and the rest of our staff. Everyone made your lives easier and instead of complaining, I'd like to see some gratitude. Also, your baby brother went to the doctor today and not one of you asked about him. And did anyone remember to ask your mother or me how our day went? I think you five have forgotten your manners and how to show appreciation since I've been away. So, I think some extra chores are in order. I'll come up with a list. Now whose been feeding Buddy?"

"Peter," said Matilda. "And he has been walking him."

"Is that his job?" Marcus asked.

"No, sir," said Jacob.

"And when we got him, what did you all promise? Do you think that was fair to Buddy or Phillip?"

"No, sir," said Bella.

"Okay, I am back, so no more goofing off. I'll come up with a chore list with your mom. Make sure Buddy has food, water, and is walked. Then get ready for karate. I will be in my study. And I think your mother should rest before dinner."

Samantha walked over to Marcus, "I'm so glad you're home. I'll check on Trey before I lay down." She kissed Marcus on the lips and left the kitchen.

Marcus said, "Put your plates in the dishwasher and I will see you at dinner." Marcus left the kitchen and the children put their plates in the dishwasher.

Matilda said, "Daddy's back."

"Yeah, I guess we had better do what we are supposed to," said Jared. They all left the kitchen. Jared fed and watered Buddy, Jacob and Matilda walked him around the patio, and Ester and Bella had a towel ready to wipe his feet when they brought him back in. The all went to their rooms, where the nannies had laid out their karate uniform and joined their trainer in the playroom.

The children were growing quickly. Trey was trying to crawl; he gets on his knees and rocks back and forth. Bella was going to 4th grade and the twins were getting ready for 5th grade. Ester was in seventh grade and Matilda was in ninth. Samantha was spending more time at the office, but was seriously thinking of selling her practice. Saul had given his blessing and thought that the Matthew Group was enough to keep her busy, especially with the children and all her volunteer work.

Marcus was getting ready to check out the island that his dad wanted to buy and wanted to take the family with him for the summer. He finished with physical therapy and had started going to the condo to swim in the indoor pool. Samantha really did not like it because she knew Renee was there. She trusted Marcus, but not Renee, who was a known troublemaker according to Mike. Sometimes it was after ten pm when he got home.

He still had not had intercourse with Samantha yet. She began to worry that he did not find her attractive sexually, anymore. He still showed passion towards her; they fooled around but he would stop right before he should have wanted him inside her. She had cornered Mike and asked him if he knew what was going on. Mike said, "Marcus needs to answer you, that is all I can say."

It was dinner time and Marcus had called and said he was going to be swimming at the condo. He had been running late from the office, but he was trying to get home to tuck the children in.

"Mike," Samantha said, "I've had enough. Come with me to the condo. I know Renee is not supposed to be there when Marcus is swimming, but I've had enough secrecy. We promised each other that there would never be any secrets between us. Get your jacket please, and let's go. I'm going to tell the children goodbye; the nannies and nurse can handle the children. I'm tired of Marcus playing his games or needing his space. He is telling me tonight what is going on."

Marcus had arrived at the condo to swim, only to find Renee in the pool— naked. When she saw him, she got out of the pool and went to him.

"What are you doing here?" he asked.

"Well," she said. "I am thinking maybe you need a little motivation to get over your problem." She pressed her wet body up to his. He caught her arms together and said, "Renee, get away from me. I should not have told you my problem. And I'll never cheat on my wife, much less, with you. Put your clothes on and get out."

Suddenly the elevator opened to the penthouse and standing in the foyer was Samantha and Mike. Samantha could see from the foyer into the living room and saw that Renee was naked, and it looked as if she had draped her naked body on Marcus. Mike said, "Shit." But before he could get to Renee, Samantha had crossed the living room and slapped Renee.

"Get out." Mike quickly picked up Renee's robe and said, "Let's get you upstairs and dressed before Samantha claws your eyes out." Samantha then turned to Marcus, "What is going on? I trusted you." With that she reached back to slap Marcus' face, but he caught her hand before she could strike him. He spoke, "it is not what you think. You know me and you know I would never cheat on you, especially with Renee."

"Then what is this? No secrets, remember?" Samantha said.

Marcus backed her up to the wall and said, "Just let me show you." He began to kiss her roughly, as if he was angry at her. She stepped back, away from him. He went towards her and tore her blouse, picked her up and slammed her against the wall in the living room. This was the roughest Marcus had ever treated her. She felt a mixture of fear but also felt turned on. Marcus reached under her skirt and tore off her pantics and unzipped his pants; his manhood was fully erect. He parted Samantha's legs and rammed himself into her. She felt that the force of his move would surely leave her bruised, but she also felt the old feelings of desire heat between her legs. He pushed twice and came with no consideration for her or her climax. His anger was scary. She pushed him back and said, "Are you raping me? I am your wife."

The glazed angry look on his face disappeared and he begin to cry. "Marcus, what is it?" Samantha said cupping his chin and turning his head to her. He picked up Samantha and carried her to their old master bedroom.

"Sam, I wanted to tell you, but I feel I have failed you and the children in so many ways."

"How is that?" she said sitting on the bed next to him.

"First," he said. "Just you and the children being Matthews. After the shooting, no matter how much security I have around you, I cannot protect you. Then after the shooting, I could not get an erection. I wanted you, but my body just would not respond. No matter what I tried I just could not get an erection. The doctors said I had PTSD and so much anger that it was going to take time for my mind and body to get back to normal. That is why I first wanted to stay at the penthouse alone, to try and work it out with the help of medication and the psychologist. But then when Trey was born, I knew no matter what that I needed to be at home with you and the children. But as your husband, I felt like a failure and I figured eventually you would leave me. I know our sex life is one of the things we have in common. Then I was embarrassed, I'm supposed to be the man to satisfy your every need and keep you and the children safe. I became angrier and that made me think if I told you, you might leave me. I knew Joseph still loved you and he'd be delighted to have you back. I promised your father that you'd never want for anything. I promised you the same thing. I started swimming here because it seemed to help relax me. Renee knew about my condition, and so did Mike and Dr. McCullough. But I told them if my ability to have an erection did not come back, I would tell you. I told Renee only because sexually she understands all kinds of techniques and she also knew me from our six months together. I confided in Mike and Dr. McCullough because Mike knows you and me and Dr. McCullough knows that you would have self-doubt and she knows your history and knows and cares for you. Renee is Renee, she used the opportunity to try and seduce me tonight, probably because she does not place a very high opinion on loyalty. But I swear nothing has ever happened between us. I'd never cheat on you. I would love you enough to give you up if I could not get my body to function as a man should to satisfy his wife. I am so sorry. I should have told you, but I felt like a failure."

Samantha said, "Marcus, yes, you should have told me. We are a team, a partnership, and you owe me the chance to help with whatever happens between us. I love you for better or for worse. We've been through worse before and we stuck together to work it out. This would have not been any different. Men, your pride and the expectations you put on yourself. But that does not matter now, from what just happened, your manhood is fully functional. I think you were a little too rough and your anger scared me."

"I am so sorry, Sam. Please, did I hurt you?"

"I'm sure I'll have some bruises tomorrow, and some soreness. But we are going to put that behind us and concentrate on making love and getting our entire relationship back on track. I think we should both continue in therapy, and I want that bitch out of this condo and our life."

Marcus picked up his phone and called Mike, "Mike, take Renee to a hotel tonight. Tell her you will send her stuff to her. After you drop her off, will you go to the mansion and stay the night with the children? Tell them that Mommy and Daddy are having a date night. Tell them that we are going to take a couple of days to spend time together, alone. Have someone send some clothes over for us and I'll see you in a few days. Handle whatever comes up, unless it is an emergency."

"Good," said Mike. "I glad Samantha knows everything. Remember, I'll always have your back. I love you two like family. See you in a couple days"

"Samantha, can we just talk for a while? Let me talk to you about my feelings and you share yours. I hope I have not messed anything up between us. I cannot change who I am, but I can change how have I reacted."

Samantha kissed Marcus long and hard. She could feel the tingling between her thighs, she could see the firmness in Marcus' pants.

"Make love to me, sweetheart," she said and leaned back on the bed and removed her shredded blouse. She dropped her skirt and removed her bra. Marcus quickly undressed and pulled the covers back. Samantha slid in and Marcus moved on top of her and kissed her passionately. He nibbled on her ears and neck, moving to her breasts, and kissed down her stomach and kissed the inside of each thigh. She reached for him and said, "Fuck me, Marcus. I am so wet and ready. Ride me until we climax together." He did not need any further invitation. Their bodies moved in unison until she said, "Oh, God," her signal that she was climaxing. She felt his breathing become heavy, and then he went rigid, signaling that he was coming also. Afterwards, she cuddled in his arms, and they talked until wee hours in the morning.

He understood what she had been thinking and she understood his fears. Finally exhausted, they feel asleep entwined in each other arms. Next morning, they slept until noon, but Marcus reached for Samantha again.

"Darling," said Samantha. "Let's take a bath together. I am a little sore."

"Of course." He jumped out of bed, his nakedness and manhood very apparent. He ran a hot bath and put chamomile in the water. Samantha came into the bathroom naked; she had a large bruise on the inside of her thigh. Marcus said, "I am so sorry." and kissed the bruise before Samantha got into the tub. The warm water made the soreness feel so much better. Marcus slide in behind her and he began to wash her body while planting kisses on her neck. She leaned back into his arms, and all seemed to be better. After the bath, they put on robes that were hanging in the bathroom.

"Marcus, do you think I could get some of your pancakes? And maybe some tea?"

"Yes, darling, like old times. "

"Yes, like old times." The doorbell rang and Marcus answered. The doorman had a bag for them sent over from the mansion. Samantha sat at the bar, and they spent the morning talking.

"Marcus, darling you realize that Trey is only three months old, and I have not gone back on birth control."

"Sam, I hope you did not get pregnant this soon after Trey, but if you do…" Samantha interrupted, "Then, love, we will have another Matthews baby. Now tell me about this island your father and you are buying. I think spending the summer there with the children is just what we need. And as far as being a Matthew, it is what I have always wanted, someone to love me for who I am.

You are my soulmate, so let's work together to keep our family safe, but raise them not to be afraid of who they are. You are a good husband and father. I am honored to be your wife. Now, how about another stack of pancakes and join me I am hungry, and you are probably starved."

"Today, let's not talk anything about negativity. Our life, as my father told me, is how you choose to live it." Marcus fixed Samantha another plate of pancakes and a chai tea and he fixed himself a plate with a cup of fruit. He seemed happier and more relaxed than Samantha had seen him since the shooting. She felt great relief knowing what the real problem was and all the speculation and self-doubt was immediately gone. She had always known that her husband was a proud and macho man and liked to be in control of every situation. He was the type of man who always prided himself on being able to take care of his family, his employees, and his business.

He was John Marcus' son, and Isabella had instilled in him the ability to show his emotions and to be a humanitarian. He was a problem solver, and she could only think how much pressure he felt and how inadequate he felt when he could not control his own mind and body. Samantha had lived her life surviving whatever life threw her way with very little resources to fix things. However, from her own mental conditions, she knew that sometimes during panic attacks, her brain controlled her. She was much more accustomed to not always being in control of oneself. That is why in the past, she had developed such a destructive behavior towards men. As a wife, she was going to encourage them staying in treatment for their mental health. She often believed that people in general did not really understand how important it was to take care of one's mental and emotional health.

The rest of the morning they talked like they did before the children. Plans of buying the island located in Exuma Cays, Bahama. It had beaches, oceanfront homes, income potential, an airplane strip, and a small village that supported the island. It was developed, but needed a medical facility to support the people there. It would be instrumental to the townspeople for jobs. The cost was twenty-four million dollars and there were parts of the project that were still underdevelopment. It would cost the Matthew's Group about ten million more to complete the project and add a medical clinic. Marcus was excited about the project and was looking forward to taking the whole family there for the summer.

"Sam," Marcus said. "Let's go out for a late lunch before we go home to the children. And then tonight, if you're feeling up to it, we will continue what we did not finish this morning."

"I am in total agreement, darling," Samantha spoke.

"Now let's get dressed and go to that little French café and then go home."

At the café, it was as if none of the prior twelve weeks had existed between them. They seemed to be in perfect harmony once again. But Samantha knew that they would need to continue treatment, you did not fix the brain that easily.

"Marcus, please go ahead and set up an appointment with the psychologist. I'd like for us to go and see him on a weekly basis. This will be important to our overall wellbeing."

Marcus picked up the phone and called Dr. Robert's office. This was the first time she knew the doctor's name and it was not a man, but a woman, which surprised her as she would have thought Marcus would have been more comfortable with a man. She was glad he had chosen a woman. A woman's perspective, she believed, would be better understanding of both of their issues and the effects the last months had had on them both. There was self-doubt on both their sides, as well as fear. On the drive home Marcus held her hand and they were like love birds; putting the sexual intimacy back into their relationship seemingly helped them both.

The children were already at the dinner table. Mike was there and they had made homemade pizza with salad. He had invited Denise to dinner, and everyone was having a rowdy time.

"Hey you guys, glad you're home." Mike said. "Just in time to try out our pizza experiment. We have three kinds; Matilda made vegetarian, the twins made meat lovers, Bella made Hawaiian, and Ester wanted just three kinds of cheeses." The children had been treated to Sprite, something that had to be Uncle Mike's suggestion, and Denise was pouring red wine for the adults. Trey was asleep in the nursery. Mike had even gotten paper plates, something that was unheard of in the Matthew's home. But Mike had created a festive air for the children, he was a good uncle to them.

"Hey, brother, how about a slice of meat lovers with some hot peppers?" Marcus asked.

"The boys seemed to think they are ready to try some hot peppers. We have milk ready just in case things do not go down as well as they think," Mike said.

"Samantha, what would you like?"

"I think I will try a slice of cheese and a slice of vegetarian." Denise poured Marcus and Samantha a glass of wine. The evening was fun. After dinner, the children went to their rooms to get ready for bed and some quiet time. Denise and Mike left the cleanup for the staff. As Samantha took Denise up to the nursery to see Trey, Mike said, "Everything all right brother?"

"Seems to be; you were right. I should have been up front with Sam," Marcus replied.

"Well, that's history now. Go forward and work on what the two of you have," he said. "By the way, Renee is leaving Saturday to go back to France. Her shoot has been over for some time and as we know, if Renee can find a way to cause trouble, she will. But after, Samantha slapped the shit out of her, I think she understands now that you're married to a pretty tough woman."

Marcus laughed, "Yep. I bet that came as a surprise to her." Denise came back down the elevator, "Marcus, he is a beauty. Samantha asked if you'd join her in the nursery before you put the other children to bed. Mike, my love, if you're ready, I think it is time for us to go. I have a lot of work to catch up on. We are buying an island and John insists I get the preliminary paperwork started."

"See you, tomorrow. You have Mason on security, so all is quiet." Mike hugged Marcus and took Denise out to his Jeep and they left for their condo.

Marcus joined Samantha in the nursery, where she was holding Trey and singing her a song, "Here is your daddy," she told Trey. Marcus went over to Trey and held his arms out to him. He flashed him his engaging smile and Marcus took him from Samantha and kissed him on the head.

"Sam, we make beautiful babies. Your eyes, my hair and skin color, and hopefully this little charmer does not inherit her aunt Penelope and Paige's personality, or we could be in trouble." Trey stretched his arms over his head and then grabbed his daddy's finger. He yawned and Samantha said, "I think he's ready to go to sleep." Marcus laid him in his crib and said, "Goodnight, my sweet angel." Samantha and Marcus left the nursery for the night nurse to take over.

They went two the boys' room and Marcus said, "Choose a book and I will read it to you if that is what you want."

"Dad," said Jared. "Jacob and I have agreed that we are too old to be read to and would like to read ourselves, if that is ok."

"Sure, little man," said Marcus. "Are you too old for your dad to kiss you goodnight?"

"Maybe on the forehead," said Jacob. So, Marcus kissed each son on the forehead and said goodnight.

"Does that mean Mommy also?" said Samantha.

Jared said, "Well, we'd like a kiss *and* a hug from you." Samantha kissed each boy on the forehead and hugged them, then gave each their favorite blankets.

"We love you boys," said Marcus. "Never get too old to let your mom and dad show you affection." He closed the door on his way out and said, "Not pass 8:30. Goodnight."

They then went to Bella, Ester, and Matilda's room. They were reading and had braided each other's hair.

"So, you three do not want me to read to you either?"

"No, Dad, we are getting too old and we like reading ourselves. Ester and Bella like to listen to music to go to sleep. They use their headphones. So, can we have a kiss and hug and stay up until ten?"

Samantha said, "Yes, I think you and Ester are old enough. Bella, you need to be asleep by nine." She kissed and hugged all three girls and Marcus gave them a tickle, then a kiss and hug.

"You three will always be my little girls, even when you're grown."

"We know Grandfather Saul always calls mommy his little girl. But Dad, we are growing up. I am fourteen," Matilda said. "And Ester is twelve, so we are old enough to put ourselves to bed."

"Well, I hope you're never too old to talk to me," said Marcus.

"Never, Dad," said Matilda.

"Goodnight girls, we love you," said Samantha.

"To the moon and back," added Marcus. They closed the door.

"Well," said Marcus, "we still have Trey who likes to be read to, sang to, and tucked in."

"Yes, and who knows? Maybe another Matthew," said Samantha.

"I really hope not yet, but I do want more children, Samantha. But I am thinking how hard your pregnancies are. Maybe we should explore other ways to have our own children. I worry about your health."

"I think I'm good for one more of your children, and if we decide we want more, we can always use a surrogate," said Samantha.

"Yes, I was thinking I'd like to have at least two more. But tonight, let's you and I finish what we started this morning," said Marcus. "If you are up to it." "Oh, I am. Up to join me in the shower?" said Samantha. Marcus joined her in the shower like old times. He let the water run over their nude bodies and lifted her up in a seated position, kissing her passionately on the mouth. Separating her teeth and probing her mouth with his tongue. Samantha felt the old tingling between her legs and wrapped her legs around Marcus's waist. He shifted her weight to better allow his manhood to enter her. They were moving in rhythm until she began to explode, and Marcus began to thrust faster until his own release began. Then it was like fireworks between them. He said, "Let me lather you up."

He began washing Samantha between her legs and then he dropped to his knees and began to kiss her stomach, working his way between her thighs. Samantha knew what was coming next and pushed his head between her legs. His tongue did its magic; licking and pulling at the lips of her core. She could no longer contain herself.

"Oh fuck, fuck," she cried out. "Darling, you're torturing me, and the water is getting cold."

"Well, step out of the shower and let me rub you off." Samantha obeyed, then reached for her robe. Marcus quickly dried off, picked up Samantha, and took her to bed.

"I love you, darling. I was a fool for not telling you."

"Marcus, it is in the past. I do have an appointment tomorrow to get back on the depo shot. We could already be pregnant, but just in case I am not, I'd liked to wait at least two years between the next one and Trey."

"I agree. I know how hard pregnancy is on you. But you did not get as sick with Trey as you did with Bella and the boys."

"Yes, but who knows what the next child of ours will be?" Marcus hugged her to him.

"I do want a girl. I'd like to have at least two more, but like I said, we need to look into surrogacy. Our embryo, but someone else carrying it." Samantha said, "Let's talk tomorrow with Dr. McCullough. Now let's get some sleep."

Next day, Marcus went with Samantha to see the doctor.

"Well," she said, "You have already taken the risk. I could give you a morning after shot, but from what you said, I do not think it'd help if you are pregnant already. Technically, it has been two days and it's usually only effective the next day."

"Dr. McCullough, I would not want the shot anyway. If I am pregnant, then so be it." Marcus had a guilty look on his face, "I know. I should have planned better, but I never expected Samantha to think I'd ever cheat on her. It was like I became enraged, and then I felt the impulse to show Sam that she was the only woman I'd ever think of having sex with."

Dr. McCullough spoke, "The mind is a funny organ and controls all emotions, so anger caused you to react, and I am glad for it. As for Samantha, well you should have told her, but what is done is done."

Samantha said, "Yes, and I love you and want to move on. We are going to continue with a psychologist, as I think it is important for our marriage," said Samantha.

"I agree," said Dr. McCullough. The nurse came in and gave Samantha her the shot.

"I hear you are leaving for the summer," said Dr. McCullough. "You're buying an island?"

Marcus spoke, "My dad found an island and he wants me to go check it out. I want my family with me."

"It sounds like a great project for the Matthew's Group. And Samantha, you sold your practice?" said Dr. McCullough.

"Yes, my largest client is the Matthew's group and with the children and all their activities and my charity work, I just think I need to unload some of my clients and make it all about the family business and the family."

"I agree," said Dr. McCullough. "It is not like you need to work at all, but I understand your need for the stimulation of the work you love. See you in three months for your next shot, unless you are pregnant. Then call the office as soon as you have your first symptom."

It was May and the children would be out of school in two weeks. Trey was crawling and four months old now. He could also say words, and of course his first word was 'dada.' The boys were excited about their new adventure and were hoping to learn snorkeling. Ester was not as enthusiastic about being gone all summer; she would miss her friends. Matilda was gathering up paints and canvases and researching the island; she was excited about the change of scenery. Bella was becoming a better dancer day by day and was looking forward to dance classes on the island. The grandparents were coming over this weekend to have some time with the children before they left. Marcus wanted to have a cookout for with his sisters, Phillipe, Rick, Scott, Denise, and Mike. Mike would be going with them to coordinate security for the family. Denise would stay behind to handle the business and coordinate with Marcus on all the other projects.

Finally, it was the day to go. The jet was ready and the baggage had been shipped ahead. All that was left to do was to board the jet with the family and start off on their new adventure. That morning Samantha had an unsettling feeling, one that she recognized before, but she was not late yet, so maybe it was nerves. The nannies and Trey's baby nurses had agreed to go. Peg was going to coordinate staff there for the family. They'd stay at the resort first, but Marcus wanted to find a home for them, if possible. There was a lot to do. Marcus had called Joseph and invited him and his family down, but it would have to be late summer, as Joseph was going to announce his run for Governor of Virginia.

Samantha and the children were exhausted by the time the plane landed on the island landing strip. Bella was the grumpiest and didn't like the long travels, so Marcus took her and they all got into the limo and headed for the resort. The nannies and nurse followed behind in a van along with a security team. Mike rode with the family, and Ester had fallen asleep on his lap. Samantha could not wait to get everyone into bed, even herself. Marcus finally had Bella asleep. He was good with her. *Better than I am*, thought Samantha. She was a daddy's girl.

It was late when they pulled up in front of the resort. Staff came out to help with the children and direct everyone to their suites. They had been expecting them as the potential new owners, so they were treated to the very best the resort accommodations. The girls shared a villa with the boys and the nannies, and the nurse shared a suite with Trey. Mike had his own suite. Marcus and Samantha had their own suite. But at this point she was so exhausted; a log would have been fine. After they said good night to the children and instructed the staff to prepare them a snack then left the nannies to take care of them. The nurse had given Trey a bath and a bottle, and he was already asleep. Marcus and Mike had laid out the plan for tomorrow, which was to look closely at the projects that was left to finish. The numbers looked good, and if Marcus liked what he saw, Samantha had a contract ready for him to sign, and a line of credit. Tonight, however, she was too tired to do more than a quick shower and hop into bed. Mike and Marcus were having a drink downstairs.

He came in an hour later and took a quick shower and got into bed and put his arms around Samantha. "Rough trip, sweetheart?"

"Just so tired," she said. He kissed her on the lips and said, "Sleep in tomorrow. I'll tell the staff to take care of the children. Mike and I are going to meet at nine to drive to the property." Samantha barely heard him; she was dozing off quickly. "Goodnight," she mumbled.

Next morning, she slept until eleven. Everyone was downstairs in the pool.

"Well, I see I was not missed," she teased the children. "I'm glad you're having a good time; Mommy was so very tired. So, everyone had a good breakfast and slept well?"

"Yes," Matilda said. "Fresh fruit and eggs."

Ester said, "I like it here, I already made a friend." The boys were too busy horsing around in the water to answer. Bella was taking a kid's yoga class. The children seemed to bounce back fast; Marcus had gotten up early to meet Mike. Samantha was the only one dragging. *Maybe something to eat and some tea would pep me up*, she thought. She headed into the restaurant and sat down and ordered. She tried to eat an omelet but just felt ill; she just settled for the tea, instead. She was not late yet; her period should start any day. But she was pretty sure she knew what was happening in her body, after four pregnancies, it was hard to ignore the signs. *Well, I'll wait before saying anything to Marcus*, she thought. If she was pregnant, Trey was just four months old and that means that there would only be eleven months between the two babies. It was going to be rough. She just knew that there is no way she could keep up with seven children without a lot of help. Marcus was Catholic and he wanted a big family. He had said at least one more. If they had anymore, then for sure they would use a surrogate. Marcus and Samantha would have to talk about this plan of his.

A nap in a lounge chair sounded good, so she found a shelter and laid down to enjoy the sun. It was one in the afternoon when Marcus woke her up. He was excited.

"Where are the children?" she asked.

"They went down to the beach area with Mike, the nannies, and security. Trey is taking a nap. How are you feeling?"

"Marcus, I'm worn out," Samantha replied.

"Do you think we are pregnant?"

"Honey, I am not late, but if I had to guess, I'd say yes." He smiled.

"I know it is not what we wanted. But if you are..."

"I said think I am. But what about the project?"

"I'd like to make an offer. The island needs some roads and a hospital, but the resort is pretty much finished. The owner either wants a partner or a buyer outright. I would want to buy it outright. I talked to Dad, and he said if that is what I want to do then go ahead. We just have to talk about living here for a while then traveling back and forth."

"Right now, Marcus, I'd like to get a salad. You go down and help Mike with the children. I just need time to wrap my head around everything."

"I know it is a lot to ask, but I think it would be great for the family." He kissed her and walked towards the beach. Samantha went into the restaurant and ordered a salad and thought about how Marcus really wanted to do this project and how it would give the family a great experience. She knew he would not do it unless she agreed. The project would provide work for the islanders and give them a much-needed medical facility. *Yes*, Samantha thought, *this is a good thing*. When the family returned from the beach, she had the contract ready for Marcus' signature. He had promised to her on the day he asked her to marry him that their life would be an adventure, and it certainly has been.

It was three, and she had given Trey a bottle while waiting for Marcus and the children to return from the beach. She sent the children with the nannies for an early dinner, while she and Marcus discussed the offer. She also wanted to hear Mike's opinion of the island and any security risk it would pose to the family. Coming through the door, she could see that Marcus had Bella on his shoulders, Ester, Matilda, and Mike following closely behind. The boys looked worn out; they would all sleep well tonight. Samantha went to the children and asked, "Did you have a good time? Do you think Daddy should buy this island for our family?" There was a tired unison from the children, "Yes, Mommy. We love it here."

"Alright, you children go with your nannies, and they will give you an early dinner after your showers. Mommy and Daddy will see you at breakfast." Marcus and Samantha gave the kids a hug and a kiss. Samantha instructed the nannies to have them use aloe on their skin, they all had a lot of sun. Mike fist bumped all the children and said, "Let's go explore the island tomorrow, if that's okay with your parents."

Marcus said, "That sounds like a great plan. You kids be ready by ten for breakfast and then we will leave after that for the tour."

"Marcus, I have the contract in the manager's office. He said we were welcome to use it," Samantha said. "Mike, I'd like you to join us, as I have questions for you about security."

They all went into the manager's office where Samantha had the contract and the plans for the resort laid out.

"So, Mike, security will not be an issue with all the guests that will be coming here for vacation?"

"No. Because it is an island, security will actually be easier to control. Marcus and I have located some land on the far side of the island that would be perfect to build a Matthew's compound. It is on the beach but would be far enough back to give you plenty of space for a couple houses. This land is separate from the resort project and would give us another 30 acres The parcels are owned by several families who are local and want to sell. There is already a house on it, but I'm sure you will want to remodel it. It already has a wall around it and is gated."

Samantha said, "Then I'll draw up separate contracts for these parcels. Marcus, I am assuming you already have their names?"

"Yes ma'am."

"Mike, would you get the folder out of the van with the information on it?" Samantha asked as Mike was leaving the room. "This will be a big undertaking, not only from the construction standpoint, but also from a cultural standpoint. The children love the beach and the warm climate, but I'm not sure they understand that we cannot be here all the time. There is school and other commitments we have made. Our families and church."

"Honey, there is nothing we can not accomplish if we are a team."

"I agree," she said. "I am in." Marcus rounded the desk where Samantha sat and kissed her passionately. He said, "It will work. How are you feeling? Pregnant?" Marcus asked.

"I know nothing's official, but I know my body and I know I am pregnant, which means another complication. Travel will be hard for me and I'm sure you will want me to be here and home also."

"I will support you in every way, Sam. Baby, kids, projects, and all." He kissed her again just as Mike came in with the folder. They worked three hours and all offers were ready to be presented.

"While Mike has the children, and the nurse has Trey, you and I will call a meeting with the developer and the owners of the other parcels. I'd like to set the meeting with the developer at nine am tomorrow and then with the three owners after that. I'd like to go into town and visit the political people of this island."

"I suggest you keep some locals on this project and make one a supervisor over the project. Use the locals as much as possible, Marcus. We want to be seen as bring money into their economy and we want to be a part of the culture here.

I do not want them to think some rich American is swooping down on this island to exploit it."

"Sam, I'd have it no other way." With that Marcus signed all the contracts and it was turning into a 100-million-dollar deal. But when you were worth 15 billion, money was not an issue. However, perception could be. Mike left with the children at ten am. Trey was with the nurse. Marcus and Samantha met with the developer and the three landowners and presented the offers that Marcus had already signed. The other parties were all eager to sign and so the deals were done.

"The next step," Samantha said, "is to meet with whoever is the representative for this small island. I know it is a bi-parliament government, but because it is so small, I am sure there are needs that the locals are lacking. It is our responsibility to make this happen as the owner of this island. Let's address education, crime, health care, housing, jobs, and whatever else is needed that is within our power to provide. Whether it's roads, farming, or something else. I do not give a damn the topic, I do not want to be seen as just people who bought an island because they could." Marcus swung Samantha around facing him, "That is why I love you so much. You passionate for people, no matter who they are. So, let's go and find that person and talk to him and see what these people, our new family, need."

With that, they left the resort and headed to the heart of the little village. Along the way, it was obvious that the locals had a different living standard than the tourists who came there. That would change. Marcus' phone rang.

"Hello, Joseph. Yes, we are in the Caribbean. Sure, fly in. Is it just you?"

Joseph said "Yes, we have a problem. It affects our families so I will fly in tomorrow to talk to you and Samantha."

"What's up with Joseph?" spoke Samantha.

"He did not say. He said he was flying in tomorrow to talk to us," Marcus replied.

"Must be important for him to leave his campaign right now," said Samantha.

"Well, whatever it is, we will help him solve it," spoke Marcus. "Now that we have met with the officials and found out the locals needs, as the new owner of an island, would you like to go see where the house is that we will live in once it is remodeled?"

"No, I trust you and the architect to figure that out. You did a good job on our home in the States. I just want the same thing in the master suite; his and her bathrooms, closet, and dressing area. And please not so large and grand, it should look more local, not a mansion." "Maybe a more modest Matthew home," he replied.

"What I want is to stop by and see the local doctor and ask him his thoughts on a better medical center. And I'd like him to do a blood pregnancy test. I am two weeks late and I have all the symptoms. We are pregnant again. I sure of it."

Marcus stopped the Jeep, "Before I get too excited, how do you feel about another baby so close to Trey?"

"Well, I feel overwhelmed and afraid. But it is what it is, a baby conceived between two people who love each other very much. Marcus, you know I was not as sick with Trey as I was with the boys. I am already feeling nauseous and loss of appetite. So, I'm thinking this baby is your little girl. So, if everything is like I think it is, I want to go back home so I can be under the care of Dr. McCullough. You and the children can stay here for the remainder of the summer."

Marcus said, "Sweetheart, we can all go home. I want to be with you."

"No," said Samantha. "I'd like to have the time without the children, including Trey. I want the time alone. Can you understand that?"

"Yes, my love. Another girl!" He broke out in a hearty laugh and leaned over and kissed her passionately.

"I guess I should say sorry. I know it is a lot to ask you to have a baby so soon after Trey."

"Marcus, I love you and there is no other way for me but to have this baby. But I am going to make the decision to tie my tubes. If you want more children than we can have Dr. McCullough remove some eggs and we can hire a surrogate. I am 35. I am not the woman who can just keep having babies. I know Catholics like having large families, and I know you said you want one more, but since money is no object, then you are going to indulge me."

"Darling, I am in complete agreement. I would not ask you to carry another baby. Now let's go see that doctor," Marcus said. Marcus and Samantha pulled up in front of a small cottage. It was stucco on the outside with a sign that said Dr. Rivera, MD. Marcus got out of the Jeep and opened the door to the small office. There was a young woman sitting at the desk. Marcus asked, "Is Dr. Rivera in?" "Yes," she said. "He's with a patient. Do you have an appointment?"

"No, but will you tell him Mr. and Mrs. Matthew are here."

"Yes, sir. You are the person who bought the island, is that right?"

"I guess news travels fast here," said Marcus.

"Yes sir, we are a small community of about 2,500 people, so word of mouth is the best source of communication. One moment please." She went into a small room. From the doorway, Marcus could see a local man who looked like he had a broken arm. The doctor had just finished wrapping it up.

"Doctor, Mr. and Mrs. Matthew are here to see you, if you have the time."

"Sure, tell them this is my last patient and I will be out in ten minutes." She closed the door and spoke to Marcus. "The doctor is finishing up with his last patient and said he would be about ten minutes."

"Thank you," said Samantha. "We will just sit over here, if you do not mind."

"Oh no, let me take you to his office. Can I get you something to drink?" she asked. "Water, please," Samantha said. She directed them to a small office and they took a seat in the chairs in front of the desk. She came back in a few minutes with two bottles of cold water. The office had a medical plaque and a license. There were pictures of children who were on his desk.

"These must be grandchildren, judging from when he graduated." He had gone to a school in Cuba. In walked a gray-headed man, who look like he was in his late 60s. He had kind eyes; Samantha noticed right away. Marcus stood and reached out to shake his hand.

"Dr. Rivera, we are the Matthews. I gather that word has already reached you that we purchased the island?"

"Yes, Mr. Matthew, it has. And I hope you plan to do more than the developer who opened the resort. We need more than jobs. The resort brought their own people in. They use locals in the most unskilled jobs."

"Please sir, my wife and I have just come from your representative's office, and we are here first to tell you that we like to build anything you need and pay for anything you need to give the locals good medical care. We would also like it to be a free clinic. We will hire the locals that would like to work for the Matthews Group, and they will have benefits, as well as training programs that we will provide for anyone who wishes to take advantage of it."

Dr. Rivera said, "Most of the young people leave as soon as they are old enough, as there are so few jobs and opportunities here. The ones that stay usually get caught up in drugs or some other criminal activity. Yes sir, with men like you guiding us we will provide a better standard of living for all the people who live here." "We want to join your community. We have children of our own, so we are dedicated to making this a very great community that we will be proud to share with them and all who live here."

Dr. Rivera said, "I did some checking on your firm and I know you are a man of your word. So welcome."

"Please, call me Marcus, and this is my wife. She is the lawyer for the firm so I know that she will make sure everything we have committed to will happen." Mr. Rivera stretched out his hand and said, "Thank you Samantha."

"One more thing, Dr. Rivera," Samantha spoke. "I'd like you to do a blood test to confirm that I am pregnant. I am two weeks late."

"Yes, dear, come this way." He showed Marcus and Samantha into the small room where the last patient was.

"Okay, let's see." He took out a syringe and drew blood from Samantha's arm. He left the room of a while and came when he returned, he said, "Yes, my dear, you are pregnant. So how late are you?"

Samantha answered, "Two weeks."

"So, you are about four weeks, maybe five weeks pregnant." "Yes, I figured that to be about right. I have very difficult pregnancies, so I am going back to the States. My husband and children will be here for the remainder of the summer. I'd love for you to come to the resort with your family and have dinner with us and meet our children." "I'd like that. It will just be me and the misses. My child is grown and a doctor in Cuba. We have two grandchildren." "Well hopefully, we will get to meet them at some point. How about Wednesday of next week, say 6 pm?" Samantha said.

"I know my wife will love meeting you and knowing all the plans you have for the community." "Thank you, sir," said Marcus. Dr. Rivera walked with them to the door.

"Congratulations on the news."

"Thank you, sir," said Marcus. Samantha leaned over and kissed his old cheek, "You'll find that we are very family-oriented, and we feel honored that we have a new family to be a part of."

"Sam, do you want to tell the children about the new baby?" said Marcus.

"After, Joseph leaves. Let's see what he needs before we tell them," said Samantha.

"I not sure how thrilled they will be," she said.

"They will get used to the idea, just like they did with Trey. And if it is a girl, like you believe, you know Jared and Jacob will be thrilled. Besides, they are going to be so busy here with me and Mike that they will have little time to think of a baby."

"But darling, I will," spoke Marcus." I am so happy." He kissed Samantha again. They were just getting back to the resort, and it was late. The children had eaten and were getting ready for bed.

"Let's say goodnight to them," said Marcus. "I'm sure Trey is already asleep." Samantha turned to Marcus, "Promise me you will spend a lot of time with Trey. It will be two months before I can hold him again."

"We will Skype every day. And yes, the children will be my priority. There are plenty of people who will take care of this project. I'm doing this for the children and Mike will be here unless you want him to go back with you." "No, I'd rather he be here with you," Samantha said.

"Mason will be just fine for me," she continued.

"Besides, I want to spend a lot of time on myself," spoke Samantha.

"Now," Marcus said. "Let's say goodnight to the children and let them know Uncle Joseph will be here tomorrow. We will check in on Trey after we get a late dinner. You must be exhausted, Sam."

"Yes, I am. You promised an adventure, darling. I did not think it would move so fast." Marcus kissed Samantha's head.

"I will try and slow it down some." Samantha smiled.

"I doubt that, but thanks for thinking about trying," spoke Samantha.

Samantha was asleep just as her head hit the pillow. She could feel Marcus' arms around her. Next morning about ten am, Joseph pulled up in a Jeep to the resort. He had just landed.

"Hi, Joseph," said Samantha.

"Where are the children?" he asked.

"They are at the pool with the nannies and the nurse. Marcus is in his office, let's go there and talk." Joseph followed Samantha to Marcus's office. The resort manager had given him the larger office and was working out of a smaller office that had been vacant. Marcus got up and reached for Joseph's hand.

"Welcome, man. How is the campaign going?" asked Marcus.

"That's what I am here for." Joseph spoke. He pulled a paper from his brief case and on the front page was a picture of him and Jared and Jacob with the caption. *Are these the love children that Mr. Claiborne has been hiding all these years?*

"Shit," said Marcus picking up the paper.

"That's why I am here. It's my opposition. He's either speculating or it has gotten out somehow."

"Yeah, it is hard to deny them as yours when you put their picture next to you," Marcus said. "We knew that this day may come."

Joseph said, "I was hoping that it would not have come this soon."

"Well," Samantha said. "We planned to tell them when they were old enough."

"Yes, but are they old enough?" asked Joseph.

"I am willing to pull out of the race, but that just will make it seem like I trying to hide the truth. But I will if you two think that's best."

"What does Emily say?" said Samantha.

"She said she would support whatever all of us decide."

Marcus said, "We'll tell the children the truth and then you tell the public the truth. And then we do as much damage control as we can. All, we should be concerned about is Jared, Jacob, and Sophia."

"I agree," said Joseph. Marcus said, "After we tell the boys, then you tell Sophia, and I contact my public relations firm. I am sure you have people who can help you on how to tell the public. We will be there for you," said Marcus.

Samantha said, "Yes. I think the truth is what needs to be told and then whatever we have to do for damage control will be done. We, as a family, will stick together. There are plenty people who have love children, it's hiding it that always gets them in trouble."

"We all knew this situation could come out, I just wished the children had been older, but I think we can make them understand," Marcus said.

"Maybe we should have told them when they were little," said Samantha. Marcus said, "It is in the past. We made decisions that we all thought best for the children. So, let's go talk to the boys."

"Let's take a walk to the beach. The air and scenery will be calming," said Samantha. Joseph, Marcus, and Samantha walked out to where the children were playing in the pool. They were having so much fun. When they saw Joseph, there was a chorus of voices.

"Uncle Joseph, when did you get here? Come swim with us." Joseph walked to the side of the pool, "You all look like you are having a blast. Maybe later."

Marcus walked to the side of the pool and said, "Jared and Jacob, would you take a walk with Uncle Joseph, me, and mommy? Let's walk down to the beach." said Marcus. Ester and Matilda said, "Can we go too?'

Marcus said, "No, we will join you later. You stay here with the nannies and help with Trey. Then we will be back and have a family meeting," said Marcus.

Bella said, "But we want to go to the beach too."

Samantha spoke, "We will go later, listen to your father."

"Yes, Mother," said the girls. The boys got out of the pool and wrapped their towels around their waists. The path to the beach was a short walk. Jacob grabbed Joseph's hand and said, "We are glad you could come down to our island to see us. Can you believe dad bought this island for us? You will have to bring Sophia here. She will love it," said Jacob.

"Yes," said Joseph, "She would love visiting here. It is beautiful." They got to some rocks that were stacked up like a wall and the boys began climbing them. Marcus said "Boys, please sit down. I'd like to talk to you and explain why Uncle Joseph is here." The boys sat down on the wall. Their faces were filled with happiness. Samantha began, "You boys know how much your dad and me and

Uncle Joseph love you."

"We know, Mommy. Why do you look so serious?" said Jared.

"Is there something wrong?"

Marcus said, "Not wrong. It is just time that you two know something that maybe you should have always known. But your mother and I made a decision, when you were born, to wait until you were older to tell you. We did it because we loved you and we wanted you and your brother to feel secure in the family." "What's going on?" said Jared. Samantha began, "You know that mommy and Uncle Joseph went to law school together and we dated in law school?"

"Yes," said Jacob. "And then you met Daddy and fell in love, then we were born, right?"

"Yes," said Marcus. "But there is more to the story than that. Mommy and Uncle Joseph had been in love and had thought they would be together and then Mommy met me and well, I knew I wanted her to be my wife the first date we had. Your mother is an amazing woman, a one-of-a-kind woman, and so easy to love that well, I loved her from the beginning."

Joseph interrupted, "And I was in Washington pursuing my career and had never really told your mommy that I wanted to marry her. So, we both dated other people."

Jacob said, "I do not understand, Uncle Joseph. If you loved Mommy, why did you not want to be with her?"

"Jacob, I thought it be good for her to go to New York and be with her dad, your grandfather Saul, and start her law practice there. I did not know really what I wanted to do, I knew I wanted to stay in DC and work in environmental law." "So," said Samantha, "we felt like we were free to date other people. So, I went out with your daddy, then your Uncle Joseph called me one day and asked me to go on a trip with him. I said 'yes', thinking that he had decided he wanted to marry me."

"But you were dating Daddy," said Jared.

"Yes, but I thought I was in love with Joseph and while Daddy was special to me, I did not love him yet, like I did Uncle Joseph," said Samantha. "Anyway, we went away together on a trip and spent several days together."

Joseph spoke then, "I loved your mother dearly, and did not know how much until I had dated Emily." Jacob said, "And then you told mom that you loved her?"

"Yes, I told her I loved her. But I had gone out with Emily and well, we were foolish and she and I went well."

Marcus said, "They had sex and Emily got pregnant with Sophia. Your mom was heartbroken and came back to New York. That's when we started seeing each other again. I had just gotten back from Spain." Both boys were very quiet. Samantha continued, "Joseph told me that he was going to do the right thing and marry Emily. Later, I found out I was pregnant and since I had been seeing your father and Joseph, I did not know who the father was. I had had sexual relations with your father and Joseph. Sometimes, adults are careless and do not think straight when it comes to love. Joseph married Emily, and your dad and I continued to date. He became very important to me, and I realized how much I loved him because we wanted the same things: a family. I never told Joseph that I was pregnant, but I told your father and he was convinced that he was your biological father. When you were born, Jared became sick and needed a blood transfusion and when they tested your dad's blood, that is when we found out that he was not your biological father. The only other man that I had been with was Joseph and he did not ever know I was pregnant."

Jacob had an angry look on his face, "So you're saying that our dad is not our dad?"

Marcus spoke up, "No, we are telling you that I am not your biological father, but you are a Matthew. It takes more than blood to be a father. I love you. You are my sons in every way. More importantly, you are a part of your mother and I loved her no matter what. She loved me after a while more than she loved Joseph."

"Dad," said Jared. "doesn't it matter? Do you love Bella and Trey more than us because they are your biological children?"

"No, they are my children. But so are Ester and Matilda and they are adopted. My heart is big enough to love you all," said Marcus. Jared said, "So why are you telling us now?"

Joseph answered, "Because I am running for governor, and someone is speculating about us. We want to make sure you know the truth."

Jacob said angrily, "So that's the only reason you told us now?"

Samantha said, "We were always going to tell you. We just wanted to wait until you were older. Please forgive me. I made the decision not to tell you sooner. I wanted us to have time to be a family."

Jared said, "We want to be alone."

"Does Sophia know that we are half brother and sister?" asked Jacob. Joseph spoke up, "Not yet. Her mother and I will tell her when I get back home. Then I will tell the truth to the people of Virginia and if they do not understand, then that is okay. What is important is you two and Sophia."

"Will you please go back to the resort while Jacob and I talk?" "Yes," said Marcus. "Just know you are my sons and I love you very much." Joseph, Samantha, and Marcus walked back up the path to the resort. Jacob was using a stick to draw in the sand. He looked sad and angry. Jared spoke up, "Jacob, tell me what you're thinking?"

"I think this is messed up. Here we think we have one dad, then we find out we have another."

"Yeah, but I think Dad has shown us the loves and cares for all his children. He never made things any different for any of us." "What about Mom? She should have told us earlier." said Jacob.

"Would that have made a difference to us? We grew up as Dad being our dad. He's always been there for us. Joseph has his own family. And you heard Mom, she wanted us to be a family and not have any division in our family. She treats the girls the same as us and Bella and Trey," said Jared.

"We may not understand it all, but Dad and Mom love us and each other. Dad was shot trying to protect his family," Jared continued.

"So, we just forgive them and go on?" said Jacob.

"Do you feel any different about Dad?" Jared asks.

"No," said Jacob.

"How about Mom?" said Jared.

"I guess not, maybe a little because she should have told us."

"I don't know," said Jacob. "I really do not know how to feel."

"And what about Joseph?" said Jared. "Do you feel any closer to him then you did? Because we now know he is our biological father, does that make a difference?" Jared continued.

"No, I still think of him as Uncle Joseph or our godfather."

"I think we may want to talk to Grandfather Saul, let's go call him."

"Yes," said Jacob. They got up and followed the path back to the resort. Everyone was having a snack. Marcus and Samantha were helping with the children. Joseph was holding Bella in his lap. Jared went to Marcus and said, "Dad, we'd like to call Grandfather Saul."

"Sure thing. Let's go to my office so you can talk in private." The boys followed Marcus into his office. "Would you like me to get Saul on the phone for you?"

"Yes, Dad. I'm not sure how we call from the island."

"Okay, just a minute. We will call on his cell phone since we are more likely to get him." Marcus dialed Saul's number and he answered right away.

"Saul, this is Marcus. I am calling from the island so I think reception will be all right. The boys have something important to talk to you about." "Okay," said Saul. "Put them on." Marcus said, "I'm going to put them on speaker and then I am going to leave the room. They have something private they'd like to talk to you about."

"Sure, sure, put them on," said Saul. Marcus punched the speaker button and left the room.

"Hi, boys. How can I help you?"

"Grandfather, did you know that Joseph is our biological father?"

"Well, yes, boys. Your mother told me at the hospital. She wanted to discuss how to handle the information. Then, when Jared needed a transfusion and it was confirmed, your father got in touch with Joseph and told him to get down to New York as soon as possible. Up until that time, no one knew for sure. Joseph had never been told anything about the pregnancy or the possibility of him being the father. So, he flew down immediately to help you get better, your mother wanted to make sure you had all the love and completeness of a family. Marcus loved you before you were born, and even though he knew that there was a question of paternity, he did not care. He loved your mother and you boys. So, after finding out he was not the biological father, he, Joseph, and your mother wanted to make sure Joseph had the opportunity to be involved with you two. He knew it would be difficult to be a full-time father as he was married to Emily, and they had Sophia. Life can get completed," said Saul. "They were trying to do what they thought would be best for both families." Jared spoke, "Did you agree with their decision?"

"Yes," said Saul. "Both families would have suffered, and it seemed like the best solution since Marcus was going to raise you. They all agreed, that when you were old enough, they would tell you," said Saul.

"What happened?" Saul asked.

"Someone has printed an article about Joseph having us as his love children, so they thought it best they tell us, and they intend to tell the truth to the public, which might cost Joseph the election."

"But he said he does not care," said Jacob.

"He wants the truth out," Saul said.

"I think the truth always wins out. I agree with Joseph. How do you boys feel about Joseph being your biological father?"

Jared spoke, "At first, we were angry. And then we could not ask for a better father than Dad."

"That's right. He'd give his life for you," Saul responded.

"Dad," said Jared. "That it is who raises you. That makes the father and he said he loves us the same as the rest of our brother and sisters."

"Marcus is an amazing man. He has a heart big enough for all you children. He takes family seriously," said Saul. "How about your feelings toward your mother and Joseph?"

"Well, we still feel the same about Joseph. He had been more of an uncle than a father, and I understand mom not wanting to complicate our lives," said Jared.

"I just do not know how to act now," said Jacob. Saul said, "Would it change how you feel toward you dad and mother and even Joseph?"

"No," they both said at the same time.

"But how do we tell people?"

"Boys, why do you have to talk about it at all?" said Saul.

"Your father will do damage control to protect you, and I am sure Joseph will also. He has a daughter, who is your half-sister. So, I am sure they have a plan," said Saul.

"Who else knows?" said Jared.

"Only Margaret and Emily, no one else," said Saul.

"Not even our other grandparents?"

"No," said Saul. "Your dad is half Spanish. Plus, there are a lot of bi-racial marriages in Joseph's family. Joseph's grandfather was married to a white French woman," said Saul.

"And look at me and Margaret. She's black and I am white. Love is love, no matter the color of one's skin. As far as handling this, it's never about the details of the past, it's how you handle the present and the future," said Saul. "Does this help?" he asked.

"Grandfather Saul, so what you are saying is that it is up to us and how we handle this situation?"

"Yes, boys. And remember, there are so many people who love you and will help you through this. Your father loves you and you love him, it does not have to change," said Saul.

"Thank you, grandfather," said Jared.

"I cannot imagine another father than the one we have."

"Boys, call me again if you want to talk some more. Sometimes life is messy. It how you react that makes the difference," he said. "I love you very much. So, call me again if you want to talk."

"Thank you, grandfather. We love you also." The boys hung up and went back out to the pool area to talk to their father, mother, and Joseph. The girls were having lunch out by the pool. The nannies and Mike and Joseph were helping them with their meal. Marcus was giving Trey her bottle and Samantha was looking on.

"Mother," asked Jared. "Can we talk to you, Dad, and Joseph. In private please.?"

"Of course," said Samantha, "Let's go inside to the café and you two can eat while we talk."

Jacob said, "I am hungry." Marcus passed Trey to the nurse and they all went to the café to eat and talk. After being served, Jared said, "After talking to grandfather, I feel better about the whole situation. I think Jacob and I understand everyone's reasoning. Grandfather Saul said it's how you go forward. Do not dwell on the past. He said it's your actions that determine your character as a man. He said he and Margaret knew," said Jared.

"Who else knows?" asked Jared. Marcus spoke up, "Your pediatrician, Dr. Wright, Dr. McCullough, and Mike. There are probably some nurses, but they would not divulge any information that involved your medical records. The Matthew's publicist was instructed to keep a lid on the information," said Marcus. "Until we were ready to tell you boys."

"So how did someone find out?" Joseph said.

"I do not think they know. I think it is speculation from my opponents," said Joseph.

"That's what happens in politics is that the other side tries to dig up dirt, no matter who it hurts."

"Well," said Jared. "I agree with you, let's tell the truth and go from there."

"You said Emily knows, but not Sophia?" said Jacob.

"She must know before you go public, Uncle Joseph."

"Yes," said Joseph. "She is the next to be told and hopefully she will be as understanding as you boys have been."

"Well, there nothing that can be done to change the circumstances," said Jared.

"I'd like to talk to her, after you tell her. Dad, Mom, it does not change how we feel. You are our parents and Joseph is still our uncle and godfather," said Jacob. "So, biology does not make the father, even though it is important to our genetics, but that's it," said Jared.

"Since we know we are bi-racial, I'm sure there will be things we will want to ask you Uncle Joseph," said Jacob. "Anyway, what about your family Uncle Joseph? And Dad, your family?" said Jared.

"Well, my parents love you and that will not change in my family. Only a few need to know. Let's handle it as it comes," said Marcus.

"As far as Joseph's family? It's up you boys how much interaction you have," said Marcus. Joseph said, "You know I love you boys. I know you do not think of me as your father, but I do think of you as my sons, and I will do anything for you to make your life easier," said Joseph. "Just like I would for Sophia. Tomorrow I will fly back to Virginia, and Emily and I will tell Sophia. Your mother and I did not mean to complicate your life," said Joseph.

"I guess we did not think about the consequences of our actions, but I did not want to lose her. I chose duty and responsibility over love." Samantha interrupted, "I could have told you I was pregnant, but I was angry."

Jared said, "We cannot go back, just forward." Marcus said, "We have raised very wise boys."

"Dad, will you take a walk with us on the beach? I'd like to talk to you about telling the girls.?"

"Would you like me to help you tell them?" said Marcus.

"Yes," Jared said. "Let's go then. We will see you later," said Marcus to Joseph and Samantha.

The boys walked out to where the girls had gotten back into to the pool. "Hey girls," Marcus called. "The boys would like you to take a walk with us on the beach."

"Sure dad, that'd be fun." They scurried out of the pool, got their beach wraps, and grabbed Marcus' hands. When they went down the path to the beach, they came to the same rocks that the boys had sat on and been told the news of their birth.

"Matilda and Ester," said Jared, "do you feel any difference between being adopted and me, Jacob, Bella, and Trey?"

"Nope," said Ester. "I cannot remember my parents."

Matilda said, "I have some memories, but Mom and Dad are our parents. I hardly ever think of being adopted. Why do you ask?"

"Yeah," Bella chimed in. "Why would they feel different? What's wrong?"

"Well," Jacob said. "We just found out that Joseph is our biological dad, and we are trying to wrap our head around the news." Matilda said, "Jared, I know you do not want to hear this, but I have known for some time. When Joseph is around, you look like him and he has always taken a special interest in you two. I never said anything because it does not matter," she said.

"Daddy is all the dad we could ever ask for," Jacob said. "What about your friends, do they ask?"

"Never," said Matilda. "When you are a Matthew, no one questions you at all. It just does not matter," she said.

"Maybe it's because of the name or it just does not matter to anyone. We are such a close family."

Marcus said, "I really do not think you will have any questions from your friends, unless you choose to tell them. The Matthew name carries a lot of weight. You are also Saul Weinstein's grandchildren. Besides, we do not care what other people say. We are the only people that matter," said Marcus.

"I love all of you. You are my children." And he hugged all five of them together.

The next morning, Joseph was scheduled to leave at ten. All of the Matthew family were downstairs having breakfast with him and seeing him off. Samantha said, "Do you want me to be at the press conference with you?"

"Emily will be there. I do not want to put you through the press and their questions about our relationship. I plan to tell them the truth and leave it at that. If they want to hold our relationship against me, then so be it. I plan to tell Sophia as soon as I get back. I just hope she takes it as well as the boys did. The children are the most important thing to me. If it costs me the campaign, then that is okay with me."

Marcus said, "We will do everything on our side to make things easier for you and the children. Anything we can do to help, please call me. I would also have your publicist reach out to ours, so that our story is the same." "You're right, the children are what's important. Whatever fall out the two families have, as long as we stick together, we will come out fine. We cannot undo the past, as Saul would say. It's how we handle now and the future." Joseph shook Marcus' hand, "You raised some amazing boys," he said.

"Yes, all my children are pretty amazing: bright, understanding, and have a great philosophy on life."

Samantha said, "Please call and let us know how things are going with Sophia." Joseph hugged Samantha and the girls and shook the hands of the boys. He kissed Trey.

"Take care," he said.

Marcus said, "You are the first to know. Sam, is it ok if I tell him the news?"

"Yes," she said. "Now that the children have gone back inside. We are expecting again. I'm going back to New York in a few weeks so that I can focus on myself. Marcus and the children are going to stay here for the remainder of the summer. I am already beginning to have the same symptoms that I had with the boys." "Congratulations," Joseph said. He kissed Samantha on the cheek and shook Marcus' hand.

"I do not know how you two keep up with so many children. Emily and I still only want the one child. So, I better go if I want to get back late this afternoon." Joseph got into the Jeep and waved and headed for the airstrip. Marcus put his arm around Samantha, "I think we should tell the children about the baby and that you will be leaving to go back to New York," he said.

"Yes," said Samantha. "Let's do it now while they are all together at the pool." They went to the pool area where the children were swimming.

"Hey guys," said Marcus. "Your mother and I have some important news to tell you. So please gather around." The children got out of the pool and came to where Marcus and Samantha were standing.

"More news?" said Bella.

"Yes," said Marcus. "Your mother will be living for New York in two weeks and all of you will be staying with me, Mike, the nannies, and the nurse. You see, mom is pregnant and it is better that she be under the care of Dr. McCullough."

"Are you kidding us?" said Ester.

"Trey is only 5 months old," said Matilda.

"Yes, but you cannot predict the things," said Marcus. "So, we will be adding another baby to our family." Jacob spoke up, "Well, I hope this baby is a boy, so we can beat the girls."

"Well, I do not care what it is as long as mom is healthy," said Matilda.

"Let's get back to the pool," said Jared.

"Congratulations, mom and dad." The children all jumped back in the pool.

"Well, that went well," said Samantha. "That's one reason I wanted them to stay here. They are enjoying the climate so much, nothing seems to phase them." "Yes, you're right," spoke Marcus. He kissed Samantha on the lips.

"Let's make the most of the time that we have together. How about you and I have some lunch together?"

"Yes, sweetheart, that sounds good. You can tell Mike and the rest of the help. I want to wait a little while before we tell your family and mine," said Samantha. "I really want to focus on me and my health," she said.

The two weeks passed quickly; it was the night before she was to leave.

"Marcus and I put the children to bed early."

"I'm going to miss you," he said. He reached across the table and took her hand. He brought it to his lips and kissed it.

"Please take care of yourself and if you need me to come home early, you know I will," he said.

"You are my heart and soul. And I feel guilty that you're pregnant again so soon."

"It is okay," she said.

"We wanted another child and at least Trey and this baby will be close in age.

They'll be good playmates with each other," Marcus said.

"I think that the age difference is getting too far apart, and I am getting too old to have any more children."

"If you really want another child, that I think surrogacy is a good idea"

"I love you," Samantha said. "I knew you wanted a big family. I just think the circumstances of the twins and the girls we did not expect."

Marcus said, "Let's go up to our room. I'd like to make love to you before you leave."

"Yes," she said.

He took her hand and went to their room. He kissed her with passion and began to nibble her ear.

"No rough sex tonight." He began to remove her clothes and kiss her breasts and neck. She began to remove his clothes, too. They were taking their time. He lifted her up and placed her on his bed. His manhood was erect, but he was holding back. He whispers, "I love you. I want to be gentle with you. I have asked a lot of you." He moved over her body, planting kisses all over. She could feel the heat rising between her legs. He hovered over her and entered her slowly. His gentle thrusting was bringing them both to climax. Once they had reached their peaks together, he held her in his arms until they both fell asleep.

The next morning, everyone joined for breakfast and the children were excited about going to the beach with the nannies. The nurse was putting Trey down for nap. Samantha kissed and hugged all the children and promised them that she would call every day.

"I know they will be fine without me," said Samantha. "They are excited about being on the island."

Marcus said, "They will miss you. You know that, but sometimes they take for granted their mother and father."

Samantha said, "That's because of how secure they feel."

"Well, if you are going to leave by ten, you better head to the plane," said Marcus. "Mike is already there. He'll fly down with you and Mason will pick you up," said Marcus.

"Now, if you need me for anything, I'll fly down as soon as the jet gets back," said Marcus. "I understand you needing some alone time, but two months is a long time to be away from you," he said.

"I know," said Samantha. "When you were in the hospital, after the shooting, it was hard to be away from you. But Hyperemesis Gravidarum is something I'd like to face alone, under the care of Dr. McCullough," spoke Samantha.

"I understand," said Marcus. He helped Samantha into the Jeep and headed toward the runway. He had his hand on her thigh and gave her a loving squeeze. *Yes, he'll miss me,* she thought, but she needed the time away from the children. Marcus could handle the children and one of them needed to be there with them. And since she'd be sick for a while, she'd rather not have the children see it. Marcus had been wonderful when she was sick with the boys, but she wanted this time to be alone. By the time they got back, hopefully she'll be through the worst part of the morning sickness.

She was dreading the flight back, as she knew that the symptoms would get worse on the flight. Mike would be there and then he would fly back to help Marcus with the children. Mason was good at security, so he'd be fine.

"Darling, I'm going to tell the family about three days after I get home so I'll have plenty of loved ones around me," she said. They arrived at the jet. "I can come with you," said Marcus. "If you want."

"No," said Samantha. "It is important that you stay with the children," she said. "Remember when you were in the hospital? They were worried about you," she said. "So one of us needs to be with them. You have a lot of things to get accomplished with the island. Please love to do not worry. Under Dr. McCullough's care, I'll be fine and all you can really do is watch me throw up about fifty times a day."

Marcus put his arms around Samantha and kissed her passionately on the lips and said, "It's whatever you want darling."

"Tell the children to help with Trey. They see him as nuisance, but with a baby around, they need to bond with him," she said.

"I understand," said Marcus. He had tears in his eyes. They embraced one more time. It was hard to leave him, but Samantha thought this was for the best, for the children, and for her. She really wanted the time alone, she understood now how Marcus felt when he was in the hospital. Sometimes, you needed to take care of yourself so you would be ready to take care of your family. Marcus said, "Joseph called this morning and said the press conference went well, but Sophia was not taking the news well. He said she did not want to share her daddy with the boys."

"Well, ask the boys to call her and tell her they will not be sharing their daddy, they have father and it is not Joseph," Samantha said.

"Yes, I think she may be a little jealous," Marcus said. He helped Samantha up the stairs to the plane and kissed her one last time. "I love you," he said. "And I'll see you soon, darling," he said. Samantha could tell he did not want her to go. She felt a little guilty about leaving her family behind, but she knew if she did not take care of herself, she would not be any good for them.

The entire trip home she stayed sick to her stomach; the plane ride did not make it any easier to keep her stomach from being ill. She could not even keep water down. She had been afraid of this and could not wait to land. Mike was so concerned that he had an ambulance at the airport to take her directly to the hospital. Once there, Dr. McCullough put her in the hospital and had the nurse hook up an IV. Mike immediately called Marcus and told him where Samantha was.

"Let me speak to her," Marcus said. Samantha got on the phone and Marcus said, "I am chartering a plane and I will be there…"

"No, sweetheart," she said. "There is nothing you can do. I am where I need to be. This is just part of this condition and as soon as the IV takes effect, I will get better. I am in good hands with Dr. McCullough. I know you think you need to be here, but it will help me more if you stay with the kids. I will stay in touch."

"How long will you be there?" he asked

"A week." she said. "Then I will go home and be on a special diet. You know this will come and go until right up to the seventh month, the worse will be under control by the time you and the kids get home."

"I cannot stand thinking I did this to you."

"Marcus, you are not responsible for my condition during pregnancy. And it is my decision to keep having children," she said. "I knew going into this marriage you wanted a big family, and so did I. So do not blame yourself. It is just the way it is," Samantha said.

"I still do not like it and if we do have anymore, we will pay a surrogate to carry the baby."

"That I will agree to," Samantha said. "I love you. Just take care of the children. Show them a good time before they have to come back and be a part of this pregnancy. They have been through enough this year without seeing me so sick," Samantha said. "Sweetheart, I need to rest but I promise you I will call my dad and let him know where I am," she said.

"Okay," he said. "I'll check on you later. Just know you are my heart." Mike's phone rang again. "Stay with her until she's at home and settled," he said.

"We will be fine with the security here. Also make sure Mason is aware and tell him he had better take care of her as if I was there." Marcus sounded threatening.

"Man, you know Mason and I love Samantha like a sister. I'll see you after I get her settled," Mike said. "I know you're worried, but I talked to the doctor, and she assured me that Samantha will be fine, the trip back brought on this severe bout of her condition and there is really nothing you or I can do for her. She's where she needs to be. I am not going anywhere until I get her home and settled. You know her dad and Margaret will take good care of her. She's right, the kids have been through so much this year and Samantha could not do much for them until she gets stable. She just wants to take care of the children and you being with them makes her feel better. So, let her do what she needs to do to take care of herself," said Mike.

"Alright, alright," Marcus said. "I love her so much."

"I got it," said Mike. "Now, go take care of the children and I'll call you later."

Marcus was pacing the floor, he was tempted to leave for New York anyway, but she had asked him to stay with the children. Jacob called, "Dad, are you coming in the pool?"

"Yes, son," he said.

***

Samantha asked Mike to call her dad and tell him she was back and in the hospital.

"Tell him I am pregnant but not to come by until tomorrow." She said, "Mike, I am too tired and sleepy to deal with my dad right now. He's not going to be happy about this, as he knows what I went through with the twins."

"Sure thing," Mike said. "He's just going to want to come, though."

"Yeah but convince him that what I need the most is to sleep, an IV, and Dr. McCullough's care. And you can go home. I am pregnant, that's all. And I have a condition that you, Marcus, nor Dad can help me with. Go home to Denise. She has not seen you in sometime and she will want to hear about the island we bought, among other things," Samantha said with a smile.

"Yeah, but I promised Marcus I would not leave you," he said.

"Well, it is like I said. I am where I need to be. So go home, call my dad, and I'll deal with my husband tomorrow. Now goodnight." Samantha yawned and was drifting into sleep. Mike left and called Saul on the way home and explained what she had said to tell him. Saul was eager to see her as expected, but agreed to Samantha's request.

"What the hell is Marcus thinking? And Samantha?" he angrily said to Mike.

"There's more story here than you know and I do not think they planned this one, but I will let Samantha tell you everything tomorrow."

"She just had Trey, what is he even three months old?" said Saul.

"I think he is almost four months but, Saul, let Samantha tell you everything, please." "Well, there is nothing about being a little pregnant" he said. "She's pregnant so thank you for calling me and I'll wait to see her tomorrow." Saul seemed to calm down when he spoke this time.

"I'll see you tomorrow, Saul. Marcus has asked me to stay until I can settle her at home," Mike explained.

"Well does Marcus not think that I can take care of my daughter? And why is he not here with Samantha?" Saul demanded. Mike explained, "Samantha asked him to stay with the children. She felt like she needed alone time to focus on herself and she asked Marcus to stay with the children and let them enjoy the summer. She felt like she would not be able to take care of them and since Marcus' accident, she's thinking of what's best for the children. So, goodnight, Saul try to get some sleep. After I leave, she will need you and Margaret."

"Goodnight," Saul said and hung up the phone. Mike, with sarcasm, said "That went well." He phoned Denise and told her he was back and would be home soon.

"Well, what happened? Not that I'm not glad you're home, but I thought you'd would be gone all summer with the new project and all."

"I'll tell you all about it when I get there. How about fixing me a steak and have a beer ready? I need it, and you," he said.

He got home and it was after ten. Denise had just finished cooking him a steak with a baked potato and salad. He sat down at the kitchen bar and popped the top on his beer and took a deep drink.

"Thanks, hon. You're not going to eat?"

"No," she said. "I ate earlier. I was not expecting you in. So, what is going on?" she asked.

"Well, Samantha is pregnant and wanted to come back," Mike said between bites of steak.

"You're kidding," said Denise. "What is Trey? Three months old?"

"Yeah," said Mike. "About that. It was not planned, and you know she has condition where she has severe nausea, so she wanted to come home. She got so sick on the flight home that I took her straight to the hospital. Dr. McCullough admitted her and I'm here for a week to make sure she gets settled at home and then I'm going back to the island," Mike explained. "Where is Marcus?" said Denise. "Did he come back also?"

"No," he said. "Samantha wanted him to stay with the children on the island. They will be home before school starts. She said she'd rather he stay with the children and show them a good time. She wants to focus and herself and felt like Marcus could not do anything for her," he said. "She said she would not be any good for the children as what she needed was Dr. McCullough. She felt like the children had been through enough with his accident," he continued.

"I called Saul and filled him in and after she gets out of the hospital, I'll to take her home and then go back to the island and help with the kids. Mason is to take over security and make sure she is safe," Mike said. "So, come here and let me give you a kiss," he said. Denise came around the bar and sat next to Mike. He leaned toward her and kissed her passionately and started unbuttoning Denise's shirt. Then he picked her up and carried her into the bedroom.

The next morning Saul got to the hospital just as Samantha had started breakfast. He went to her bed and kissed her on the head and sat down next to her.

"Now tell your dad what's going on?" Samantha blushed and began the story of Marcus's accident.

"Well, Dad." she said. "After Marcus's accident he was recovering but one of his side effects from his brain injury was he was not able to get an erection. That is why he spent time at the condo swimming, which he thought might help him relax and start being normal again. He had lost all confidence; he was passionate but could never get his body to cooperate with his desire. He put a lot of pressure on himself, and the doctor said he'd regain the ability to have an erection, but he was going to have to wait until his brain and his body would connect," she said. "But he never told me, as he knew that sex was important to our relationship. He felt if he could not get his ability to have an erection, well he lost what he thought a man should be like," she explained.

"He had also let his old girlfriend stay at the condo, Renee the model he dated for a while in France. Well, Dad, I knew he was keeping something from me, so I had Mike take me to the condo where I was going to confront him. Renee was supposed to leave when he was using the pool, but this time she was there and she was trying to seduce him," Samantha said. "I never thought about him cheating on me. I knew he loved me and his family and would do nothing to jeopardize our marriage. So, I got angry when I saw Renee there. He had not told me for fear I would be jealous," she said. "Anyway, Mike threw her out and I confronted Marcus," she said. "But just like the doctor told him, he was able to get an erection. I tried to slap him. I was angry that he thought that I would be so shallow," she said. "Anyway, we talked it through and he agreed that he should have told me, and that having Renee stay around was a mistake. Renee is a troublemaker and just for fun she was trying to seduce him, since he left her," Samantha said.

"So, I am pregnant. And I know it is too soon after Trey, but what is done is done. I came back to focus on myself and let Marcus stay with the children. I need Dr. McCullough's care. There is nothing he can do, so I asked him stay with the children. You know they've been through hell when he had his accident," she said.

"So, I got really sick on the plane and Mike brought me here. I was so dehydrated that Dr. McCullough admitted me," she said. "Dad. Marcus wanted to come back with me, but I insisted he stay. No one can help me, and I would be no good to care for the children. They are having such fun on the island we bought, I want them to have a relaxing summer before school starts back up," Samantha said.

"Well," Saul said. "You always bring a little excitement to my life. Margaret and I will be here for you," he said.

"I know, Dad, but there is really nothing anyone can do," she said.

"So why is Mike staying?"

"Marcus asked him to stay until I was released from the hospital. Mason is going to take his place," she explained. "He's just doing what Marcus asked then he will go back and help with the children."

"All right then," said Saul. "Is there anything you need?" he asked.

"It would be great if you and Margaret could pack me a bag and bring it to the hospital," she asked.

"You got it kid. I'll call Margaret and pick her up and we will go by the mansion and bring it back here," he said.

"Thanks, Dad."

The phone rang and it was Mike. "How are you today?" he asked.

"I feel much better. Please spend time with Denise and just pick me up on Friday when I am released from the hospital."

"You know Marcus will have my head," said Mike.

"I'll take care of Marcus. Like I said, there is nothing you can do. My dad stopped by, and he and Margaret are picking up what I need from my house."

"Okay, but I will still check on you in a couple days," Mike answered.

"You know I am concerned also," he answered. "As is Denise."

"Thank you," Samantha said. "I've got to go, this is Marcus. I need to take this," Samantha said.

"Darling, how are you?" Marcus asked.

"Much better now that I am here. Dr McCullough has me on fluids and a strict diet. How are the children?" she asked.

"They are having a blast, even Trey is enjoying the pool," he said.

"I think he's trying to crawl and say 'dada,'" Marcus said. "I hate that you will miss that, sweetheart," he said.

"Yes, I know, but it cannot be helped. I am where I need to be. Also, my dad came by, and he and Margaret are bringing some things from the house for me," Samantha answered. "And I told Mike to take a few days off and spend some time with Denise."

"Sam, you have no security there?" he sounded alarmed.

"Marcus, no one knows I am here. And I'll be out of here Friday. Mike will pick me up. He also said that he and Denise would check on me in a couple days. I am well taken care of, sweetheart," she answered.

"Sam, I do not like you not having security with you. You are a Matthew and anything can happen," he scolded.

"Marcus, please I am a big girl. I will be fine. Please let me make these decisions and you take care of the children," she said. "And I will call the children tomorrow when I am feeling better. Love, you are helping me by just doing what I asked," she said rather strongly back to him.

"I love you so much, and if anything happened to you, I could never forgive myself," he sounded worried. "I'm already the reason you're there now and not here with me and the children," he said.

"Marcus, love, I am where I need to be. Stop worrying and I'll call you tomorrow. Right now, I'm going to take a nap," she said.

"Well, you are so independent, I guess I have no choice but to agree to what you have asked. Sweetheart, have a good nap and if you need anything call Mike, and if your health changes, please call me and I will be on the next plane out. The children have their nannies and a nurse, so they will be fine," he said.

"I love you, Marcus. But I am fine, and yes, if I need anything I'll call my dad or Mike. You are a worry wart, but I understand after what happened to you. I get it, but just trust me, love," she said.

"I guess I have to, as you are very stubborn. I love you. Call me tomorrow and I'll put the children on a zoom call and let them talk to you," he said.

"That'd be great, love. I'll talk to you tomorrow. Now go have fun and tend to your island; you have so much more to do than I have," she answered.

"Talk tomorrow," and she hung up the phone. She thought, *He just cannot help but worry after his incident.* She wanted him to continue with counseling so he could relax and allow her and the children some freedom. He had changed so much since the incident, and she did not want to live her life in fear just because she was a Matthew.

Marcus hung up and called Mike and said, "I have talked to Samantha. I know she told you to take a few days off, but I want you have security posted outside the hospital and the lobby. She does not need to know, but I'd feel better until she is safely at home," he said.

"Okay," said Mike. "I am on it."

Marcus hung up and went back to the children who had gone to the pool. They liked the pool better than the beach. *I guess it is the sand*, he thought. Anyway, the nannies could watch them, and the nurse had put Trey down for a nap. So now he could get some work done. He called Denise and gave her instructions on the plans for the construction of the island and the house he wanted to remodel. He also asked that she send the Matthew's architect down so he could draw up the plans for the new house and other things he would need to start the projects he had proposed. He was going to use as much local labor as possible. He invited her down when Mike came back for a few weeks. She said she'd get right on everything he requested and said she'd enjoy a couple of weeks in the sun. Denise also said that everything at home with the company was under control. Marcus hung up and started making calls to different suppliers and labor sources so he could have most of the work started before he left at the end of the summer. He wanted to get as much started as he could as he wanted to spend most of his time at home, especially now that another baby was on the way. He was worried about Samantha getting pregnant so soon after Trey and felt a strong responsibility for the pregnancy since he should have asked if she had started birth control. But what was done was done; all he could do was give Samantha the space she had asked for.

On Friday, Mike came at ten to pick up Samantha and take her to the mansion as he promised. He had been glad that he had gotten to spend time with Denise and was flying back to the island early Saturday morning. Samantha was ready to go.

"You look much better," Mike said as he helped her into the car.

"Yes, and I'm ready to go home. Please look after Marcus and the children. I know he wants to be by my side during this stage of my pregnancy, but like I tell him each time he calls, he is helping me the most with the children and allowing me to focus on getting my eating and health under control before he and the children come back," she said.

"Yeah, but you know Marcus. He feels so responsible and protective. It is hard for him to be away from you," Mike explained. They arrived at the mansion to find that Saul and Margaret were there waiting.

"It's hard for my dad to get the message, also. That is why I have not told John Marcus and Isabella I am back," she said.

"You have a lot of people who love you and simply want to help out, but I see that you are right. A week in the hospital has helped you so much. Everyone, including Marcus, just need to back off and allow you to do what is best for you," Mike said. He got her bag and opened the door to his Jeep. He was immediately greeted by Saul and Margaret.

"Dad, you and Margaret do not have to come over every day. I will be fine. All I want is to keep to my diet, medications, get messages, and take care of myself before the family gets back," she said.

"I know, darling, I just wanted to tell you that Joseph called. His political numbers have gone up since the news came out about the twins."

"I did not know he had told you yet. I have not had a chance to tell you," said Samantha.

"Yes, he called and asked my advice. I told him since he is building his career, just tell the truth and see what his constituents decide. I also said to never underestimate the voters' desire for the truth. After all, it was a love story; one everyone accepts for the sake of the boys. Unlike me, who manufactured your paternity, I do not want anyone to question your paternity because I did not want those despicable people in your life. My reputation and career were already established. My desire was to protect you," he said.

"And you have, Dad. Now you can do two more things. Tell John Marcus, Isabella, and Rick the circumstances of me being home and about the twins. Marcus will call them now that I am home," she said.

"I made you a salad. I will keep your dad from running over here every day. You will call when you need us," Margaret said. Samantha kissed them both on the cheek.

"I think I'll go up for a nap. Mike, please call Marcus and tell him you have delivered me home. I'll call Mason after my nap and let him know I am home," she yawned. "Then I will call Marcus and the children."

"Too late. He already called Mason and he is on his way and will be staying in the guest house until Marcus gets home," Mike said.

"I should have known. My independence is hard for Marcus to understand," said Samantha.

"It is not your independence; it is just the after effects of Mr. Carr shooting him. He's like his father. His family's safety is everything to him. But I will get out of your hair," said Mike and he left to spend one last evening with Denise.

"Honey, if you need me call, please," Saul said.

"Come on, old man. She's tired and she asked to have her time," Margaret said. Samantha kissed them both and they left. She went upstairs to nap.

When she woke, she called Marcus.

"Hello, sweetheart. I'm sure Mike called you and told you I would call after my nap. I just had to sleep when I got home. I'm just seem so tired these days."

"Yes, Mike called and said you are feeling better. I sure miss you, Sam, and the children do also. Do you want me to get them? They are almost finished with dinner."

"No, darling. I'll call them tomorrow after breakfast. How are you?"

"Well, good. Getting a lot done and spending a lot of time with the children and counting the days until we get home." Marcus sounded tired and anxious.

"Marcus, I hope you understand that I need to get my condition under control before I can be of any use to the children or you."

"Yes, I am trying to understand, but I just want to take care of you," he complained.

"Yes, but remember how you needed time to get yourself recuperated after the shooting? Well, I need the same," Samantha explained.

"I just feel like it is my responsibility to protect you and care for you, Sam. If something happened…" Samantha interrupted him.

"I'll call you or Mason or Dad. My dad called your parents and Rick and told them I was home and everything that is going on with the twins and the new baby."

"Yes. Mother said he and Margaret stopped by and told her everything. She said dad was at the club and she explained everything to him. They already knew about the twins, she said that all you had to do is look at the boys and Joseph. They know he was the biological father. My parents are very opened-minded and do not care, as long as we are all happy. She knew we would tell them when we were ready to. I told her we were waiting for the boys to get old enough to understand, but since Joseph was suspected, and the issue had been raised, that it was time to bring it out in the open. She agreed. She's excited to have another grandchild. Mom said dad is hoping for another granddaughter," Marcus explained.

"I knew it would make no difference to them, or Rick," Samantha said.

"They are concerned about you, Sam, and want you to call them when you are ready. Joseph called to tell me that his numbers were up after the announcement. I invited him and his family down for a week. I'm hoping it would help Sophia if we were all together as a family," Marcus spoke.

"Thank you, darling. I think that is a good idea. Marcus, I love you so much, but right now it is time I eat. So, kisses to you and the children." She hung up the phone.

The days passed quickly. She was going on her second month of pregnancy and continued to follow her diet. She worked with a yoga instructor and practiced meditation. She began going to the condo and swimming in the indoor pool. Margaret and Saul came by at least once a week for dinner and a game of chess. Samantha went to John Marcus and Isabella's home and had dinner every other week. Marcus's sisters were planning a baby shower. Rick was working at the Matthew's construction office. He brought Samantha some work to keep her in the loop on the latest projects that the firm had taken on. Scott and Rick had her over for dinner and were very supportive of the pregnancy. Mason drove her to every function and doctor's appointment, and he and Samantha had gotten to know each other better. Denise had flown down to the island to help with the hiring of a project manager for the island project. Marcus called to tell her that Joseph and his family had visited the island for a week and Sophia had fallen in love with the island just as the children had. She was beginning to accept that her father was the biological father of the boys, and even though they all got along, she still treated them as friends, and not as her brothers. The twins made it apparent to her that Marcus was their father, and knowing that Joseph was their biological father, they still treated him the same.

Marcus was busy getting all the plans in place so he would only have to come back only once. He wanted to spend most of the time with Samantha and the new baby. Emily was showing that she was the dedicated politician's wife and so everything seemed pretty much normal. The phone rang just after dinner one evening.

"Hello, Sam. How are you doing, love?" Marcus asked.

"I am good. I have really got my condition under control," she said.

"How are you and the children?"

"We are missing you and counting the days until we come home, and I can hold you in my arms. I hate sleeping alone," he said.

"Yes, that is the hardest part, but I am hoping by the fifth or sixth month, I'll be over the severe nausea. Thank you for understanding. I know it has been hard for us both to be away from each other, but it was for the best. When you get home, I will be three and a half months along and Dr. McCullough will do an ultrasound and we can see what the baby is. How is Trey doing?" Samantha asked.

"He's pulling up. He seems to want to do everything quickly. He can say 'dada' and 'mama.' He tries to say the boys' names, but it's just babble. The girls enjoy fixing his hair and he enjoys swimming in the pool. The older children have started enjoying the beach. They are there now. Do you want me to have them call you when they get back?" he asked.

"No, I'll call them in the morning after breakfast." "Sam, I'll have this project wrapped up in three weeks. My plan is to come back then. That will give the children a week before school starts."

"I'd love that, Marcus. I am ready for my family to come home. I miss you and the children, and I am ready for us to get back to normal. I certainly cannot wait to make love to you again. We can also talk about preventing more pregnancies and talk to Dr. McCullough about my eggs and surrogate. I'm almost 35 and I know my body is finished having children. I know you want one more, and I understand that. We both wanted a large Catholic family. I just do not have the body to do that." She spoke with emotion.

"Sam, that is alright. What is money for if we cannot have what we want? But most of all, I want you healthy. I would be lost without you. You're my heart, my soul, the love of my life, and my best friend," he said with conviction. "When I was in the hospital, all I could think about was how happy I was that you came into my life. So, do you know approximately when this baby is due?" he asked.

"The way I have it figured, about the middle of December. We will know more when Dr. McCullough does the ultrasound," Samantha explained.

"A Christmas baby. We do not have one of those yet, that will be a nice Christmas gift to unwrap Sam," he laughed.

"I'm not sure the unwrapping will be that great for me, but I hope it is another girl; we have plenty of boys to worry about," Samantha teased.

"Yeah, I guess I'll have to get a shotgun for when they hit 13 years old," Marcus threatened. He thought that Samantha sounded so relaxed, and it was a comfort to him to hear her laugh and joke.

"Goodbye, sweetheart. I need to help get the children ready for bed. Mike has been a great help with the children. They all swim like fish. Trey is not there yet but he loves the water," he said.

"See you soon. And tell the children I love them, and I will call tomorrow after dinner," she said as she hung up the phone. The next day Samantha called the children and Marcus answered the phone.

"Hello sweetheart, we just finished breakfast. Jared, go get the iPad so you and the children can see and talk with your mom," he instructed. "How are you feeling this morning, Sam?"

"Good. I am waiting for my yoga instructor. She'll be here in an hour," she said.

"It is going to be a busy morning here. I am trying to get everything finished before I get home. I think I might have to come back one more time, but I want to time it around the baby. Here is Jared, and then I think they are ready to come home and see their mom. Jared, are you ready to talk to Mom"?

"Yes, dad, we are all ready to talk to Momma," he answered. "Mom, how are you? I've been thinking of you," he said.

"Yes, we are ready to come home," said Jacob.

"Mom, you will not believe how much Trey has grown. He's really smart," said Ester.

"Yes, he's smart and I think he misses you as much as we do," said Matilda.

"We all miss you so much, Mommy!" Bella exclaimed.

"Who is ready to start school?" Samantha asked.

"We all are. I need someone better than Dad and Mike to play chess with," Jared answered. "I need Grandfather Saul, he's better than the two of them. Doc is better than Dad, who is better than Mike, but Grandfather is better than Doc," Jared explained.

"So, you've gotten to know the doctor there?" Samantha asked.

"Yes, he's been showing us a lot of medical stuff. I decided I'd like to be a doctor," Jared answered.

"Not me. I want to be in construction, like Dad," said Jacob.

"I miss my friends," Ester said.

"I miss my art classes; I think I want to do something with art," said Matilda.

"I get to go to dance class out here and I love it," said Bella.

"It sounds like you all have been busy, and I am glad you ready to come home. I was afraid you would never want to come back," Samantha said.

"Mom, nothing's the same without you," Jared said.

"Yeah. How is Buddy? I'm sure he misses us," Jacob answered.

"He does, and he will be so glad to see you guys. Peter has been doing a good job with him, but it is not the same as having you guys here to play with him," Samantha answered.

"Let me see Trey, please," said Samantha, and Marcus, who was holding him, put him closer to the screen. Trey laughed out loud when Samantha said, "Mama."

"Well, he did not forget me," said Samantha.

"And these children will never forget their mom," said Marcus.

"Well, I was afraid they would not want to come home," she said.

"They miss their mother. I miss you and cannot wait to hold you in my arms again."

"Me too. I have kisses for everyone. Well, the yoga instructor is here. I need to go," she explained. There was a chorus of "I love you"s and "bye"s from the children.

"Goodbye, sweetheart. We will talk tomorrow," Marcus said.

"Thank you, darling. I love you for understanding me and my need to be alone." She hung up the phone and joined the yoga instructor on the third-floor gym.

The days were going fast, and Marcus and the children were due home August first, which gave them two weeks before school started. Mike would bring them to the mansion. Samantha could hardly wait to see the children and be in Marcus' arms.

It was the first, and Samantha was feeling so much better that her and Dr. McCullough thought the worst of her symptoms were over. She was going on her fourth month and symptoms usually lasted until after the fifth month. But her plan to take care of herself seemed to be working as long as she stuck to her plan. She felt very confident that the worst was over.

Marcus and the children were to arrive at two. She knew the children would be tired and hungry. She had planned a late lunch for them and could hardly wait to see them. Marcus came through the door carrying Trey; the rest of the children were behind him. Buddy was so excited that he was jumping up on the boys. Everyone had kisses and hugs for Samantha. Marcus kissed Samantha passionately.

"Wow, the baby is growing. Are we still on for the ultrasound?"

"Yes. Tomorrow we get to see the sex of the baby. Come children, let's eat a late lunch. I have all your favorites prepared." The children hurried into the dining room.

"I knew they'd be hungry," she said. There was lasagna, a green salad, rolls, chocolate chip cookies, and milk. They sat down and started passing the lasagna around, and Mike was eating with them. The children were eating very rapidly and gulping down their milk.

"Children, slow down. I know you're hungry, but the food is not going anywhere. Just slow down," Samantha said. She had a salad and some mashed potatoes to stay on her diet.

"Sweetheart, would you and Mike like a glass of wine?"

"No, Sam. I think Mike and I could use a beer. Then I think we could all use a nap," spoke Marcus.

"I'm going to head home; maybe Denise is there. She knew I was coming in. I'll see you tomorrow," Mike said.

"Take the rest of the week. I am here, and so is Mason."

"Thanks. I could use some down time," Mike replied.

"Tell Denise that she can take the rest of the week, too. I'm sure you'll want to catch up with her," he smiled.

"Yep. I'm sure you got some catching up to do also. I'd like to know the sex of the baby if you want to share it," said Mike.

"Yeah, we will give you and the family a call," Marcus replied.

The nurse had already taken Trey up to the nursery and the nannies were taking the children to their rooms.

"Are you ready for a nap, among other things, Sam?"

"You bet," said Samantha. They left the table and went up in the elevator to the second floor, where their suite was. Marcus could not keep his hands off Samantha. He started by undressing her and rubbing her rounding stomach. Then he kissed it and slowly moved her to the bed. His erection was apparent, but he was moving more slowly than usual.

"Are you sure, Sam? I do not want to hurt you," he said. She kissed him back, "I've been waiting two months for you to get back." He removed his clothes and slowly removed Samantha's.

"Darling, I want to take it slow. I do not want to do anything to upset you physically.

"I won't break, Marcus; I have missed your passion."

"I know, but it was my passion that got you pregnant," he said. He began kissing her stomach and down between her legs. He pulled her legs apart and placed his mouth on her pussy and listened to Samantha groan. Then he moved to her neck and kissed her as he rubbed his penis across the lips of her vagina. Slowly, he entered.

"Darling, I have so much to thank you for. You are a good mother and wife, and now you're giving me a third child that symbolizes the love I have for you." Marcus was making love to her, not the normal aggressive sex he normally would have after being away so long from her.

"Darling, I am pregnant. We did not plan this, but I love you. Having this baby so soon after Trey is just part of being married to you."

"I know. But I should have told you so we could have been careful and used birth control. All I was thinking of proving to you that I was still a man," he said. "Please forgive me for being so arrogant."

"Stop talking and make love to me. It is done. I love you and forgive you," she said. Marcus was making love to her which was fine with her. He began to enter her faster and faster, until she reached climax and was moaning loudly. After they finished, Marcus rolled off her and began to talk.

"It is not that I love Bella and Trey more than the other children, but they are me and you, just as this baby is. I can see you and me in them, that's all it means. Already the boys are beginning to look like Joseph, and the girls look like their parents. Can you understand that?" said Marcus.

"I totally understand. I see you in them and the next one will look like us," she said.

"You're a very generous man with your love, Marcus, and I love you for that," she said.

"Well, I should have thought more carefully. That is why I'd like one more child, but we will use a surrogate. I would never put you through another pregnancy," he explained.

"Well tomorrow, after the ultrasound, we can talk to Dr. McCullough. I knew you wanted a large family before we got married," she said. "And I do also. Now, let's talk about a nap. Let's get some sleep." Marcus held her close to him and she was so happy to have him back.

"Sam, what time's the doctor appointment?" he asked

"Ten o'clock," she said yawning.

"That's perfect, Sam. I plan to spend the rest of the week with you and the children," Marcus said. Soon, they were both asleep.

Marcus and Samantha were up early to have breakfast with the children. The children were making plans. Jared was spending the day at Saul's house to play chess, Jacob and the girls were making plans with Isabella do some shopping for school, and Trey was almost walking and was racing around in his walker, getting into everything. The nurse would be caring for them. The nannies were making workbooks and reports to do for the children to get them prepared for school. Everyone had their day planned. Samantha's doctor appointment was at ten. Marcus had decided to drive her himself. He felt more relaxed about his family now that he was home.

They arrived at the doctor's office at a quarter to ten. The nurse was ready for them, and Samantha and Marcus went right in. Dr. McCullough was waiting for them. The ultrasound machine was all set up. The nurse took her vitals and helped her on the table.

"Are you ready to see the baby? I guess you want to know the sex of your child."

"Yes. I cannot wait. Samantha and I do not care, as long as the baby is healthy." Marcus said. Dr. McCullough raised Samantha's shirt and put the cold gel on her stomach, then the monitor.

"Well, here is the heartbeat and the fetus looks a little small to be almost five months. I'd like you to gain a couple of pounds. Start having a shake every day if you can hold it down," she said. "Now, I can see what looks like a penis, yes, the outline is definitely a boy. You're having boy, Marcus," Dr. McCullough said. "I'm certain of that."

"A boy," said Marcus, and he kissed Samantha on the lips.

"Thank you, darling. A boy so we can name him George after my grandfather. My father's dad," he was gleaning in surprise.

"I love the name George. It's important to keep names in the family."

"Let's go to lunch and celebrate our boy," Marcus said.

"Before you go, I'd like you to come in my office. Let's talk about Samantha and any further pregnancies," said Dr. McCullough. She left the room and went to her office. Samantha wiped the gel from her stomach and knocked on Dr. McCullough's office door.

"Come in and have a seat." She had a serious look on her face.

"Marcus, I know you are Catholic and want more children, but she does not need to have any more children."

"We have decided to have one more child, but we are going to use a surrogate," he replied.

"I think that is a great idea," said Dr. McCullough.

"We are hoping you can help us with this idea." She thought a minute.

"I think I know someone who could use the money. She is in med school and is struggling with student loans. She about 26 and is a hard worker. Does not drink, date, or smoke. She is dedicated to getting through school. Her family is poor and unable to help her. She has interned for me and I would like to help her," she explained.

"She very proud and will not take handouts. But something like this, well she would earn the money. What do you think?" Dr. McCullough asked.

"I'd like to meet her. Would you Samantha?" he asked.

"I suppose you'd want to do Invitro ferritization?" she asked.

"Yes, after the baby is born, when you think Sam is ready. We would use her eggs and my sperm, all we need her to do is be a surrogate and carry the baby. It may be selfish of me, but to see our own child means a lot to me," he explained.

"Dr. McCullough, I know Marcus loves all our children, but I understand his need to see himself and me in our own offspring. Can you understand that, Dr. McCullough?" Samantha asked.

"Yes, people use surrogates of many reasons. Some people cannot carry a baby, some people's career hinges on their figures, like models and such," said Dr. McCullough. "I'll arrange a meeting with her and you can explain your reasons," she said to Marcus.

"Good. If she agrees, I'll have my attorney, not Sam, but one that specializes in this field draw up an agreement," he said.

"Well, it will be expensive, but I know you can afford it," said Dr. McCullough.

"I'll call her and see what she says, and if she agrees to a meeting, I will set it up."

"Thank you," Samantha said. "Call us whenever you talk to her. We would want to wait until this baby is six months old. Then we would have two children under the age of three, but with help, I think we can do it."

"We talked about this a lot, and I understand that she may not be able to carry the baby or even get pregnant. So, if it happens, it happens. Right, Marcus?" she asked.

"Yes, I will be content with what we have. So, call her and let's see if she is even interested."

"Sam, how about that celebration? And we will start those shakes today," he said, and with that statement they left Dr. McCullough's office and waited for her call.

Marcus called his and Samantha's parents. They were overjoyed that they were having a boy and were very attentive to Samantha the next two months. Samantha was gaining weight and was right on track with her weight up to eight months. Then she started dilating; the baby was trying to come early. Dr. McCullough told her the muscles the uterus were weak. She was going to have to go on bed rest and see if she could at least get to thirty-two weeks or more. Marcus was so worried, he hardly left the house. He distracted himself by spending all his time with the children.

Margaret came by and brought her food and said this had happened to her and she made it through. Her third child was born with no problems. She went to church and prayed for Samantha. Saul was worried. He knew how much Samantha wanted this boy. A miscarriage would devastate her. He knew she had regretted her abortion she had many years ago.

Marcus' parents were bringing her books and magazines for her to read and Marcus' sisters brought her gifts. That's the only way they knew how to show their concern. The children would visit her each day and brought her drawings and music to listen to. They would sing songs to her. Even Trey, who was going on one, knew something was wrong with his mama. He would lay on the bed with her and talk to her as much as a one-year-old could. Samantha would read to him and that helped to pass the time.

Dr. McCullough came by every day to check on her since she lived in the neighborhood.

"Something is wrong, I am feeling pain in my back and I am starting to have contractions. We need to go to the hospital," Samantha said to Marcus one day.

"Yes, darling. Let me call Dr. McCullough. Lay down, please." He frantically called the doctor and told her Samantha's condition.

"Call an ambulance. I want an IV started immediately. She is going into labor and they will know what to do. I am leaving for the hospital and will meet you there." Marcus called 911 and asked for an ambulance, gave them the address, and told them what the doctor had said.

"The paramedics will be right there. Tell her to stay calm and if she has the urge to push, do not. How many weeks is she?" the operator asked.

"About thirty-four weeks" he said.

"Has her water broke? Any bleeding?"

"No. Her water has not broken and there is no bleeding."

"I will stay on the phone with you until the ambulance and the paramedics get there."

"Yes, please," he said. Marcus laid the phone down as he was instructed and told Samantha to lie down, and he got her a glass of water.

"Honey, you must drink two glasses of water to prevent dehydration," Marcus said. He picked back up the phone and told the dispatcher.

"Now that's good," she said. "Time the contractions until the paramedics get there." Marcus looked at his watch. It had been 10:30 when she had her first contraction. Her second one had come fifteen minutes later, than she had another one ten minutes later. So far, she had not had another contraction, but her back was still aching.

Marcus was talking in a whisper. "It is too soon. I can't deliver a premature baby. Hell, I cannot deliver a baby at all. I am a construction worker." "Mr. Matthew, I know who you are. Hopefully you won't to have to deliver this baby. The paramedics should be pulling in now, so lay the phone down and let them in." Marcus took the stairs as he thought it would be faster than the elevator, and raced to the door to let the paramedics in. He saw the bed and the equipment they were carrying and decided that the elevator would be quicker.

"She's on the second floor," he said. By now, the children were alarmed and the staff was trying to quiet them down. The paramedics immediately examined her and asked how many weeks she was.

"Thirty-four weeks," Marcus said. They started and IV with Terbutaline, a drug administered to stop contractions, and asked how far apart her contractions were.

"She had one at 10:30, then another one fifteen minutes later, and then another ten minutes later. She has not had another one since the last one," he said.

"Okay. That is good. We will give her a shot of Ativan to calm her down. I guess you want to go to the Matthew's Hospital?"

"Yes, and her doctor is meeting us there." They loaded Samantha on the gurney and covered her with a blanket took her downstairs and loaded her into the ambulance. As Marcus was going out the door he yelled out, "Call her dad and Mike and tell them what is going on. I love you kids, but I have to go with Mommy and make sure she and the baby are alright." Then he got into the ambulance with the paramedics, and they left for the hospital.

"Samantha, just stay calm. I am so sorry I put you through this. I love you so much."

"Darling, we both wanted him, but we just cannot lose him—not when we have come this far."

"It will be alright, I have faith." Marcus bowed his head and prayed. "I promise you never again," he said.

"We have already agreed to that. Just hold my hand."

"We are almost there. It appears that the contractions have slowed down," the paramedic said. They pulled up to the hospital and got the gurney out. Dr. McCullough was waiting in the emergency entrance for her.

"Let's get her in a room so I can examine her," she said. The nurses took over and moved her in the room. Marcus thanked the paramedics and went in the room where Samantha was being examined.

"When was her last contraction?" Dr. McCullough asked Marcus.

"About 45 minutes ago," he said.

"So the medicine they gave her is slowing them down. Now we just need to get her to her room and keep giving her the medicine and try to stop the contractions. I'm going to give her several drugs to ensure that the baby, if born, will be healthy. Nurse, give her calcium, magnesium sulfates, an antibiotic, a shot of progesterone in the uterus, and corticosteroids tocolytics for 48 hours. That should buy us some time."

"Do whatever you have to do. I do not want to lose her, or my son," Marcus said. They wheeled her bed to her room and put a gown on her and made her as comfortable as possible. Dr. McCullough asked, "Did they give you something for stress?"

"Yes," said Samantha.

"Do you need something else?" said Dr. McCullough.

"No, I have calmed down now, I think I was on the verge of a panic attack and was feeling very stressed out."

"Samantha, what were you doing when the pain started?" the doctor asked.

"I had just put Trey down and was figuring out how close in age the two youngest kids were and if I could have the time for both of them and then have another baby and if I could handle all of them equally," she explained. "Then I was thinking how much I would have to rely on their nurse and nannies and if they would know who their mother really was."

"So, you worked yourself up to a panic attack with your future thoughts which not even happened yet?" the doctor said.

"Pretty much," said Samantha.

"Have you shared these thoughts with Marcus?" the doctor asked.

"No, not really, he is so happy to have a boy and a large family. I just want him to be happy," Samantha said.

"Well, I think you need to tell Marcus your thoughts on having George and Trey and another child. I also want you to start with a psychologist again. I have one in mind. I will call her and set up an appointment immediately," she said very seriously. Then she turned to Marcus, "You also need to attend some of these sessions and listen to your wife's fears." She said it like she was lecturing a teenager.

Marcus replied, "Whatever I have to do I will. Just save my son and wife; right now that is all I care about."

Dr. McCullough replied, "So far, it is a good sign that the contractions have stopped. The next forty-eight hours will tell us and be critical. Then if they stay this way, I am going to keep her and try to get her to two more weeks. She is forty weeks (about nine months) and if she goes into labor and delivers then at least the baby will be full term, but small. The last month is primarily for the baby to gain weight, so we can hope she can go a little longer before she delivers."

"So, two weeks after the forty-eight hours and we can have a healthy baby," said Marcus.

"Yes, that is right," she said.

"Thank you, doctor. I will pray that we get through the forty-eight hours and then the two weeks, I am so grateful to have you here," said Marcus.

"Oh, you will get my bill Mr. Matthew, I can already see a new clinic or a new wing to the hospital," Dr. McCullough said laughingly. "Anything you want," he said. "What I really want is Samantha to please herself and not always think of you. She is codependent and that is something I want her to work on. And you, sir, need to listen more to your wife before you make your plans," she scolded. Marcus looked sheepish and said, "I have a tendency to make decisions without asking my wife. I feel as I have to take care of her and my family. My dad has always been headstrong but my mother always seems to stop him if he got too carried away."

"Well, Samantha is not your mother and your learned behavior from your dad will be brought out in therapy and the both of you will learn who you are as a couple," she said. "Now I am going to leave and check on my other expectant mother, I am on tonight so I will check back later," she said and left the room.

In came Saul. He went to Samantha. "Are you alright?" he asked with a worried look on his face.

"Yes, Dad. I am feeling better," she said.

"Well Margaret is with the children, and I called Isabella, and she said she will go over tomorrow and help out with the children. She sends her love," he said.

"Thanks, Dad," said Samantha.

"No thank you needed, I only want you to be healthy and well," said Saul. "Marcus, I will talk to you later," Saul growled.

Marcus said, "Yes sir, I know you will, and I deserve a good tongue lashing. If you will stay, I like to go to the chapel for a little while and call my dad."

Samantha said, "Go ahead, sweetheart, and call and check on the children, please." Marcus came to Samantha and kissed her on the head and said, "You know you are the most important person to me. Life would not be the same for me without you by my side and I am sorry if I not listening to you as much as I should. I promise to do better, please, Samantha, forgive me," he said humbly.

"Marcus I really want what you want, we are perfect together and I want a man who takes care of his family. You have always tried to protect me and the children. I think this is more about doing some more work on myself. I think it is very important that I start believing that I do not have to be a perfect mother, wife, and attorney. I think I need to let that idea go and just do the best I can and know it is good enough. I hold myself to high a standard. I have all my life. I have wanted to make sure that I am better than where I came from. I am not my biological parents or my stepmother. I was damaged early in my life, and I want to be loved so badly for who I am that I overdo it sometimes," she said.

"Sam, I loved you from the first time I saw you. Nothing you have been through will ever change that. I love you for the woman you have become," he said.

"Go, darling. Call your parents and the children and say a prayer for me and our son and the family you and I have created," she said. "I love my life. It is better than I could have imagined and I am thankful for that."

Saul pulled up a chair and held her hand. "Samantha Amanda Weinstein, I love you, warts and all. I am honored to be your dad," said Saul, he wiped away a tear. "I am here now, Marcus will call your parents and your children, I am sure Margaret has them all asleep in bed."

When Marcus left the room, it was 12 o'clock. He called Margaret who was still up and answered right away. "Marcus," she said, "how is Samantha and the baby?"

"They are resting, the contractions have stopped, and we will know more in the next forty-eight hours the doctor said."

"Good, everyone here is asleep. I got this handled, give Samantha my love and tell her the children are fine."

"Thank you, Margaret," Marcus said. "You have always been here for my family," he said.

"Of course," she said, "now tell my husband that he needs to come here, I am waiting up for him."

"I will tell him. Have a blessed night," he said. He called Isabella next and woke her up.

"Son, is Samantha alright? And the baby?" she asked. "You sound so tired."

"Yes, I am but I am where I need to be."

"That is right, my boy," said John Marcus. "Your wife needs you and your son. Marcus, I am proud of the man you have become," he said.

"Thanks Dad, I try, but sometimes I do not listen enough to my wife," Marcus said. "Darling, you will learn more every year to use your ears and less of your mouth," his mother said. "Do you think your father and I have not changed and grown through the years? Marriage is like a tree: it needs good soil, water, and love and it will grow straight to the heavens," said Isabella. "Now say a prayer and God will listen," his mother said.

"Yes, mother," said Marcus. "I am on my way to the Chapel now, goodnight," and he hung up. Marcus entered the Chapel; no one was there this time of day. He sat in a pew and pulled out the kneeling bench, then put his knees on it and bowed his head.

"God," he said. "I know I am a sinner, but by your grace, you have forgiven me. I have asked for a lot from you, and I am here today to ask for your help once again. My wife and unborn son are in the hospital .Please let her have the time she needs to produce a boy healthy and full of life. You sacrificed your own son for my son, and for that I am eternally grateful. Please use your everlasting grace and place your hand on my wife and unborn son. Thank you for giving your son and thank you for the eternal love you have for those who believe. Amen." Marcus crossed himself, then dropped a hundred-dollar bill in the offering box. He felt better. He went back to Samantha's room to see if any progress had been made.

Saul looked tired so Marcus said, "Go home and get some rest. Margaret is sitting up waiting for you.

Saul said to Samantha, "Darling daughter, are you alright enough for me to go home to Margaret so she will go to bed?

"Yes, Dad, I am where I need to be. Go home; you look tired," she said. Saul got up from the chair he was sitting in and kissed Samantha on the head and said, "I will see you tomorrow and if anything happens tonight, please have Marcus call me."

"Dad, you will be the first one he will call. I love you. Go home and sleep. You and Margaret will have your hands full with the children tomorrow." Saul left the room and drove to the mansion where Margaret was waiting for him.

Samantha said, "I know, darling, you will not leave, so I had them bring a bed in for you. I have not had another contraction, so the medicine must be working. I am tired so I am going to sleep. Come and kiss me, and you go to bed, as well," she said.

Marcus got up from his chair and kissed her on the lips with as much passion as he felt. "I love you, darling. I said a prayer for you and my unborn son. I believe everything will be okay."

"Yes," Samantha said. "I believe so, too." She crunched down into the bed and pull the covers over herself. Marcus turned off the lights, then took off his shirt and belt before laying down in the bed the hospital provided for him. He too went to sleep at once. The next morning around six, a nurse came in to check Samantha's vitals and to administer more medicine into her IV.

"Sorry to wake you," she said, "but it is time for another round of the medications Dr. McCullough had ordered."

"I know that you're only doing your job and I thank you for that," Samantha said. Marcus woke up and listened to the conversation. He felt refreshed even though he had only had about five hours of sleep.

"Well, everything looks good. No contractions during the night?" she asked.

"None," replied Samantha. "The medicine seems to be working."

"Good," said the nurse. "They will be bringing in your breakfast around seven. Let me get the bedpan and let you relieve yourself. Would you like a wet washcloth so you can tidy up?"

"Yes, please. Marcus, will you call home and have them put a bag together of things I will need for a two-week stay at the hospital? I am sure Margaret has already started that," Samantha said.

"Of course, darling. I will call right now."

Marcus called and Margaret answered. "Yes, Marcus, is everything okay?"

"Yes, so far so good. Sam wants you to pack a bag for her and have someone bring it over to her."

"It is already done and Mike is on his way with it as we speak," she said.

"Thank you," said Marcus. "How are the kids?"

"They are all sleeping in this morning. Saul is still asleep, as well. The staff is up and doing their jobs; Peg has the chef preparing breakfast. I called their school and explained the situation to tell them the children will be taking today off and will be back tomorrow. They will have their homework ready this afternoon and Saul is going to pick it up on his way to the hospital. Peg and I have got everything under control here. How is Samantha?" she asked.

"No contractions and the doctor said if we can just get through the 48 hours, she believes Sam will make it through the next two weeks. So we are very hopeful," he said.

"Good," she said before hanging up.

"Mike is bringing your things this morning," Marcus said to Samantha. "Would you like to see him or should I meet him downstairs?"

"No, he is like family, I'd like to see him," she said. "I think we need to call Joseph and let him know what is going on. He may want to come and help with the boys for a few days. He has not seen them in several weeks. What do you think, Marcus?"

Before he could answer, the phone rang. It was Joseph.

"How are you, man?" asked Joseph.

"We were just thinking of calling you," Marcus replied.

"What's up?" Joseph asked.

"Sam went into pre-term labor last night so we are at the hospital, but the contractions have stopped. She will be in the hospital for two more weeks."

"I am so sorry," said Joseph. "Give her my love. I guess I'll come see the boys, if that's okay with you."

"Yes," said Marcus. "I think they would enjoy seeing you. What's up with you?"

"Well, I won the election, so I'm Governor of Virginia for the next four years. I called to invite the two of you to the swearing-in ceremony in January and the ball afterwards. I will send you all the details and you two can let me know. I am so sorry about Samantha. I will plan to fly down this week for a couple days."

"The weekend would probably be better," Marcus said. "They are in school now and that takes up most of their day. Just let me know so I can ask them if they mind you visiting them."

"Of course," said Joseph. "Just plan for the weekend, and if there is an issue, please call me. I do now want to exceed my boundaries with them," he said.

"I will let you know," said Marcus.

"Once again, I am so sorry for you and Samantha. I know things will be okay. She's a fighter," said Joseph.

"That I know. Hopefully we will see you this weekend," said Marcus before hanging up the phone.

"Honey, Joseph called to tell us he is the new Governor of Virginia, and we are invited to the swearing-in ceremony and the ball afterwards. It is in January," he said.

"I will have to send him a note of congratulations," Samantha responded. "I'd like to go if everything is alright with our baby and the family, if you think it is okay for me to go."

"Darling," Marcus said, "All I am thinking about is how if in three months if everything is alright with our son and family, I will take you anywhere you want to go." There was a knock on the door and Mike stuck his head in to ask if he could come in for a few minutes.

Samantha said, "Yes, Mike, and thank you for bringing my things."

"Marcus, I brought some things for you, too. I thought you could use a change of clothes," Mike said.

"Thanks, man. How are the kids?" Marcus asked.

"Eating breakfast when I left and excited to have a day off from school, and of course, asking about their mother," he replied.

"Tell them she is doing well, and the baby is, as well. I will be home tomorrow when the 48 hours are up.

"So, Samantha," said Mike. "Things are going well with you and the baby?" he asked.

"Yes, so far so good," she answered.

"Good," he said as he sat the suitcases down in the corner of the room. "I am glad to hear that. Denise said she has the office covered and you're not needed for anything," he reported.

"Come in and have a seat; they should bring breakfast soon," Marcus said. "Have you eaten?"

"Yes, Denise fixed me breakfast before she left for the office," Mike said.

"Well, I'll get you a cup of coffee," Marcus said as he pushed the intercom button.

The aide answered: "Can I help you?"

"Yes, this is Mr. Matthew. Could you add a pot of coffee to breakfast, along with a second cup, please? I have a friend here," he said into the intercom. "Mike, everything alright in security?" Marcus asked.

"Yep, I have everything buttoned up. You don't even have to think about it," he said. "I have Mason at the house and a man in the hallway of the hospital. Your family is safe."

"Good," Marcus replied. "Since the incident with Mr. Carr I just worry about someone else I may have pissed off accidentally.

"I think that man was a one-time thing, and it has been over a year. Last I heard he was still in the psychiatric hospital and they would notify me if he was ever released," Mike answered.

"That's comforting," Marcus said. There was a knock at the door and an aide came in pushing a cart of food, then began serving them breakfast. The first tray she set on the table across from Samantha's bed and said, "Mrs. Matthew, you are restricted from caffeine, so I brought you milk, instead." She lifted the cover off Samantha's plate, then served Marcus and pour him and Mike coffee. "There is cream and sugar, if you want it," she added.

"No, we both take it black, but thank you. This looks so good."

"Well, if there is anything else I can get you, please just call on the intercom. I will come back later to take the trays away," she said, then left the room. In walked Dr. McCullough and opened the computer screen to check on the information the nurse input for her to read.

"Well," she started, "it looks like the medication is working, so a day and a half from now will be 48 hours. If there are no more contractions, we just might get those two weeks we need to get to 40 weeks. Then we will just wait until that boy of yours is ready to join us. Samantha, how are you feeling?" Dr. McCullough asked.

"I feel like I want to get this pregnancy over with and go home so I can get back to my life," Samantha answered.

"Well, I can understand that," the doctor answered. "Marcus, did you get any sleep?"

"Yes, about five hours. Enough," he said.

"Mike, it is good to see you," Dr. McCullough said.

"Yes, it is good to hear news about Samantha.

"Well, I have one more patient to check on, then I am going home for some much-needed rest, but if I am needed, they will call me," she said to reassure Marcus and Samantha.

"Thank you," said Marcus. "Hopefully the scare is over and Sam will get through the next two weeks. I will be so glad when my son is born."

"Well," Mike said, "I am going to see the children before I go home. Anything you want me to tell them when I see them?" he asked.

Marcus said, "Tell them I love them and Daddy will be home tomorrow to see them."

"Tell them," said Samantha, "that Mommy will call them this afternoon on Daddy's phone."

"Gotcha," said Mike. "See you later. If you need anything, call me. Marcus, take a shower. You look like hell."

"Gee, with a friend like you—"

Mike left before he could finish.

"Chicken!" Marcus yelled out after him.

"You two are like brothers," Samantha commented.

"Yes, I love him as I would a brother, of course. I have known him practically all my life and he has helped me out of—let's say some unusual—scrapes through the years," he said.

"I can only imagine," Samantha replied. The door opened and Saul came in with a beautiful bouquet of flowers.

"How's my girl today?" he asked.

"Good, Dad," Samantha replied as he leaned over to give her a kiss. He presented her with the flowers. "These are beautiful. Marcus, will you ask the aide to bring me a vase, please?"

"Let me take them and put them in a vase," he said. Marcus took the flowers from Samantha and as he walked by Saul, he gave him a hug. Saul hugged him and patted him on the back, then Marcus went to find a vase.

"So how are the children?" asked Samantha.

"Well, the older children are easy. Jared has been beating me at chess and Jacob has been building some kind of model skyscraper he intends to build once he is head of the company. The older girls have been in the kitchen with Margaret baking all afternoon."

"And Bella?" asked Samantha.

"Well, she's a handful, and a chatterbox, as always. She's so clever, I'd guess she might be a lawyer someday. She loves to argue to get her way—definitely a master negotiator. She's more hard-headed than her sisters. I'm not sure how you two manage her," Saul responded.

"Sounds like you and Margaret are busy."

"Yeah, I stayed until Isabella arrived to rescue Margaret. Isabella has a way with Bella. She said she acts just like Marcus, so she knows all Bella's tricks and how to outsmart `her," said Saul. "I told her that's great, but let's hope this next one takes after my daughter because I am sure she was much calmer as a child," he said jokingly.

"I'm not sure this one will be any tamer," Samantha said. "He is already trying to come into this world before he is ready. It feels like he is as impulsive as his father," Samantha joked.

"Well, you look better than last night," Saul said.

"I feel better," said Samantha.

The 48 hours went by quickly with no contractions. Samantha was able to get up and take a shower and put on her own gowns. She did as she was instructed, taking short walks down the hall. Marcus went home as promised to see the children. Samantha called them every day to see what was going on. She was anxious to get home. John Marcus, Penelope, and Paige came by with more flowers and balloons to cheer her up. Rick and Scott brought her a milkshake, which she enjoyed very much. Phillipe even came by with a pasta dish that he had cooked at his restaurant, claiming she had to be tired of hospital food. Marcus even snuck Bella up to her room so Samantha could see her youngest child. Bella was so happy to see her mama, she kept excitedly hugging her.

Samantha felt very loved and lucky to have such a loving family. The final day marking 40 weeks (about 9 months) arrive and the time was great for the baby to come. Another week passed and still no baby. An ultrasound revealed that he was breech and had not changed position yet. Dr. McCullough became concerned and said she was going to try to reposition the baby, otherwise she was suggesting surgery.

So the next day, under light anesthetic, she stretched Samantha's uterus and was able to get him in the position of feet-first, which she was still not happy about. Before she could say much more, the mucus plug gave way. Samantha's water broke and the contractions began, and they were coming fast.

"Get her up to delivery; she's already at five and I think this is going to be a fast delivery. Marcus, you better get gowned up—looks like we are having a baby today." It was November 1st. Marcus got into his gown and followed the nurse into the delivery room where Samantha was already in stirrups ready for delivery.

"Dr. McCullough, this is going to be a record delivery. She is in active labor; expect to see the feet any minute. Samantha, it will be important to get his head out quickly. So, when I say give your biggest push, you do that," the nurse said. Samantha looked exhausted, but she was determined to get this boy out safely. Marcus was very encouraging and loving, but nervous.

"Darling, I am here. Take my hand and squeeze if you need to," he said. "Samantha, push hard. Here he comes."

With that, George the second was born screaming his head off. Healthy and about 7 pounds but 21 inches long. Marcus cut the cord, and after the nurses cleaned him up and wrapped him in a blanker, they handed him to Marcus. He was beaming.

"George," he said, "you have given your parents hell—especially your mother." He handed the baby to Samantha.

"He's beautiful," she said. "He looks like you and Bella."

Marcus said, "He is beautiful like his mother." The nurses and Dr. McCullough quickly cleaned up Samantha and she was rolled back to her room where all she wanted to do was sleep. Dr. McCullough came in later before she went home to check on Samantha.

"Let's see what tomorrow brings, but if everything goes well, I am thinking two days and you can go home with George. Dr. Wright has checked him out and he is fine. Long, but lean and probably needs to gain a pound, but that will come. By his looks, he will be tall like his father," she said.

"Well, I wish at least one of our children will look like their mother," said Samantha.

Marcus chuckled. "Our son would hate being as short as his mother. Bella has your hair."

"Yes, and she will probably hate me for that. It's always been tough to deal with," said Samantha.

"But I love your hair," said Marcus, "and we make beautiful children."

"That we do," said Samantha.

"Yes," said Dr. McCullough. "Last time I saw her she was model material."

"The only problem is," said Marcus, "she has a personality like her old man, and I am not sure that is a good thing."

"It got me to marry you, didn't it, sweetheart?"

"Yes, it did, and I have loved every minute of our marriage," he said.

"Okay, you two. Remember, no sex for twelve weeks. We will do the tubule in six weeks and harvest the eggs then," said Dr. McCullough. "Goodnight you two. See you tomorrow."

"Goodnight," Marcus said. "And thanks."

"Goodnight," said Samantha. "Thank you. I could not have my son without you."

Marcus said, "The nurse will bring George by for his last feeding. I would like to give him his bottle. Then I will go home to be with the children and tell your parents and mine that their new grandson is born."

"Sounds good to me," said Samantha. "I could use some sleep and peace before I go home. The nurse brought the baby in and put him in Samantha's arms then gave her a bottle of breast milk. Samantha unwrapped her newest son and said, "He is just so beautiful. You can already see how much he resembles you and Bella. His hair is dark, and his eyes are a crystal blue. He is starting to get restless and probably is about to yell for his bottle. Marcus, take your son and the bottle, please."

Marcus reached for his son and the bottle and ran the nipple over George's lips. He latched on immediately. Marcus said, "Son, you gave us quite a scare. I hope this is not a sign of what is to come from you. I hope you are not totally like your dad." George just hungrily sucked his bottle. He finished it in seconds. "Slow down, take life a little slower. There is no rush. First, you want to come early, not you want to suck down your bottle like there's no tomorrow." Marcus put George on his shoulder and burped him.

He sat in the rocker and continued talking to him. He was so proud to have his own biological son. It wasn't that he loved him more, but Bella, George, and Trey represented Samantha and him. He felt a closer bond with Samantha. There was no one else mixed in—no Joseph or parents that had died. No one that they had to share another person with. No Joseph or pictures of parents who had died to mix into the family. It was hard to explain, but he would talk to the psychologist about his feelings and what they meant for the sake of his children. Samantha was asleep—she had a rough day. It had been a scary and painful birth. Marcus kissed Samantha lightly on the forehead so as not to disturb her and whispered, "I love you dearly. Thank you for my son."

He kissed his son and took him back to the private nursery. The nurse was there and ready to take him. Mason was posted in the hallway. Security was always a priority to Marcus. "Congratulations, Marcus, on your son," Mason said. "You must be so very proud to have another son."

"Yes," said Marcus. "This one gave us hell and I am afraid he will be a lot like him older sister—demanding and impulsive. Always in a hurry. Are you here all night?" asked Marcus.

"Yes, sir. I have the night shift and will be relieved about six in the morning."

"Well, thank you for keeping an eye on my son and wife. I always feel better when someone else is watching over my family, especially if I am not here. I am headed home to be with the other children so I can tell them about their new brother at breakfast in the morning. Goodnight," said Marcus.

"Goodnight, sir. I have got your back. I will watch your wife and son as if they were my own," said Mason. Marcus entered the elevator and went down to the hospital lobby. He got in his car and left for home. Entering the mansion, Buddy greeted him at the door. Marcus patted him on the head and told him it was bedtime. All was quiet, and he took the elevator to the second floor and checked on each child who was sleeping peacefully. He went into his suite. The maids had cleaned the bed and the room. He undressed and got into bed and pulled the covers up around his shoulders.

It is so nice to be in my own bed, he thought. He fell asleep as soon as his head hit the pillow. Next morning, he was up at six, showered and dressed. He wanted some time to himself before the children came down at seven. He went to the kitchen where Peg had fresh coffee and an omelet ready. Somehow, she always knew when he was home. Peg had been with him for fifteen years and was more of a friend than part of the staff.

She said, "Well, how is your new son?"

"He's very long and looks a lot like Bella and Trey," he said.

"So, we are getting another Bella and Trey?" she asked.

"I am afraid so," Marcus responded.

"Well, Lord help us watch the three of them," Peg replied.

"Yes, we will definitely need another nanny and nurse."

"Well, we have room for them. I will call the agency and start the interview process so one will be available for Samantha to approve."

"Thank you," said Marcus. "She will be home in three days. I am going to take my coffee and breakfast in the den. I would like to have time to read the paper and collect my thoughts before the children come down to breakfast," Marcus explained.

Peg said, "I understand. The paper is on the table and I will bring you a pot of coffee in a few minutes."

Marcus thanked her then left for the den. The children came down at seven for breakfast.

"How is Mom?" asked Esther.

"She is tired, but good. She will be home in three days, so I want you kids to get ready for her," said Marcus.

"How is our new brother, George?" Jacob asked.

"Well, he looks like Bella and is very long and thin, so he needs to gain weight," Marcus said. "But he is good, and he will come home when Mom comes home."

"He will probably be like Bella—a little terror," Jared said.

"Well, we can only hope," said Marcus, "but you boys as big brothers can help keep him and Trey directed towards the right path.

"Yeah, if he will listen. Bella does not listen. She does her own thing," said Jacob.

"Bella's okay," said Matilda. "She just likes to be a leader. You even encourage her sometimes."

"Well," said Marcus. "There will be no more bossiness from you Bella. You need to learn your place as a child in this household. We have a new baby in the house, which will be a lot of work for all of us. Mom will hire another nanny and nurse to help out."

"Yes, sir," Bella responded with a giggle. "Speaking of nannies," she continued, "we really do not need a nanny anymore. I am almost nine now, Dad. We all know how to take care of ourselves.

"The nannies are here to help your parents out," Marcus replied. "None of you can drive so they are here to help with that."

"Dad, we have a driver, and Mike is always here to help us out or provide security. It is a waste of money," Jacob said.

Matilda interrupted, "I like having a nanny and I am older than you. Sometimes when Mom isn't here, they help us with our homework. Mike and the driver would not know how to do that. You're just acting like a dummy like you always do."

"Alright, you children need to stop arguing and focus on eating your breakfast and getting ready for school," Marcus snapped. "Matilda, apologize to Jacob. We do not use the word 'dummy', that is an upsetting word."

"I'm sorry," Matilda said to Jacob. "I know you are far from a dummy."

Margaret and Saul came down to breakfast.

"Sorry we are late, kids. We overslept and our alarm didn't go off," said Margaret. "I see your dad is here, so you kids are taken care of."

"Yes," said Jared. "And Mom will be home in three days, so Grandmother, you can probably go home if you want."

"Well, we will wait until your mother gets home and see how she feels," said Margaret.

"Are you tired of us being here?" Saul asked.

"No," said Jared. "I like beating you at chess. I need some better competition. So far I have beaten you and Joseph when he was here, Mike, and everyone at school."

"I'll play you, Jared. Let's see if you can beat me," said Marcus.

"I am going to enter you in a chess competition," said Saul. "That will be the best teacher.

"I think I'm already good enough to beat the doctor on the island. Dad, I decided what I want to be when I grow up: a doctor," said Jared. "One that specializes in the brain."

"Not me," said Jacob. "I want to take over Dad's. company and build skyscrapers."

"I want to be a graphic artist," said Matilda.

"Well, I want to be a teacher," Ester chimed in.

"And I'll be a dancer, actress, and a lawyer!" Bella shouted with glee.

"Right now, you all need to brush your teeth, grab your bookbags, and get in the car for school," Marcus replied.

The kids asked to be excused and started to leave the table.

Jared said, "Dad, here's a piece of paper from our guidance counselor saying Jacob and I should skip a grade because our currently class isn't challenging enough."

"I will talk to your mom about it when she gets out of the hospital," Marcus said. "Now go get ready." The boys hurried out of the room.

About ten minutes later, the children reentered the room, ready for school.

"Go get into the Suburban," Marcus instructed. "I will get my coat and meet you outside."

"Bye," the kids yelled to Saul and Margaret.

"Have a good day, my loves!" Margaret called after them.

"And stay out of trouble! Especially you Jacob," Saul teased. Marcus grabbed his coat from the hall closet and left to get into the Suburban with the driver and the kids.

"Does everyone have their seatbelts on?" asked Pete the driver.

"Yes, sir," the kids answered. With that, Pete started the car and drove them to school. The kids were talking amongst themselves.

Matilda said, "My birthday is coming up. Dad, can I have a sleepover? All my friends are having them. Please, I really want this birthday party."

"Let me talk to your mother today and I will let you know at dinner. How does that sound?" Marcus asked.

"Thanks, Dad. I'm sure Mom will agree."

The driver pulled up in front of the school and went around the car to open the doors. "Have a great day at school," said Marcus.

"Tell Mom we love her," said Ester.

"Bye, Dad," said a chorus of voices. "We love you."

"I love you too," Marcus replied. "Learn something and tell me about it at dinner. I will be here to pick you up." After they got out of the van, Marcus told the driver to take him to the office. He wanted to check on progress on the island house. He also wanted to asked Samantha about spending two months there and having all the family come to see his latest project. Denise was in the office and surprised to see Marcus.

"Well, hello, new dad. How are Samantha and the newest Matthew doing?" Denise inquired.

"Great," said Marcus. "I have another son now and he looks just like Bella."

"Well, how is Samantha doing?" she asked. "And what brings you to the office?"

"I wanted to check on the progress of the island house," said Marcus.

"It is right on schedule to be finished in May. Why do you ask?" Denise asked curiously.

"I want to spend two months of the children's vacation there if Samantha feels up to it, along with the grandparents and the rest of the Matthew group if Samantha completely agrees to it. And I want you to send the designer there to put the house in place and completely stock it by the first of June. That should not be a problem. The new houses we are building in the medium price range will also be finished in May. All she has to do is put the model home together and our sales agent in it, then we will start selling. Denise, contact Dr. McCullough and find out what she thinks about a new clinic being built by the Matthew group. Give her what she wants," Marcus instructed.

"Got you, boss," said Denise. "Anything else?"

"Yes, while we are gone, I want you to upgrade some things on our home here and see if anyone in our subdivision wants any maintenance or upgrades," he responded.

"That will be done," said Denise. "We will be busy this summer. I might have to add some subs to payroll."

"That's fine. The market is very hot right now so the subdivision should sell out fast. I want you to create a position for Jacob three times a week after school," said Marcus. "He said he wants to get into the construction business, and I want him to start learning."

"Is this a paid position?" asked Denise.

"Set it up like a paid internship. I will talk to his school and see if he can get credit for it. I think he is getting bored with his classes at school. They are wanting to have him and Jared skip a grade, so if Samantha agrees, I think we need to create some extra work for him," said Marcus.

"So, instead of 5th grade, they will go to 6th in the fall."

"Yes, that is right. We have very smart boys and we need to let them have more to do," Marcus said.

`

"No, he wants to be a doctor and play competition chess, so Saul is helping him with that. While we are on the island, I will talk to the doctor who oversees the new clinic about an internship there," explained Marcus.

"Sounds as if you have two smart kids," said Denise.

"Yes, and the smart ones need to stay busy," said Marcus.

"You're right," said Denise. "Now there is a project in Spain that needs your personal attention. We have some labor disputes, and the workers are talking strike. I am not sure what their issue is. It is not wages, but I figure in a couple months you can go there and have it straightened out."

"Book the jet, then contact my grandmother and see if there is anything she needs on the villa. Let her know I am coming, please," said Marcus. "Also, call her when I know the exact dates after I talk to Samantha."

"Is that all?" Denise asked.

"Yes, that covers all the projects we have going right now."

"Thanks for stopping by and tell Samantha congratulations. I will stop by the house to see her and the baby when she has had the time to get settled," said Denise.

"Thank you," said Marcus. "I will tell her, and if you need me, just call. Thanks for keeping everything together here at the office. You're doing a great job."

"Thank you. This is what you pay me for," she smiled as she answered.

"I am on my way to the hospital to see my wife and son. See you when I can get away from the family," said Marcus.

Denise said, "Take your time. I have got it covered here."

"See you later," said Marcus as he went out the door. He got in the car and instructed the driver to take him to the hospital.

Marcus got off the elevator on the second floor. Mike was in the hallway. "Hi," he said to Marcus.

"Anything going on?" Marcus asked.

"No, all is quiet," said Mike.

"I thought you sent one of your other guys here to be in the hallway," said Marcus.

"it's Samantha. I would rather do it myself," he said. "I stuck my head in there to see if she needed anything, but she said no. I guess you want the same procedure when she leaves Friday."

"Yes, the baby and the nurse will leave from the side door, and you will take them home. Samantha and I will leave from the front. Have my publicist here to answer questions. There will be questions about Jared and Jacob's paternity, I suspect. But she can handle it. Have Mason cover us and the Suburban out front so we can leave quickly," Marcus instructed.

"You got it," said Mike.

"Thanks, man," said Marcus. He then went into Samantha's suite to find her showered and with her makeup on. "You look beautiful, my love," he said to her, then went to sit on the side of the bed beside her. He kissed her passionately and held her in his arms. She could feel that tingle between her legs.

Will I ever get enough of this man? She thought to herself.

The kissing became more intense, and Marcus's penis became hard. He held Samantha tighter and pressed himself against her.

"I want you so bad," he whispered sharply.

"Sweetheart, we must wait, remember?" she said. "What is going on at home? I'd like to catch up before I go home tomorrow."

"Fine," Marcus sighed. "The guidance counselor at school has suggested that the twins skip a year. I have created an internship for Jacob that he will start as soon as Denise sets it up and contacts the school for approval. I want to set up another one for Jared with the island doctor so he can start in the summer. I would love to take the whole family to the island house and have the grandparents and the uncles and aunts visit to see what we have bought, along with all the work that is going on," said Marcus. "Of course, only if you approve."

"I think that is a wonderful idea. I also think we should let the boys skip a year and bring in a tutor to give them some prep classes for high school. I know they can handle it; we have some very smart boys," she said.

"Then Matilda wants to have a sleepover with her friends."

"I like that idea but set a limit to fifteen girls. Is that alright with you?" Samantha asked.

"Yes, darling. I think I'd rather than having them giggling all night at our house than someone else's," he said. "How is my boy?"

"Very demanding like his father," she spoke. "He will be here in fifteen minutes so you can give him a bottle. Right now, he has to be fed every two hours, and the way he eats, he will gain the needed weight in no time. Dr. Wright was here this morning and said he is healthy and ready to be discharged tomorrow."

"All the children have let me know what they are interested in as far as careers. Matilda is interested in graphic design, and she will paint on the side. I guess she does not want to be a starving artist."

"That's funny, but smart," said Samantha.

"In a few years, she can go to France and spend some time studying there. Ester wants to get a teacher," he said.

"I can see that," said Samantha. She over-organized the children, especially Isabella.

"Jared wants to be a doctor and play competition chess. Saul is looking into that. Jacob wants to take over the business and build a skyscraper," Marcus continued.

"Well, what do you think of your son taking over for you?" she asked.

"I think once he gets through his education, including an MBA, and traveled, then we will see," he said. "Bella wants to be a dancer and a lawyer. She's quite argumentative."

"She's impatient and hard-headed like her father," Samantha laughed.

"No, I disagree," said Marcus. "Sam, she is like her mother: determined to get to the next step in life. While we are at the island, I am going to have the house repaired and remodeled. The girls are wanting separate bedrooms."

"And if we're planning another baby, we need to make room for a nursery," Samantha said. "I talked to Dr. McCullough, and she said the medical student was on board with the surrogacy. She wants us to clear her student debt of $80,000 and take the $150,000, but she wants to continue her classes and cut back her hours. Dr. McCullough has set up a meeting in a month."

"If we like her," Marcus said, "I will have the attorney draw up the paperwork and we will try the surrogacy route when George is six months old."

"Here's your boy," said the nurse. "Hungry, as usual." She handed the fussy baby and the bottle to Marcus. He sat down in the rocker and talked to George as if the child could understand. Samantha knew he felt some difference with his own biological children—not more love—but a sense of pride about his two children being a product of his genetics. Marcus had a big heart and could take in the love for all his children. The ones that were not his biological children were just as much his own. That is just who he is.

Dr. McCullough signed the discharge papers and they left through the front while Mike and the nurse left from the side with the baby. There was a crowd of reporters all asking questions about the paternity of Jacob and Jared. Everything was handled by the publicist from the company. Mason cleared the path and they hurried to get into the car. Some of the reporters followed them, but the entrance to the mansion was blocked by the subdivision's security team. Mike had sent extra security in case there was a persistent group.

They pulled into the driveway of the mansion and were greeted by Peg and the butler, Peter. "Welcome home," they said. The baby was taken to the nursery with the nurse.

"I have a cup of chai tea ready with a sandwich," said Peg.

Marcus said, "Mike and I will go and pick up the children, just in case reporters have gone to the school. Mike, put extra security on the children until the story concerning the twins dies down. That's why I would like to take the family away to the island for two months, so the publicist can handle the publicity around the boys' paternity."

"I think that's a good idea. Children are born out of love relationships all the time. We are just rich; they see us differently," Samantha said. "I'm calling my dad and having him put a stop to this nonsense."

"Well," said Marcus, "I think I have it handled; you do what you feel is right." Samantha dialed her dad and told him what happened at the hospital.

"Darling, girl. I will make some calls to the owners of the rag magazines and the New York Times and have them call their dogs off. I am glad you are home. How are you feeling?" he asked.

"Glad to be home," she said. "A little tired, but thanks for your help. I will see you soon. I love you, Dad."

"I love you, too. You do not need to worry about anything. I got you always," he said.

"Well, I think I will have that cup of tea and go to the nursery to see George. Tomorrow we will introduce him to the children. Speaking of children, who went to pick them up from school?"

"Mike went to pick them up and was going to stop for ice cream with them so you and the baby could get settled before the children got home and bombarded you with questions," Marcus explained.

"That's nice of him," said Samantha. "And greatly appreciated. And you, what are you going to do?"

"Well, I am going to check with the chef and ask him to make a special dinner for tonight. Then I am going up to see my George and spend time with him until dinner."

"Alright, and you will see the other children at dinner?" she asked.

"Of course, Sam. Do not think I am making a difference in the children, please. I love them all equally. George and Trey are babies and requires more attention than the others. I have thought about how I will divide my time between all the children, work, my wife, and extended family, as well finding time for myself. I decided that I will that them to work on projects, but I never want you to make me feel guilty because I am proud to see that Bella and Trey and George are represented of our love together. Not you and Joseph or Matilda and Ester's parents who had no choice to love them as parents. Their mother and father died because of their mother's selfish gambling problem and the fact that their mother was too proud to tell me about it. I was the one person she knew could have helped her out. That kills me every day to think about, but people do selfish things to people they love. I should have told you I was struggling with my confidence concerning my ability to get an erection, then my anger boiled over and I practically raped my wife. People do selfish things. Yes, I wanted to be the twins' father, and if Jared had not gotten sick, I might not have called Joseph. I would have gone on pretending they were biologically mine, and the girls were so young when they were orphaned, but we kept their parents' photo by their bed. If I hadn't told them stories about their mother and father, maybe they would have forgotten them with time. They hardly speak of them, and when was the last time we took them to visit their parents' graves or their grandmothers? They love being Matthews and I am not taking that stability away from them. Then you find out you're expecting George, my son. I was overjoyed to see our love duplicated into another child of our own. I knew how hard another pregnancy would be on you and I knew you would go through with it and not put yourself through a second abortion. But I did try to give you space like you asked, and I even told you before we were married if I am ever smothering you to let me know and I will try to do better," Marcus said lovingly.

"He continued, "I understand that these pregnancies have been hard for you. You sold your practice and you have hardly any time to practice law anymore. And now I am asking for another child to see if you can divide your time with. And your faith, you hardly ever get to practice it as I have the kids tied up in Catholic school and church. I promised your father we would immerse them in some Jewish faith…well, we started with the boys, but I never followed through like I said I would. I am a pretty shitty son-in-law. And yes, I am a multi-billionaire, my family has lots of money—big deal! We have been married for almost ten years, so I shower you with gifts and surprises. This mansion, I built it for you, but it reflects more of me than you, and the beach house, that house also reflects more me than you. I am sorry, Sam. If you think I have lost interest in you, if you think I do not find you sexy, you are crazy. I cannot stop thinking about you every day. I hang around the house because I want to be I the middle of my family life and still have my occasional project."

"Are you finished?" asked Samantha.

Marcus had a tear run down his face and he quickly wiped it away with his shirt sleeve. "Yes, Sam. I am finished."

"I remember a man who asked me to paint a picture of how I wanted life to be, and I painted this picture, except for the law part. It is pretty much what I painted. What I have learned during counseling is that through this journey, I have forgotten myself. So there will be some changes, and except for the accident, I would not change a thing. Now, I am going to make some suggestions along the way, and we are going to include more of me and what I find important into my life. It is never too late. I'm so glad we had this talk, and I want us to have a meeting with our counselor so I can lay out what I am talking about," she said. "You are my heart and soul, and I have one question to ask: will you marry me again on our tenth wedding anniversary?"

"Hell yes," he responded, and he grabbed Samantha and twirled her around in his arms and kissed her with a deep passion. She could feel the firmness in his pants pressing up against her legs and she was aroused, feeling the magic come to life between her legs.

She pushed him back. "Twelve weeks," she said. "Dr. McCullough said twelve weeks, and no matter how much I love you, we are waiting twelve weeks, understood?" She smiled at him.

Marcus chuckled. "Yes, ma'am. I know I am used to getting what I want with my boyish charm and good looks. My dimples and devilish sex appeal. But I promise to abide by the rules of fair play."

"Now there is that cocky, arrogant man that I fell head over heels in love with," she said.

Mike opened the door and said, "Hello, we are home!"

"Children, I am so glad to see you. Daddy, say hello to the children, then we are going to get some milk and a healthy snack and sit in the kitchen while Daddy feeds the baby and changes his diaper. Doesn't that sound fun?" Samantha asked.

"No," the children said in unison.

"Say bye to Uncle Mike and thank him for the ice cream, then follow me to the kitchen," she instructed.

"Thank you, Uncle Mike for the ice cream, bye!" And they hurried to the kitchen to meet their mother.

"Did you get yourself in the doghouse somehow?" asked Mike.

"No, I think my wife just put me in my place," he responded.

"Well, it's about time. I hope she continues to do so. Samantha has grown since George was born. You gave her time and she used it to find that part of herself that has space for her personal life. It's a good thing, Marcus, so let's go change that dirty diaper and feed that little guy in the nursery. And never say that I'm not your brother, cause if you do, I'll kick your ass," said Mike. "And you know I can," he boasted. They went up to the nursery to see the baby. George was laying in his crib.

Marcus picked up George carefully. The nurse had bottles ready to go. "I'll handle the diaper," Mike said. Marcus handed the baby over. Mike said, "Let's see what we are dealing with in your diapers." He laid George down on the changing table and opened the diaper. "Holy shit," he said. "This is a freaking mess. He pooped!"

The nurse said, "I will change his diaper, but usually when his parents visit, they change his diapers."

"No, I got this. Hand me some wipes and I can do this," Marcus said, laughing as he took over the changing table. "Son, did you leave your dad a treat? It's like yellow paste!" The nurse had wipes ready for Marcus. Then George peed on Marcus. "Son, that was an ambush!" He put his hand over George's penis to block the pee, then continued changing him. The nurse handed him a bottle after he finished up and washed his hands. He sat in the rocker with his son, who hungrily latched on to the bottle. He never struggled to feed himself.

Mike said to Marcus, "He's a smart one."

"Yes," Marcus replied. "He has a smart mother."

"Yeah, which makes up for the father," Mike retorted.

"Thanks man, and who graduated top of the class?" Marcus laughed,

The nurse cleaned up the changing table, amused by the men's banter. They talked to George as if the infant understood what they were saying, telling him about their day. She thought it was adorable. She left them to take her break, telling them she would return in half an hour.

"Take your time," said Marcus. "We've got this, right Mike?"

Meanwhile, Samantha was in the kitchen with the older five children. "How about some carrots or apples?" she asked the kids.

"Yes, please," said Jacob. "And peanut butter."

"You got it," said Samantha, as she put five plates with apple slice and a spoon of peanut butter on each plate. The cook had already sliced the apples and kept healthy snacks available in the fridge for the children when they wanted a snack. "Matilda," Samantha said, "Dad said you want to have a sleepover. That's great. How many girls are we talking about?"

Matilda looked up. "Fifteen."

"That's fine," said Samantha, "and do you have activities and snacks in mind?"

"Yes, pizza. And we are going to give each other facials, watch movies, eat snacks, and hang out," said Matilda.

"And how late are you thinking of staying up?"

"Well, I think 1:00 AM is our goal. Sleeping bags in the movie room or playroom I think would be better."

"Let's do homemade pizza," said Samantha. "And let each girl make their own."

"That's a great idea, Mom!"

"I will let Miss Peg know after you send your invitations out. I will pick up the cake. Do you want ice cream, as well?"

"Yes, please, and cones. A chocolate cake with white icing, "

"You got it. How about decorations?" Samantha asked.

"I think just balloons. Enough so each girl can take some home," said Matilda.

"Well, we will go shopping this weekend for party bags and invitations so you can get them out Monday," said Samantha.

"That sounds great, Mom. My first sleepover!"

"Well, you're turning sixteen, I think you are plenty old enough."

"Can I come?" Ester asked.

"If Mom says alright, then I don't mind," Matilda replied.

"What about me?" Bella asked.

"It's your party," said Samantha. "If you want your sisters there, that is fine with me.

"Yay!" shouted Ester. "My first sleepover! Maybe I can have one on my birthday!"

"I want one too!" said Bella.

"We will see," said Samantha.

"Well, we will just hide on our room," said Jacob

"Other than having pizza, we can stay in our room," said Jared.

"I'll have the cook fix your pizza and send it up to your room with some fresh fruit and carrot and celery sticks. You can have your dinner there and we can move the game system up to your room if you want."

"That would be great, Mom. That was we won't have to deal with so many girls in one place," said Jacob.

"Okay, drink your milk and time for homework. Jared, your dad and I are going to talk to your guidance counselor about skipping a grade if you and Jacob really want to," she said.

"We do, Mom. Our classes are so easy."

"We are also going to add a tutor to your program and have you take some classes to see if you can get high school credits. They have to make an exception because of your age, but if you think you can do the work then we will see what we can do. And dad has worked out internships for each of you to work based on your career choices. I think they will be helpful to your career paths."

"Mom, what about us?" asked Matilda.

"I think we can get tutors for you girls, and you can work on other things to help with your career paths. I think both of you should be candy stripers. That looks good on a resume. Ester will be fourteen soon and you are almost sixteen, so you are at a good age to start working at one of the clinics we sponsor. Bella, you might need to wait another year. Now bear in mind, children, as you get more life experiences, your choices may change. Jacob, probably not yours—you have been building things since you were little. Jared, medicine is a rigorous program and there are so many different avenues of medicine you might explore. You love to explore. Look into research; there are different fields you can explore; you like to research. I could see you as a research scientist. I have always been fascinated with genetics. Sometimes life throws challenges and opportunity in your path. And then there is love that might completely change your life. But I am proud of you and your dad, and I will do everything we can to support whatever decisions you make as you grow up. You will soon get more ideas and experiences that will shape your choices," she explained.

"Mom, did you always know you wanted to be a lawyer?" Jared asked.

"Yes, but I had many obstacles thrown in my way," she said. "Most of which I did not see coming. You know I am adopted, and until Saul came into the picture, life was hard. Then meeting Joseph almost turned my path around. I loved him and though we would be together forever. Then you dad rescued me, and we began to love each other, even though he claims he wanted me from the first time he met me. And you know he has that Matthew determination—when he wants something, he gets it, no matter what obstacles are thrown in his way. He is a good father and I love him with all my heart. Now you know about how I loved Joseph and he loved me, and I thought I would marry him, but he was involved with Emily, and one careless act can change your life forever. So, Emily got pregnant, and now Joseph's duty is to marry her and raise Sophia. Marcus believed that it was only right that he was involved in your life. Jared, you know that you were very sick when you were born. Your dad called Joseph and told him what was going on and that he was your biological father. We needed him to save you. He came at once, no questions asked. You see, I had sex with both men about the same time. I was always attracted and interested in your dad, and I had not seen Joseph in two years, but he called out of the blue. I went running to him and thought that he would ask to marry me. He took me on a whirlwind trip because the news he had to tell me was hard for him. He knew it would hurt me to the core of my soul, so I never told him that he could be your biological father. Your dad did not care who the father was. He loved you because you were a part of me. You know the rest of the story. Your dad always wanted a big family, and his heart is large enough to include all of you children," said Samantha.

She continued, "So we have George and Trey now, and he wants one more of his own children. You know how hard it is on me to have children, so we hired a surrogate who will carry our embryo and have another biological child for us. I know this is a lot of information for you children to understand, but I want you to know the truth about what kind of men your dad and Joseph are. Honorable men. You are surrounded by honorable and good people who have accepted the truth and form no judgment except for loving you for who you are. Someday, I hope that Sophia can see that, also. She just does not want to share her dad; what she does not understand is that knowing the truth did not change your opinions of the man you know as your dad. Nurture over nature makes a father," said Samantha. "Alright, let's go to your rooms and start studying. You can go for a walk if after if you want; it's such a pretty day. Spring is coming quick this year. Just stay in the area that security is watching."

"Yes, Mom. That will be great," said Jared. The kids went outside to play, and a ball rolled out the back gate. Jared volunteered to go get it, even though they had been told not to. The nannies were out on the play area with them, and of course security was there, but Jared snuck out the back gate to get the ball. He was snatched by a man that was in the woods before security could react. He grabbed Jared, jumped into a car, and zoomed off. This was the first time a Matthew had been kidnapped. Mike was still in the nursery when the call came in.

"Get all the men on it immediately," he said. "But do not leave the family exposed. Put extra security on all the Matthew family and Saul and Margaret."

Marcus was listening as Mike was giving order. The children and the nannies ran back to the house and were crying that someone had taken Jared. Marcus raced to the elevator to the first floor and called the police. They came immediately and everyone was doing a search of the woods. Samantha was trying to console the children when Saul and Margaret showed up. "How can we help? Just be here for the children?" they asked.

Isabella called; she had just seen it on the news. Her and John Marcus had already offered a million-dollar reward for information on the whereabouts of their grandson. Mike called the hospital where Mr. Carr was hospitalized and asked if he was still there.

"Yes, he's still in his room."

Mike ordered a security watch on Mr. Carr. Mike sat Marcus and Samantha down and asked them to think about who could possibly want to get back at the Matthew family.

Samantha said she saw Kenneth at the wedding, and he waved at her. She said it unnerved her and she looked around to see if Joseph was there, as well. With all the excitement, she forgot to say anything about him being there. Kenneth was there with a guest who was evidently on the approved list.

Mike said, "Get the film footage of the wedding and let's identify the woman he was with. Normally in these types of cases, we have three days to find Jared unharmed."

"It's all my fault," cried Samantha. She started having a panic attack, so Martha took her upstairs and the nannies took the kids to their rooms. Mason was assigned to stay in the house. Marcus was stationed at the phone in case a call came in concerning a ransom. Joseph called and said he just got the news and would be there as soon as his jet was ready.

"How could Jared breach security?" Marcus asked.

Mike said, "I told you that back gate should have been taken out. It was always the weakest spot in our efforts to keep your children safe."

"Get that fucking gate removed so there is not a security breach," demanded Marcus.

"The camera footage showed it was a man with his faced covered, and he jumped into a black Impala. No license plate. We already have a description of the car out. We also need a description out for Kenneth and the woman from the wedding photo. Samantha said that she had bleached blonde hair. Marcus, can you name the woman that Kenneth was with? It had to be a family member otherwise they would not have been at the actual wedding."

"After reviewing the security tape, I found that is my cousin Shelia. She's my dad's niece. She has been very unstable since her mother died. She has blown through her mother's fortune and Dad put her on an allowance. She travels around Europe with different men and has become an alcoholic. She comes back to her mother's mansion when she runs out of money and waits for her next allowance check. Dad keeps up the mansion, so she has a place to crash. She has become the outcast of the family. She has been in several treatment centers and been in psychiatric care facilities. My guess is she hooked up with him at a bar somewhere in the city, and when she grew tired of him, my guess is she gave him the boot and put him out," Marcus explained. Marcus called Shelia and she answered the phone—her voice made it clear she had not been drinking. "Shelia, this is Marcus."

"Well, hello, cousin."

"Shelia, listen to me. You were with Kenneth McMahan at the wedding, correct?"

"Yes, he insisted that he wanted to be my escort. So, I bought him a suit and we came to your wedding. What is going on, Marcus?" she asked, confused.

"I think Kenneth kidnapped Jared and I need all the information I can get to find him."

"Marcus, he always talked about how he lost his business and everything he owned because you put him out of business after he got Samantha pregnant then insisted she get an abortion. At that time, I was so out of it that I did not pay much attention to him. When he left, he didn't say where he was going. You think he took Jared to get back at you? He never said where he was going when he left my house. Marcus, I have cleaned up my act and I'm pregnant, but I do not know who the father is, and I don't care. The baby is mine. It has given me hope and some reason to have purpose again," she responded.

"Shelia, I am happy for you, but I need to go in case Jared or someone calls."

"Marcus, call and let me know when your son has been found, please. "

"Someone, will, Shelia. I promise. I am glad that you have found purpose in life," Marcus said.

"It is Kenneth, I am sure of it," Mike said. "I have my guys looking for him." There was a knock at the door and a police detective entered with several policemen.

"It is difficult to get through your gate, Mr. Matthew," he commented.

"Yes, I designed it that way. Most of the residents here, including me, value their privacy. Now let's get down to why I called. My son Jared has been kidnapped. Here is his picture, and here is the man who did it. He has a grudge against me, and my security team is investigating his whereabouts now. We know he is from Tennessee and my father has alerted the media. We have lines designated for any calls and we are running down any leads. That should bring you up to speed. If there is anything you can do to help, I would greatly appreciate it," Marcus explained.

"Mr. Matthew, do you know if he wants any money from you?"

"I do not know," said Marcus. "We are waiting for that call, and so far, it has not come in. It has been five hours since he was grabbed, and I want him found in the next ten hours. That is probably all the time we have. I have a line available for me in case Kenneth or my son calls. My head of security can answer any questions you might have. I am going to check on my wife, excuse me, detective," said Marcus.

"Certainly," said Detective Poole, then he began to ask Mike some additional questions. Marcus went to see Samantha; she was in their suite lying down. Marcus went to put his arms around her and said, "We will find him. It's my fault. I told them they could go out and play nonsense. I was the one who wanted the gate in the backyard. Mike warned me that it was security risk, so if anyone takes blame, it should be me. I ordered that we undercut Kenneth's construction bids and buy up all his loans. I bankrupted him. I was pissed at what he did. He is a parasite that preys on women. I will find Jared. Please."

Margaret urged Samantha to eat and offered to stay up in the suite with her. "I will take care of Samantha. Saul has the children. You find Jared," she said.

"I will," said Marcus. He went back down to the den where Mike had set up base and all the phones were being monitored. Each tip was traced, confirmed, and followed up on, and so far, nothing had led to anything that was helpful. It had been fifteen hours since Jared went missing. Marcus had checked on the children and they were quite upset. Saul was doing everything possible to distract them. Peg was making sure everybody had food and drinks. The staff wash helping as much as they could. Everyone was waiting, hoping for a call. Eighteen hours had passed, then a call came in from Tennessee.

It was Jared. "Dad, I do not know where I am, but we drove a long distance and Kenneth went out to get food. He tied me up, but Mike had showed me and Jacob about knots and how to tie and untie them, so I was able to get free. There is a land line in this cabin, that's where I'm calling from."

"We have his location," Mike said. "I will notify the helicopter pilot to get ready to move. He is in Columbia, Tennessee surrounded by woods.

"Jared, is the door locked from the outside?" Marcus asked.

"Yes, I have already tried it."

"Is there a window, Jared?" Mike asked.

"Yes," Jared replied.

"Can you take a chair or something to break the glass?"

"Yes," said Jared.

"Then do that," Marcus instructed. Jared laid down the phone, took a chair and broke the glass.

"It's done," Jared said.

"Now put a blanket on the windowsill to keep from getting cut and push something against the window so you can climb out. The map I have says there is a road after you climb up a steep hill. Go up that hill and flag a car down. Have them take you to the nearest police station. It looks like there is one five miles from you. Explain who you are and what has happened. We are on our way, son," Marcus said. "Now hurry, son. I love you. You have been brave, now go before he gets back." Marcus told the detective to notify the police in Tennessee and tell them the location Jared was calling from. "Let's go, Mike. Joseph, we will take the helicopter. It will be faster, and we can land at the location. Peg, tell Samantha we found him, and we are on our way to get him," he said. The three men left, and Peg went up and told Samantha. She went down to the children and filled them in, then called Isabella and John Marcus.

"Thank God," they said. Samantha told them about Shelia and asked them to call her as she had tried to help. Mike and Marcus boarded the helicopter on their way to Tennessee. Mike said it would probably take two hours to get there. Then another call came from a Tennessee number. Mike quickly determined it was coming in from the police station.

"May I speak to Mr. Matthew?" a voice said on the other line. "This is Detective Brooks and I have Jared Matthew here. He said he is your son and was kidnapped. He caught a ride from an old man who picked him up about five miles from here."

"We will be there in about two hours by helicopter and will have all the details for you," Marcus said. "Please let me speak to my son, and my head of security will call you on another line. His name is Mike. We know who it was and where he is living. Let me speak to my son, please." The detective gave the phone to Jared.

"Jared, son, it is so good to hear your voice," said Marcus. "You are so brave."

"Dad, I wasn't afraid of him. Actually, I felt sad for him. He said he lost everything because of a mistake he made. He asked a lot about our family, about Mom and Joseph especially. He said some magazine was paying him $500,000 for a story about our family."

"Are you alright?" asked Marcus. "Not hurt, I hope."

"No, Dad. Just a few scratches from going out the window and getting through the woods. It was easy to find the road and flag down a truck. An old man took me to the police station and explained to the detective where he picked me up. He left his name and number in case the detective wanted to ask him more questions. I guess all I really am is hungry. They are getting me a couple of hamburgers and fries and a lemonade. Not something Mom would approve of, but heck, I am hungry," said Jared.

"I think right now Mom would not care what you ate. All she cares about is that you are unharmed," said Marcus.

"Please call her, Dad, and tell her I am okay, and I love her."

"I will, Jared. We will be there in another hour; you just stay put. When we get there, we are going to land in the police parking lot," Marcus explained.

"You must be in the company helicopter," said Jared.

"Yes, we are. I love you, Jared, and I am proud of you. Uncle Joseph is here, and he would like to talk to you. Mike is going to give all the details on this Kenneth man to the police. Here is Joseph. Again, I am so proud of you handling this situation like an adult," Marcus said.

Joseph took the phone and said to Jared, "Wow, what an adventure you've had. I'm. just thankful you're okay. I have to say, I was really scared for you, but you handle yourself really well."

"Well," said Jared. "Uncle Mike is constantly teaching us self-defense techniques. He even teaches the girls. I just recalled a lot of what he taught me and kept the man talking. I am not sure her is all there mentally. Joseph, he seemed really broken in spirit. He said he had not seen his daughter since she was born. His mother will not let him see her. She lives in Florida," he said.

"We will be there in thirty minutes," Joseph said. "I love you, son."

"Jared, you're a good man," said Mike. "You really used your skills. Now, while you're eating, write down everything you saw and heard from the time you were abducted, okay?"

"Yes, sir," said Jared.

"Good, man, we will see you in about twenty minutes. I love you, Jared, and I'm so proud of you," Mike said.

They landed in the police parking lot. Marcus was the first to see Jared. He picked him up and hugged him and kissed him on the cheek.

"God, I am so glad to see you," said Marcus.

"Come on, Dad, put me down," Jared said as he wiped his sleeve across his cheek to wipe away the kiss.

"Sorry, son," said Marcus. "I forgot you're too old to be hugged and kissed like that."

"Well, that's okay. Just this time," said Jared. "But I'm sure glad you're here, Dad. And this is all over." Joseph extended his hand and Jared shook it.

"You are really changing quickly into a man," Joseph said.

"I am glad you remembered your training in an actual scenario of a real kidnapping," Mike said. "Now do you have everything you remember written down?"

"Yes," said Jared. "Here it is, Uncle Mike."

"Great," said Mike. "Now let's catch this guy." Marcus hugged Mike.

"I owe you, man," said Marcus.

"For doing my job?" asked Mike. "And loving this kid like he was my own? Your children will always be my first priority. That and the family. Now let me talk to the police."

Kenneth got back to the cabin and opened the door to find the rope laying on the floor. He looked around the cabin and could not find Jared. Then he saw the broken window. "Shit," he said as he hurried out the door and got into the Impala. He headed for the Alabama border. "I'll need to get rid of this car soon," he thought out loud. He pulled over quickly and opened the trunk and got a temporary tag out to place on the back window of his car. "If I can get to the Mexican border, I can disappear into Mexico." But as luck would have it, there was a roadblock set up at the border and the police were checking driver's licenses. He tried to pull his car out of the link, but it was too late. The police spotted him and soon, he was surrounded and pulled from the car. Before he could say anything, he was handcuffed, read his Miranda rights, and placed in the backseat of a police car. The officer in charge radioed Detective Brooks and said, "We have the suspect and we are on our way in."

Detective Brooks went to Marcus and said, "Mr. Matthew, we have him. I think it is best that you let us handle it from here, and we will be in touch."

"No. I'm not leaving until I see that son-of-a-bitch," said Marcus angrily. *No one tells Marcus Matthew what to do when it came to his children,* he thought.

"Marcus, I will stay behind and wrap things up," said Mike. "Joseph, please take Marcus and Jared back to the helicopter and get them out of here." "I will, unless you need me here," said Joseph.

"No," said the detective. "This is cut and dry. We will hold him until we can expedite him to New York."

"Let's go, Jared," said Joseph. He called Samantha from the helicopter.

"Jared, let's go home," said Marcus.

"I know you're angry," said Jared. "But let the police handle it from here. I'm tired and I could use another burger before we get home and Mom vetoes the junk food.

Marcus snapped out of his anger and said, "Let's go, son. We will stop on the way and get some good. We can land in the parking lot of Burger King, since we cannot go through the drive-thru," he laughed. Jared took Marcus by the hand, and they went out to the helicopter with Joseph trailing behind. Joseph thought it was true what they say: nurture over nature. Marcus was Jared's father, and he was just an uncle. He was happy he could be included in the boys' lives. Marcus instructed the pilot to find a Burger King that they could safely land in, and they all went in for a burger. During their dinner, Jared called Samantha and said, "Mom, I am okay and on my way home."

Samantha could hardly speak; she began crying as soon as she heard Jared's voice. Jared tried to comfort his mom, but it was useless; she was crying so hard. He gave the phone to Marcus and said, "Dad, maybe you can get through to Mom. I can't even understand her."

"Sam darling, listen to me. Jared is okay. I am so proud of him. He handles himself like a man. We are on our way back as soon as we get him something to eat. I must confess, we are having junk food," Marcus said, trying to distract her with humor.

She laughed. "I see. As soon as Mom's not around, what do they say? Mice will play."

"Something like that," said Marcus. "I love you, and Jared says he loves you, but he is busy eating Burger King."

"Well, I don't really care what he eats as long as he is on his way home to me."

"We're on our way. We will be there in about three hours. See you soon, and let the family know," said Marcus.

"I will," she said, then hung up the phone. She went into the playroom first and told Margaret, Saul, and the children. Then she called Isabella and Joh. Marcus to tell them that they were all on their way back. Everyone felt great relief. Samantha thought to herself, *We need to find a way to make the children understand this is a rare event so they are not afraid to play outside again.*

Marcus paid for the food and gave the cashier an extra $200, a hundred for her and a hundred for the owner for allowing them to park their helicopter in the parking lot. The owner did not want to accept it after hearing Jared's story, but Marcus insisted.

"Jared, that man who picked you up on the side of the road and took you to the police station, we need to do something for him," Marcus said to Jared.

"These people just wanted to help me, but whatever you want to do, I will support you," said Jared. The pilot landed the helicopter on top of the Matthew's office building. Marcus, Jared, and Joseph met Mason at the car that he was driving to pick them up and take them back to the mansion where Samantha and the children were waiting. Saul and Margaret had gone home to give them some privacy. When Jared walked into the front door, he was met by his mother, even though it was one in the morning. It had been a long day, but Samantha stayed up to see her son and hug him.

"I love you so much," she said with tears in her eyes. "I am so glad you're safe."

"Mom, I'm okay. Mike trained us well. I don't think you realize how much effort Uncle Mike has put in to make sure we know how to handle situations like this."

"I understand," said Samantha. "But I was so afraid, and I feel responsible. Because of me and decisions I made in the past, my family was put in danger."

"Well it was me that went after Kenneth out of anger after what he did to you," said Marcus.

"Well," Jared said, "I went out the back gate when I knew I wasn't supposed to."

"And I didn't have the back gate removed when Mike told me the gate caused a breach in the security system he had established, mainly because the cameras couldn't pick up images with the woods being so thick," said Marcus.

Joseph said, "You can all blame yourselves, but like Jared said, I think he had some mental issues, so maybe no matter what had taken place, he never acted like a responsible adult so who knows how he would have acted? I think that pretty much, a parasitic man was thriving from the abuse of women. He definitely needs help and now he will be forced to get it. I am sure there are other women who will be safer for that reason. The mother of his child must have some serious concerns if he is not able to see his own daughter. The courts would never allow that unless there was evidence that he was dangerous to his daughter."

Jared said, "Mom, Dad. I'm tired and would like to go to bed. I want to talk with my brothers and sisters and tell them that I believe this was an isolated incident. I don't want them to be afraid."

Samantha hugged Jared and said, "I'm so proud of you. Yes, go to bed. We will talk tomorrow."

Joseph said, "Unless someone needs me, I'm going to be, as well. I will stay one more day, then I need to get back home to my family and all the meetings I need to attend as governor.

"Goodnight," said Marcus.

"Yes, goodnight," said Samantha. Marcus kissed Samantha and said, "I am going to tuck Jared in, then I'll check on the rest of the children. "You go up, Sam. I will be up shortly."

She kissed him back. "See you in a few. I really need you tonight," she said. Marcus and Jared took the back stairs to the children's wing. After he tucked Jared in and checked on Jacob and the girls, he went to the nursery to see Trey and George. The nurse was there and greeted Marcus telling him she was grateful that Jared was brought home unharmed. She said the baby had been asleep for hours but should be awake in a few minutes for his bottle.

"I'd like to give George his bottle," said Marcus.

"Of course," she said. She gave Marcus the bottle and he picked George up and rocked him as he fed him. It was apparent to the nurse that Marcus was visibly shaken by the incident and found comfort in feeding his youngest son. After he burped George and laid him back down, he went to Samantha who was waiting for him in bed.

"Darling, let's go to bed" she said. "The children will be up early with lots of questions and I want to call the psychologist to get some advice on how to respond to them."

Marcus yawned and said, "I'm so tired, let's go to bed." He turned out the lights and cuddled Samantha and said, "I love you." In minutes, they were both in a deep sleep. Jacob was the first one up and climbed into bed with Jared and wrapped his arms around his twin. Jared woke up and said, "I'm alright, brother. I will talk to you and the girls at breakfast. Right now, I would like to sleep a little longer. So Jacob and Jared went back to sleep in Jared's bed. At breakfast, everyone was full of questions. The most Jared would say was that this was an isolated incident and that he did not want them to live in fear. He also said that Mike's training had really taught him how to handle this situation and he would take Mike's training even more seriously. He wanted the four of them to do so, as well.

Samantha had called the psychologist and she said she would come by that afternoon to speak with the children. Joseph told the children how brave he thought Jared has been.

Marcus said, "I want you children to follow the security rules that Mike had set up for you. The back gate will be removed today, and you will not be allowed into the woods without supervision."

The children then got ready for school, as Marcus wanted them to have as normal of a day as possible. Mike called to say he was on his way back and had booked a flight for noon. He had everything under control and would talk to Marcus, Joseph, and Samantha as soon as he got home. Marcus and Joseph drove the children to school. Trey and George were oblivious to what was going on and spent much of his day in the nursery. Samantha went back up to take a nap. She still had not recovered emotionally from Jared's kidnapping.

Things got back to normal pretty quick. Spring break was coming up and Isabella and John Marcus wanted to take the children to Spain so they could visit their grandmother. She was feeling poorly and Isabella thought seeing the children would cheer her up. She also wanted to see her sister who had never married and lived with their mother when she wasn't working. Their dad had died several years ago and had only known the older children. Isabella's family had a very large vineyard that produced fine wines and olive oil. Isabella wanted the children to explore the vineyard and she wanted Marcus to have repairs made to the family home. So, Marcus booked the jet for spring break and took Mike with him. The kids were excited to see their grandmother again and she was excited to meet George and Trey. Samantha walked the vineyards and olive groves. Grandmother had workers take the older children through the whole process from picking grapes to bottling the wine. Matilda was asked to design this year's label. She was so excited and spent her last week designing the label. Marcus hired some locals to make repairs and put a local in charge of the crew that would do the repairs. He had Samantha look at the books and she hired a bookkeeper to help grandmother out. Even though his mother's twin lived with her from time to time, with her modeling career, it was not enough to help her out. So, Samantha hired someone to act as her companion. She wrote up a contract defining her duties and the scope of her responsibility. On their way back, Marcus brought the surrogate up to Samantha. George was almost three months old mow.

"Sam, are you planning anything for Bella's upcoming birthday?" he asked.

"Just the family and a few friends. I thought we could all go to the zoo and have the zoo set up one of their parties."

"Well," said Marcus. "We talked to Cindy the medical student. You had your tubes tied and we have the fertile eggs. We have the contract drawn up and I waited the twelve weeks as Dr. McCullough suggested, so tonight my dear, let's you and I slip off to the condo for a date night.

"Sounds like a plan, but you promised that the surrogate would not be implanted until George was six months old. That would make him fifteen months old when the new baby is born. Bella will be ten and a half, Matilda nearly seventeen, Ester fifteen, and our boys, almost twelve. I am good with these ages with a newborn around," said Samantha.

The pilot landed the plane and the nannies loaded the girls into the waiting cars to take them home. Marcus and Samantha packed an overnight bag and kissed the kids goodbye. "Goodnight, we will see you tomorrow. Mom and Dad are going to have a date night," Marcus said.

Marcus pulled the car in front of the Matthew's building and tossed the keys to the valet. They were acting like newlyweds, kissing passionately as they removed their clothes in the penthouse elevator and jumping into the indoor pool of the penthouse. Marcus's erection was not deterred by the chilly pool water. He had not turned on the heater in the pool yet. Samantha had suggested they go into the hot tub where they continued their foreplay. Finally, Marcus had had enough and picked Samantha up and laid her wet on the rug on the floor in the master suite. He then flipped the fireplace on and covered her body with kisses, finally reaching the lips of her vagina, licking with his tongue. "Sam, what do you want?" he asked.

"Fuck me, sweetheart. After nine years of marriage, you know what I want," she laughed.

He sat back on his knees and said, "Marry me on our tenth anniversary?" he asked.

"Yes," she said. "Now stop torturing me."

"First open this box," he said, then pulled it out from under the bed. Samantha opened it and it held a canary diamond bracelet with ten one carat stones and a two-carat canary diamond, all set in platinum.

"They are spectacular," Samantha said. "But are they an early anniversary gift?"

"No, my love. They are ideas of what's yet to come," he boasted. "Now put them on and I will fuck you. Then once you are dried off, I'm going to find those handcuffs and we are going to repeat our first night together. But this time, there will be no running off to Joseph."

Once they were both dry, Marcus proceeded to find the handcuffs and cuff Samantha to the bedposts. She lay on her back, each arm cuffed to a bedpost so she could not more.

"You're all mine now," Marcus said mischievously. We began kissing her neck, then slowly made his way down to her wet pussy. He licked and kissed her beautiful pink vagina until she oozed cum and was begging him to stop.

"It's too much," she said, breathing heavily.

"Cum one more time for me, darling," he said. He continues licking and sucking on her clit and labia until she released one more glorious orgasm, and then they snuggled in each other's arms once they both reached completion.

Returning to the mansion at seven, Samantha and Marcus felt like newlyweds and acted more affectionate than usual. They told the children that date night would be happening once a month. They asked the children about their weekend and if they were feeling ready to go back to school. The girls were ready, but the boys seemed disgruntled and bored. There were no emotional signs of distress from Jared's kidnapping during the Spain trip, and Jared's reaction to the kidnapping made the children unafraid and already back to playing in the backyard under the close eye of their nannies and security. The back gate had been removed and the fence now extended around the manmade pond that the children often boated in. Ester had ridden her horse Dusty that was kept in the barn around the pasture with the other resident horses. Samantha had decided to take the children to the Brooklyn Zoo and thought that a two-day weekend aboard the bullet train would further help them resolve any fear they have about being amongst the public. This would be in celebration of Bella's tenth birthday. Eighteen invitations went out to the family about the zoo trip. All the family members had accepted, and some were going to make the full two-day excursion. Saul and Margaret saw it as a great opportunity to display their mixed-race union as now Jared and Jacob's biological father had been identified as Joseph. They also thought it was a great opportunity to show how tightly connected the Matthews were. Phillipe had agreed to cater the outing at the zoo and bring the cake. He had recently opened his new line of food trucks and wanted to make connections with the zoo. He said 39% of his profits would go to the zoo to show his support.

Samantha had given $500,000 to the zoo as a contribution to keep it open and make it free for underprivileged children. The board at the zoo asked her to be part of the board, and she asked if her daughter Matilda could take her place instead. Although the board had never allowed a teenager to work before, they thought it would be great PR to have her on board to get a fresh perspective on how the zoo should be run. Also, if a Matthew was involved, they could always count on the family's further support, along with the tight-knit group of wealthy friends they would bring with them. The children were excited about the train ride. They had never taken a trip on public transportation. Of course, Mike and Denise went as guests, but Mike was there for security, also. The trip showed the children another part of New York that they had been sheltered from. The party at the zoo was more than eventful. The children were able to get close to the hippos, and all the animals in general, without making any real exceptions for the Matthews. Even the nannies were left behind, which created more work for Samantha and Marcus as they had to care for Trey and George. Marcus carried Trey in a baby carrier on his back to give him a good view of everything. All the extended family took turns carrying him and showing off the children. Paige and Penelope had taken the train ride along with the children and were such a good help with the younger ones. Mike and Denise spent most of their time with the older children. Saul loved playing chess with Jared on the trip in the service car of the train. John Marcus and Jacob were busy trying to figure out how to build better shelters for the zoo animals. Isabella made comments about staying closer to the picnic table reserved for the party. She and Ester found the smell of the animals off-putting. She and Isabella spent most of their time together. Ester loved shopping trips with Isabella. Phillipe had provided an extraordinary Italian meal. He created a cake that began with a hippo, then the second layer was other zoo animals, and the top layer was a monkey with "Happy Birthday Bella" written on top. He provided servers to make it easier on the family and of course, he was serving wine from Isabella's family vineyards. His food truck was a big success and people stood in line to sample his Italian cuisine that he made affordable for everyone. Not only was he extending his food truck line, but he was also opening another restaurant in the Bronx. He and his mother had found their place within the Matthew clan. Being the son of John Marcus Mathew had opened many doors for him.

Samantha had called Dr. McCullough and requested another meeting with Cindy, the med student who was going to be the surrogate for their last baby. Her and Marcus wanted to make it known that no matter what the outcome was, they were always there for her. Marcus has agreed to fund her medical school education in exchange for her doing the residency at the hospital that carried the Matthew's name. They wanted to really get to know her before she was implanted with the first egg in three months, so they had made arrangements for her to spend time with the family and children so they understood their sibling was just not bought, but was doing good for all the people involved. Samantha wanted to start planning the vow renewal that Marcus wanted to celebrate their tenth anniversary. She called Rick and told him she wanted a wedding at a garden. He said, "Honey, tell Marcus to get the checkbook out because this is just what I needed now that I'm retired. Scott and I are driving each other crazy."

Scott had even rented a small office and took on some new clients to get some time away from Rick and his boundless energy. He had redecorated their condo and their friend's condo and needed a diversion. So, he began researching places to have the wedding outside and Samantha provided him with a list of family and close friends that would be invited.

The telephone rang. It was Rick. "Hey, darling, what about having your renewal at the rose garden at the Brooklyn Botanical Garden? I can reserve the Palm House and the Pool Terrace, it is the iconic glass-walled Palm House. You can get lost in the luxury of nature."

"That sounds wonderful. Can we get it next year in June?" Samantha asked.

"Yes, if I reserve it now. They wanted a $5,000 deposit, which I wrote them a check for today because I knew you would say yes. It provides the perfect setting for an unforgettable event and may at least equal your wedding. Provided you're not pregnant and go into labor leaving me to handle the hundreds of guests," Rick teased.

"You loved it," she said.

"Yes, you know I like to be the star of the show whenever I can," he said. "Tell me more. We can gather at the Palm House for your reception and party in the Atrium. The Atrium was designed by Lillian and Amy Goldman. A stunning ecological event place. Tall crystal vases filled with different colored roses and foliage will decorate the center of each table. The tables will be round and covered with white linen tablecloths and white linen napkins. The china will be white with crystal glasses. The finest silverware and servers will be present to serve your guests. There is room for a dance floor. There is a small white umbrella on stands where the reflecting pool and the ceremony could be under a rose canopy at the end of the pool. Then there are white lights strung up all the dome ladders and around the dome. I put lanterns with candles that can maybe sit on the steps. All the chairs are white ladder backs with kind of an oriental scroll. Marcus could wear his trademark black stove pipe pants with a matching vest. A fedora hat. The older boys wear striped, gray vests with stove pipe pants and fedoras. Trey and George can wear striped pants with a solid vest and suspenders. So the boys are dressed in grey and Marcus in black. Since this is a renewal, the kids could stand up for you."

"Okay" said Samantha. "I'm seeing it so far."

"Now for you, let's go sexy. Something to remind Marcus of why he still has interest in you after six kids. You would wear a mermaid gown featuring a trendy strapless neckline with an illusion of shoulder long sleeves that detach. The dress is made of sequin embroidery, lace appliques places over the sequin net with underlining detailed with floral motifs paired with a full tulle skirt. That shows off the dramatic sleeve. The color is a soft beige. I will have the designer bring over a sketch. As for the girls, Ester would be in a Boho tulle twirling dress, in dusty pink trimmed in beige ruffles in three quarter length. Bella would wear a white Bohemian flower tulle dress. Matilda would wear a boho style tulle lace flower top with a blush pink tulle bottom with an underskirt. Each girl would wear a flower band in their hair, and you would have tiny roses pinned in your long curly hair, maybe styled down to one side. The girls can all wear strappy sandals in beige, and you can wear a strappy heel sandal. Well, what do you think? Phillipe can cater it and make the cakes. Your mother-in-law can provide her world-famous wines. Maybe Adele can sing after the dinner, and of course, we would need to hire an orchestra for dancing."

Samantha screamed into the phone, "I love it! You know me too well."

"Yes, I gotcha girl. The venue can hold up to 250, as the list grows, and I know it will. So, we will get the invitations out in January for the June event. I'll let my man Marcus plan the honeymoon. So, I figure $259,000 will cover all of it. It's perfect. Talk to Phillipe about the dinner, maybe something light like fish and hors d'oeuvres. Marcus will need to talk to Adele and Elton in case they are busy, but I think they have both retired so that shouldn't be a problem. I am going to start with a set designer next week and you and Marcus need to talk to a priest and rabbi. I guess you will want to add some Jewish traditions in to please Saul. So, with your approval, I'll start setting everything up," he said.

"I approve," shouted Samantha excitedly. "I'll tell Marcus about it tonight at dinner. The girls will be excited. The boys will live with it. Yes, start right away."

"Gotcha, girl," and he hung up. That night at dinner Samantha told the family about the plans for the renewal with such enthusiasm, Marcus smiled and said, "I better get busy with planning a honeymoon and design a little something to go with that set of rings on that beautiful finger of yours."

The girls were excited about a new dress and getting to stay up late. The boys did not have much to say and really wanted to change the subject to talk about a history project they were working on. After dinner and the children were in bed, Samantha called Dr. McCullough and set up another appointment with Cindy.

"When, sweetheart?" the doctor asked.

"For next week," said Samantha.

"That sounds good, yes," said Marcus.

"I think it's time we get started," Samantha said. Dr. McCullough put Cindy on the medication to help her body accept the implanted embryo. After two weeks, Cindy, Marcus, and Samantha met at Dr. McCullough's office for the first implantation of the first embryo. Marcus and Samantha were going to be with her at every appointment and assured her she would never go through any procedure alone. Marcus had already cleared her student debt and paid for the remainder of her medical school. They had asked her to stay in the guest house and provided her with a driver and security when she went to school. Her hours were long and concerned Dr. McCullough, who was not surprised when she started to bleed which means the implantation didn't take. She as allowed to finish her period and after two months, they would try again.

Cindy was devastated. Marcus spent time with her comforting her and taking her places with him when she could spare some time from classes. He even arranged for her to take a relaxation break in California to soak up the sun. Cindy's parents were killed in a car accident when she was eleven and she had been raised by her older sister and her husband. Cindy's sister Lisa lost her husband in the Iraq war and was raising three children on her own. Marcus put the family in one of his nicer houses and said she could live there for free as long as she'd like. He also put money away for her three children's college education and they were becoming a part of the Matthew family. Often, Samantha's girls played with Lisa's three girls, as they were close in age. The girls were also indulged in Isabella's shopping sprees and Margaret's cooking classes. Pierre had taken an interest in the children, and Cindy and Samantha babysat the girls sometimes when Lisa and Pierre were out. They usually ended up at his restaurant cooking together. They both had cooking in common. Lisa was part Italian, and she was teaching Pierre Italian cooking techniques.

After two months, the procedure was tried again. But once again, Cindy started to bleed, and they were forced to wait another two weeks. Christmas was coming up, so they decided to wait until after the holidays so that Cindy could cut back on her school schedule and try again. She was feeling very disheartened and told Marcus that perhaps they needed to find another surrogate. She was willing to return the money, but Marcus said, "It's just money and it's only good if I can spend it on a good cause."

They soon received good news. The third implantation worked and Cindy was pregnant. The family was so happy! It was now March and Samantha was getting ready for June's nuptials.

After six weeks, a call in the night brought disappointment when Cindy was rushed to the hospital for a miscarriage. Dr. McCullough called Samantha and Marcus into her office. "Emotionally, I don't think she can do this again," she said. Marcus went in to talk to Cindy and Lisa was there with her sister. Marcus sat on Cindy's bed and hugged her and said, "I think you've had enough. We will start looking at another surrogate."

"My sister and I have been talking," Cindy said, "and research says the best candidate is someone who has already given birth. So, my sister wants to be your surrogate. She has an easy time getting pregnant and has easy pregnancies. So, if you, Samantha, and Dr. McCullough agree, she wants to do it for you. You made such a difference in our family and we want to help you. Marcus agreed to talk to Samantha and Dr. McCullough about it. It was May, and Samantha was in a frenzy to make everything perfect for the upcoming renewal of vows that Marcus so wanted. Rick had been such a help. The list had grown to the limit of 250 guests. Samantha and Marcus kept adding to the list until Rick called a halt to inviting more people, as it was far too late to send out more invitations and adjust the arrangements for more people.

Marcus had hired the Italian composer, Andrea Bocelli. He was coming with his son, Matteo Bocelli, to sing for Samantha as a gift. He was also planning a new ring designed by a European designer of an eternity ring that also featured the birthstones of the children, along with Marcus and Samantha's birth stones, leaving room for a stone for the new baby they were hoping for. Samantha and Marcus had met with Lisa and agreed to try one last time using Lisa as a surrogate this time. Dr. McCullough had used the last three embryos and implanted them all in Lisa. Because of her age, she had to use drugs to increase her fertility, and they figured they had a better chance by using all three embryos. Samantha and Marcus had agreed that this was the last attempt, and if it didn't happen, it wasn't meant to be.

This was a more relaxed attitude and a more acceptance of the blessing of children they already had. Bella was ten years old now and as talkative as ever. George was trying to walk already and his first birthday would be celebrated after his parents returned from their honeymoon. The boys had started their new grade and were finding it more challenging, along with the tutors and the college pre-courses. Both girls were busy with the wedding plans and were loving the fittings for the different outfits. Samantha had let them get special dresses for the reception that they could change in to. Marcus had bought the girls their first real pearl necklaces and earrings and planned to give them to them right before they got their dresses for the vow renewal. He had a small pearl ring fashioned for each of them, as well. The boys were more difficult to shop for to commemorate the occasion, so he had men's small chain bracelets designed for all three boys with their initials on them, He had made one for himself with the date and the initials of all their children, along with his and Samantha's, and room for the new baby if that worked out.

It had been since the middle of May since the implantation took place. It was June first now and wo weeks had passed, but it was still too soon to know anything. Marcus had planned a three-week cruise on his yacht down the Atlantic Ocean to the coast of South America as a getaway for him and the bride. After they got back from their trip, they were hoping they would know the news of the baby, and perhaps even do a sonogram to make sure it was alright if the best should happen. The day of the prenuptials was exciting and nerve-wracking for everyone except the boys, who were bored and fidgety. Marcus had given all his gifts to the children except the ring he designed for Samantha, by Laurence Graff, who was known for his collection of rare diamonds. Adele started the ceremony with a song. The priest and the rabbi started the ceremony and Samantha was overcome with love when she saw the ring that Marcus had designed for her. After the vows, Elton played "Your Song" as they left to change into their clothes for the reception and festivities. The older children were delighted to be able to stay up later than normally allowed. The nurses had taken the baby and put him to bed. He was quite fussy by the time Mason drove them back to the mansion.

Marcus and Samantha danced the night away and the festivities lasted until two in the morning. Mike then drove them where Isabella was docked and they spent their second wedding night wrapped in the love and lust they had felt a renewed energy for. Later in the day, they left for their long trip. The nannies and the grandparents had all taken turns with visiting and helping the children. Lisa telephoned Dr. McCullough and said she just knew she was pregnant but wanted a blood test to confirm. It had been four weeks since the implantation and she knew the signs of pregnancy from her own experience. Dr. McCullough called the yacht and had the news that Lisa was pregnant relayed to Marcus and Samantha. They were overjoyed and sent Lisa a giant bouquet of roses. This meant that if all went well with the pregnancy that a new life would be expected in February of next year. That was perfect, as George would be walking by then. He might even be off bottles and diapers soon, too. The honeymoon was everything the couple had hoped for. Their renewal contributed to their newfound energy to take on their ever-growing family.

Now it had been nine weeks since Lisa had been determined pregnant. Marcus wanted a sonogram. He wanted to know the sex of the baby and make sure it was developing as it should. He called Dr. McCullough and asked her to schedule one. He called Lisa and asked if she minded and offered to pick her up. Him and Samantha wanted her to feel their love and gratitude for her contribution to their family. Dr. McCullough rubbed the familiar cold gel onto Lisa; she was larger than normal for how far along she was. When she turned the monitor screen so everyone in the room could she, she gasped after she placed the instrument on her stomach.

"Well, I hope you two are ready for this news," said Dr. McCullough. "But even if you aren't…you're having triplets and they are all boys. Everything looks perfectly developed."

"I need to sit down," Samantha said. Marcus was literally jumping around the room as if he was playing basketball.

"I cannot believe it," he said. He went between all three women and took turns hugging them. Dr. McCullough was trying to go over the extra care that Lisa needed to follow and realized the only person listening was Lisa, who was getting dressed and getting the diet instructions and a chart of what to be watching for the babies development. Instructions to rest and stay off her feet as much as possible and watch for any swelling as the added weight can cause this condition. She gave Lisa stronger pre-natal vitamins and scheduled her next appointment.

Marcus wanted to take everyone out for a late lunch and talk about sending Lisa more help with her own children and a small staff to cook and clean and help with the kids. Samantha finally found her voice and said, "Do we dare tell anyone yet?"

Lisa said, "Let's get past the fourth month and then you should tell your parents and children only. Let's keep this close to our vest until we get to the sixth month, Then I feel we would be clearly safe to tell the world."

"Yes, agreed," Samantha said. "Marcus, you must promise."

He said, "I will try but it's going to be hard not to tell. But Sam, I have three named I'd like to try out on you, and we will need to call Mary to start the addition of another nursery, as Trey and George still need theirs."

"Yes," said Samantha. "So, what are the names?"

"Samuel, after you. Michael for Mike, and Adam for Saul," he said.

Samantha said, "I love those names! So, I guess, yes! We are having triplets!"